Praise for the Dark Warrior novels by
DONNA GRANT

MIDNIGHT'S KISS

5 Stars TOP PICK! "[Grant] blends ancient gods, love, desire, and evil-doers into a world you will want to revisit over and over again."

—*Night Owl Reviews*

5 Blue Ribbons! "This story is one you will remember long after the last page is read. A definite keeper!"

—*Romance Junkies*

4 Stars! "The world of the Immortal Warriors is a thoroughly engaging one, blending powerful ancient gods, fiery desire, and touchingly human love, which readers will surely want to revisit."

—*RT Book Reviews*

4 Feathers! "*Midnight's Kiss* is a game changer—one that will set the rest of the series in motion."

—*Under the Covers*

MIDNIGHT'S CAPTIVE

5 Blue Ribbons! "Packed with originality, imagination, humor, Scotland, Highlanders, magic, surprising plot twists, intrigue, sizzling sensuality, suspense, tender romance, and true love, this story has something for everyone." —*Romance Junkies*

4 1/2 Stars! "Grant has crafted a chemistry between her wounded alpha and surprisingly capable heroine that will, no doubt, enthrall series fans and newcomers alike." —*RT Book Reviews*

MIDNIGHT'S WARRIOR

4 Stars! "Super storyteller Grant returns . . . A rich variety of previous protagonists adds a wonderful familiarity to the books." —*RT Books Reviews*

5 Stars! "Ms. Grant brings together two people who are afraid to fall in love and then ignites sparks between them." —*Single Title Reviews*

MIDNIGHT'S SEDUCTION

"Sizzling love scenes and engaging characters fill the pages of this fast-paced and immersive novel."
—*Publishers Weekly*

4 Stars! "Grant again proves that she is a stellar writer and a force to be reckoned with."
—*RT Book Reviews*

5 Blue Ribbons! "A deliciously sexy, adventuresome paranormal romance that will keep you glued to the pages . . ." —*Romance Junkies*

5 Stars! "Ms. Grant mixes adventure, magic and sweet love to create the perfect romance story."
—*Single Title Reviews*

MIDNIGHT'S LOVER

"Paranormal elements and scorching romance are cleverly intertwined in this tale of a damaged hero and resilient heroine."   —*Publishers Weekly*

5 Blue Ribbons! "An exciting, adventure-packed tale, *Midnight's Lover* is a story that captivates you from the very first page."   —*Romance Junkies*

5 Stars! "Ms. Grant weaves a sweet love story into a story filled with action, adventure and the exploration of personal pain."   —*Single Title Reviews*

4 Stars! "It's good vs. evil Druid in the next installment of Grant's Dark Warrior series. The stakes get higher as discerning one's true loyalties becomes harder. Grant's compelling characters and the continued presence of previous protagonists are key reasons why these books are so gripping. Another exciting and thrilling chapter!"   —*RT Book Reviews*

4.5 Stars Top Pick! "This is one series you'll want to make sure to read from the start . . . they just keep getting better . . . mmmm! A must read for sure!"
            —*Night Owl Reviews*

4.5 Feathers! "If you're looking for an author who brings heat and heart in one tightly-written package, then Donna Grant will be a gift that makes your jaw drop. You don't want to miss *Midnight's Lover*."
            —*Under the Covers*

NOVELS BY DONNA GRANT

THE DARK KINGS SERIES
Darkest Flame
Dark Heat

THE DARK WARRIOR SERIES
Midnight's Master
Midnight's Lover
Midnight's Seduction
Midnight's Warrior
Midnight's Kiss
Midnight's Captive
Midnight's Temptation
Midnight's Promise

THE DARK SWORD SERIES
Dangerous Highlander
Forbidden Highlander
Wicked Highlander
Untamed Highlander
Shadow Highlander
Darkest Highlander

FROM ST. MARTIN'S PAPERBACKS

FIRE RISING

DONNA GRANT

St. Martin's Paperbacks

This is a work of fiction. All of the characters, organizations, and events portrayed in this novel are either products of the author's imagination or are used fictitiously.

FIRE RISING

Copyright © 2014 by Donna Grant.
Excerpt from *Burning Desire* copyright © 2014 by Donna Grant.

For information address St. Martin's Press, 175 Fifth Avenue, New York, NY 10010.

ISBN: 978-1-250-04137-1

Printed in the United States of America

St. Martin's Paperbacks edition / June 2014

St. Martin's Paperbacks are published by St. Martin's Press, 175 Fifth Avenue, New York, NY 10010.

10 9 8 7 6 5 4 3 2 1

To my readers—
the adventure continues . . .

ACKNOWLEDGMENTS

Thanks so much to my amazing editor Monique Patterson, and everyone at SMP who was involved in getting this book ready. Y'all rock!

To my agent, Louise Fury, who keeps me on my toes. Hats off to my team—Melissa Bradley, Stephanie Dalvit, and Leah Suttle. Words can't say how much I adore y'all.

A special thanks to my family for the never-ending support.

And to my husband, Steve. For everything! I love you, Sexy!

PROLOGUE

May 2014
The Rose and Crown pub
Oban, Scotland

Sammi wiped the last part of the highly polished bar as the front door opened and Daniel came rushing into the pub. She wondered at his harried expression and the sweat beading his face. When he locked the door and turned to her with wild eyes filled with sorrow and remorse, she knew something was dreadfully wrong.

"What is it?" she asked cautiously.

Daniel meandered through the tables as if he couldn't decide whether to hurry or wait and made his way to the back of the bar. His eyes darted about and his face was flushed. "We need to leave. Now."

"I just shut down for the night." Sammi reached for a glass before she tilted a lever and watched the dark ale fill half the glass before she shut it off and lifted the glass to her lips. She drank several swallows as she thought about her ex-lover and his peculiar actions.

Their affair had been wild—and short. She knew Daniel wasn't the type to stick around forever, nor was he the guy she would settle down with. Not that there was such a guy.

Or that she would even let anyone get that close.

But he had a keen business sense. Even as their quick affair died down, their friendship grew until he was a part of her business. His connections to distributors and suppliers cut her costs by a third, saving her a lot more than she thought possible.

"Sammi, I mean it," he said, ire deepening his voice as he reached for her arm.

She dodged him to prop an elbow on the bar, her look daring him to try and force her. Her ears still rang from the noise of the night, and her mouth watered for the lobster sandwich waiting for her in the pub's small kitchen.

"Tell me what's going on first."

"Dammit. We doona have time." He raked a hand through his thinning, dark hair and let out a string of curses. "We need to leave now."

"I've still got the floors to clean, which was your job tonight if you'll remember the schedule. You know. The schedule I put up last week? The one you agreed to. You might see it if you spent more time here. What's up with that, by the way? You've scarcely been around lately."

He swallowed and nervously glanced at the door. "I'll tell you everything once we're on the road. Go pack a bag as quick as you can."

Sammi nearly snorted her ale through her nose at his

absurd request. "What?" she asked incredulously after she stopped coughing. "Why do I need to pack a bag?"

"They're coming, Sammi. We've got to leave!" Daniel shouted violently. "Now!"

A tingle of apprehension ran down her spine. "Who is coming? I'm not moving until you tell me, so you might as well spit it out."

He put both hands on the bar and hung his head as if the weight of the world rested on his shoulders. "I was an idiot. I . . . I got in with some bad people when I was a lad. Had no choice really. Everyone in my family does some sort of job for them. I kept working with them because the money was so good. And easy."

"What people?" she asked hesitantly, unsure if she really wanted to know. Sammi set down her glass and glanced at the door Daniel had locked as apprehension began to grow.

"Their name doesna matter. They're organized crime."

Her blood ran cold at his words. "What did you do for them?"

"Laundered money. Through the pub."

"*My* pub?" It was like she had been kicked in the stomach. The man she'd trusted to share the accounting of her business had laundered money for the Mob. It was too surreal to even grasp.

Daniel lifted his head, his blue eyes filled with guilt. "We both made money off it. I made sure of it."

"Oh, God." This was going from bad to worse. She knew it, yet she still found herself asking, "What have you done?"

Daniel pushed off the bar and took her hands in his.

"I skimmed some of their money. Just a little, Sammi, but I wanted to make sure you were set. You struggled with the pub after your mum's death, not to mention me using the pub for the money laundering. It's the least I could do for you."

She didn't know what to say. The man before her, the man she had shared her bed and her business with, was a stranger. However, the fact he was scared put her on high alert.

"They found out you took the money, didn't they?"

He nodded woodenly. "I was supposed to meet them two hours ago."

"Supposed to? You mean you didn't?" She could only stare in complete shock.

"Do you know what these people do to those who steal from them?"

Sammi looked around her pub as realization sank in. She had scraped together money, and with a little help from her mother, she had managed to acquire the pub five years ago. It was her life. The dark, smooth wood of the bar, the bottles of liquor lining the shelves, and the smell of food cooking in the back were the only things she looked forward to every day.

She was going to lose it all. Because of an idiot she had trusted. "I've seen enough movies to know."

"They'll come for me. You can't be here when they do. They'll . . . you don't want to know what they will do to you."

No, she really didn't. But she also didn't want to walk away from her pub. It was hers, and she would fight for it. First, she had to stay alive. "How long will we be gone?"

Daniel frowned, his dark brows lowering over his eyes. "We won't ever come back. Their reach is long. If we remain in one place too long they'll catch us. No credit cards, no mobile phones. We need to disappear and find new identities."

The room began to spin, just as her life was doing. She had woken that morning thinking about going down to the docks tomorrow to get first pick of the freshest seafood in all of Scotland.

"All of my money is in the bank."

"We can no' chance it," Daniel said. "Take what you have here. We'll improvise. I've got some money stashed in the warehouse. You know the one I bought under that fake name."

She did know, but she couldn't see how they would get there without the Mob finding them first. And how was she supposed to survive without her credit cards, bank, or her mobile? The thought of being on the run left her shaken, unsettled.

Dazed.

"Move," Daniel said as he shoved her to the swinging door that separated the pub from the back.

Sammi glanced into the brightly lit kitchen and the lobster sandwich waiting for her on a white plate atop the stainless steel counter. Instead, she turned to the right and passed the door to her office and started up the stairs that led to her flat.

There was no need to turn on any lights. The streetlamps shining in shed enough for her to see her way clearly to her bedroom.

At three in the morning, Oban was the quietest. How many nights had she fallen asleep listening to the sound of the water as it lapped against the docks? How many times had she woken to the squawks from the gulls as a ship docked? How many drinks had she served the people of Oban?

All of that was going to be left behind. It didn't seem fair. Maybe she wouldn't go. Daniel was the one who had stolen the money. He was the one they would be after.

"Who am I kidding?" she asked herself.

They would probably shoot her rather than look at her. Even if she feigned ignorance, she was sure they wouldn't let her go.

She didn't want to die, so Sammi did what she had to do—as always. After grabbing a bag from under her bed, she pulled open several drawers and was about to start stuffing clothes in when she heard a vehicle pull up.

Sammi hastily rushed to the other side of her loft that faced the parking lot and sidled against the wall next to the window. She hesitated for just a second before she carefully peered through the sheer gold curtains.

That is when she caught sight of the Lexus SUV and the three burly men who stepped out and flanked a tall, impressively dressed man who was obviously their leader.

He paused to button his suit jacket and glanced up at her window. She couldn't tell much about him other than he had dark, clean-cut hair.

"Shit. Shit, shit, shit," she mumbled as she ducked and crawled away from the window as fast as she could.

She had to get down to Daniel so they could get out the back before—

Her thoughts came to a screeching halt with the sound of the pub door crashing open. There was no way they could get out now. Sammi stood at the top of the stairs, her heart beating a slow, sickening rhythm.

This was the night she was going to die. The realization turned her blood to ice. She glanced at the phone, wishing she had returned Jane's phone call as she had planned to do earlier that day.

Jane, the half-sister who had walked into her life so suddenly two years ago. It had been impossible not to like Jane. No matter how Sammi tried, she and Jane had become closer than she had let anyone after her mother died.

Sammi's thoughts halted as Daniel cried out in pain. Adrenaline spiked as she flattened herself against the wall in case someone glanced up the stairs.

"You should've known better than to steal from me," came a cultured English accent from below. "I might have been more lenient had you come when I summoned you."

"Ow . . . I," Daniel said around large puffs of air. "I was going to bring you the new tallies from the latest batch I've laundered."

"How much did you take this time?"

Sammi cringed when Daniel hesitated.

"Danny," the man said, a hint of malice and something even darker infusing his voice. "I suggest you answer me."

"I on-only took ten thousand."

"And what have you done with my money?"

The sound of footsteps approaching had Sammi backing farther away from the stairs. She didn't hear

Daniel's response as she focused on whoever might come up after her.

Several tense minutes passed before the man walked away. Sammi let out a relieved sigh, but when Daniel let out another scream, she knew she couldn't wait around forever.

She licked her lips as she looked across the space to the windows on either side of her bed. If she could get to them, she could use the water pipes to slide down. But that was a big if.

"Where is Miss Miller?" the leader asked.

She was really beginning to hate that sophisticated tone of his.

Daniel refused to answer. A moment later she heard the unmistakable sound of a fist meeting a body. Daniel coughed, his wheezing breath telling her the punch had landed in his stomach.

"I'll ask once more, Danny. Where is Miss Miller?"

"She's not a part of this," he said.

Sammi closed her eyes as she heard another punch being thrown.

"Right his chair, Fabian," the leader said.

A chair scraped against her floor, then there was nothing but silence. Sammi's imagination ran rampant with what could be going on.

"Danny?"

"She's not here," Daniel barked angrily. "Sammi took a couple of days off."

There was a snort. "You mean you sent her away so you wouldn't have to explain yourself to her, right?"

"Whatever you say, Mr.—"

Daniel was cut off with another punch to his face.

Sammi opened her eyes and looked at the windows again. Her time was running out. The men wouldn't take Daniel's word for it. They would search the entire pub. If she wanted to see the sun rise, she couldn't remain.

She drew in a deep breath and released it at the same time she dashed across the open doorway. Her thought had been speed, not stealth. A mistake she realized all too soon when a board creaked beneath her foot. She froze, and that's when she heard the leader send someone to search upstairs.

Sammi's hands shook as she tried to unlock the window. The adrenaline kept her from falling apart, but it was the panic that caused her to fumble.

She got it open when the first thug bounded up the stairs. With the lights out he couldn't see her, but that didn't stop him from firing off several shots around the room—one coming entirely too close.

While he groped for the lights, she wedged the window open enough so she could slip out. She had a grip on the pipes with her legs and one hand so she could lower the window until it was nearly shut.

Luck was on her side, because at that moment the lights flicked on.

Sammi heard voices out in front of the pub and quickly slid down the pipes as fear pushed her. She landed hard on the ground, tweaking her ankle. After a hasty look over her shoulder, she ran between empty crates and into the water with nary a sound just as footsteps running toward her grew louder.

Even in the dark water, she huddled against the dock, afraid they would see her. They were there waiting for her to make a noise and reveal herself, but she refused to do something so foolish.

Sammi shivered from the cool water and the terror gripping her. Any moment her life could be snuffed out, ending before she had accomplished any of her goals.

They walked to the edge of the docks and stood there searching the black water. The silence was the hardest. She silently begged them to talk, to say anything to break the quiet.

She got her wish when they began firing several rounds that zinged all around her like tiny missiles. After what seemed like hours, the leader called to his men and they walked off. Sammi waited until she heard their SUV engine turn over, and then she started to climb out of the water.

That's when her pub blew up.

Sammi was forcefully thrown back into the sea by the impact. She looked up through the rippling waves and saw the flames shooting into the dark sky. It wasn't until she started swimming that she felt a twinge in her shoulder.

She broke the surface and drew in a ragged breath, letting her burning lungs take in huge mouthfuls of air. People were running about, shouting as they tried to put out the fire so the rest of the street didn't go up in flames as well.

Sammi swam father down the dock away from her pub and climbed unsteadily up the ladder. Only then did she touch her shoulder and hiss in a breath at the contact.

She fisted her hands, only to bite back a curse. When

she glanced down at her palms, she found they were bleeding and raw from her journey down the pipes.

The adrenaline was putting off most of the pain, but that wouldn't last long. She needed to put some distance between her and Oban before the real pain slammed into her.

CHAPTER
ONE

"Hey, sis, it's me."

Sammi rolled her eyes at her too bright tone as she drove her fourth stolen car. That would never do. She had to make Jane think it was an unplanned—and quick—visit.

If her half-sister got wind that she was in trouble, Jane would try to help. And that's the last thing Sammi wanted her to do.

The truth was, she was desperate for some rest. True rest. Not the kind she'd been getting for the last four weeks where she slept for a few minutes at a time because there wasn't a place she felt safe enough to give into the sleep her body needed to help it heal.

"Jane. It's me," Sammi said with a big smile. It quickly faded as she groaned. "I don't know how to be casual. She's going to see right through me."

Nothing had been easy since she ran away from the docks. She didn't want to chance using her credit cards out of fear the Mob might find her. She couldn't even access her bank account for the same reason. At least Daniel's money had been where he had said it was. That alone was what kept her alive.

She resorted to stealing cars that would be better off becoming a pile of metal than a mode of transportation. But she shouldn't complain. The piece of shite she was driving now had managed to go fifty miles without breaking down.

"Just get me to Dreagan, P.O.S., and I won't be tempted to torch you."

As if to let Sammi know she wasn't in control, the 1982 Morris Marina sputtered before the engine revved again.

Sammi forgot about the car and went back to finding a way to greet Jane without causing suspicion. She had gone through two more scenarios when she slowed the car as she came upon the turn Jane had told her about over a year ago, when she'd invited Sammi to a party after her and Banan's wedding.

Another invitation she had made up an excuse not to attend. What kind of person was she to lie and not go to her sister's wedding party?

She didn't know how she remembered it since Sammi had been taking orders at the pub while on the phone, but somehow she had. And she was most thankful.

Slowing the car, Sammi drove down the long, winding road with two mountains flanking either side of her. On one occasion she thought she glimpsed someone in the dense trees, but it must have been her imagination, which was on overdrive since the incident, as she now called what had happened in Oban.

Sammi felt some of the tension leave her shoulders as Dreagan Industries came into view. Jane had invited her several times, but she had never been able to leave the pub. Now, as she took in the spectacular views, Sammi wished she would have.

She parked the car and wondered where the house was. Jane lived on the property, but all Sammi saw were buildings used for the production of Dreagan's famous whisky.

For several minutes, she simply took in the white buildings with their red roofs, the sounds of the stills, and the tranquility that seemed to be a part of Dreagan itself as she got out of the car.

Jane had said Dreagan consisted of sixty thousand acres. From what Sammi could see, there wasn't a part of it that didn't take her breath away.

For the first time in over a month, Sammi didn't feel that tickle on the back of her neck that said she was being watched. A look around confirmed that there were no suspicious cars, no dubious men who might be following her.

Maybe here she could finally relax. If for only a few days. She wouldn't stay longer and bring the Mob to Jane's doorstep. Not to mention Sammi was certain Jane's husband, Banan, wouldn't appreciate bad men coming and destroying the beauty of Dreagan.

"Are you here for the job too?"

Sammi jerked, startled by the voice behind her. The movement pulled at her slow-healing wound, causing her to hold her left arm against her side for protection. She turned to find a young woman with glossy black hair falling over one shoulder.

The woman's black eyes glanced down to Sammi's arm, concern clouding her face. "Are you hurt? Can I help?"

Sammi swallowed and gradually loosened her arm. "I'll be all right, thanks."

"You didn't see how pale you were."

"American, right?" Sammi asked to change the subject.

The woman briefly looked away as she nodded. "My mother was from South Africa while my father had dual citizenship with the US and Spain."

"How interesting." As a bartender, Sammi had a knack for spotting people who had a story to tell, and she could see that this woman was one of them.

She took a step closer and shoved her mane of midnight hair off her shoulder. "At least let me help you inside so you can collect yourself before the interview."

Sammi instantly liked the woman, American accent and all. There was just something about her that told Sammi the woman was as kindhearted as the day was long.

"I'm not here for the interview," Sammi told her.

The woman paused before she gave a little laugh. "Well, I'm glad. I really need this job."

"Forget any competition. You have a natural ability with people. If the job involves that, they'd be fools not to give it to you."

The woman beamed, her large black eyes crinkling in the corners. "Thank you. I'm Lily, by the way. Lily Ross."

"It's nice to meet you, Lily. I'm Sammi."

Lily moved her purse to her other shoulder, causing

the sleeve of her sweater that was at least three sizes too big to fall and reveal a huge bruise on her arm.

"That's one hell of a bruise," Sammi remarked.

Lily laughed as she moved her sweater over it. "I'm as clumsy as they come. A laundry basket filled high and shoes in the middle of the floor, and I'm a catastrophe waiting to happen."

"You should get along with Jane famously." Sammi made a mental note not to have anything breakable around when Lily and Jane were together.

Lily looked Sammi up and down, a frown marring her forehead. "You need to sit. Shall I help you inside?"

"I think I'll be okay, but I will walk with you."

They had only gone a few steps when Lily asked, "How do you know I would be a good fit to interact with people?"

"It's a gift I've always had. I can look at a person and just know. I used to run a pub, and I learned quickly that only certain kinds of people could work there and be successful. People like you."

Lily smiled as she looked at the ground.

When she didn't say anything, Sammi decided to push her a little. "What kind of job is it you'll be interviewing for?"

"Oh, it's nothing too important. It's for the gift shop."

"So you would be selling the Dreagan whisky to tourists?"

"I would."

"It's perfect for you. Be confident when you go in. And remember, it is an important job, because it'll be yours."

Lily's smile widened, making the charming girl into

a real beauty. She wore very little makeup and her clothes were too big and very drab.

Sammi, who had never had a close girlfriend, suddenly wanted to go shopping with Lily and outfit her with proper attire. Something bright and bold to complement her coloring. It must have been all the weeks hiding from the Mob that was messing with her mind.

It was a good thing they came to the door of the shop before Sammi did something really stupid and offer to bring Lily shopping, which might truly offend the woman. Lily might enjoy dressing as a sixty-year-old. Some women were just like that.

Despite her attire, Lily was a striking beauty with her black hair, black eyes, and mocha skin. The same couldn't be said for her, but Sammi had learned to work with her stubborn hair and pale complexion early in life, thanks to her mother.

As soon as they entered the shop, Sammi looked around at the shelves that covered the walls and were filled with bottles of Dreagan whisky.

Some of the glass bottles where in small, colored casks denoting an added flavor in the whisky, while others were in the tall, rounded tins. There were other bottles that where about half the size, and still others that looked like some kind of cream liquor.

At the far back wall was shelving enclosed in glass with the bottles proudly displayed.

"Those would be the fifty-year-old scotches, and ones that are even older. They're highly prized by collectors, and highly priced as well," Lily said.

A woman with long, brunette hair with the top half

pulled away from her face came around the counter and smiled at Lily. "You know your whisky."

Lily turned to the woman and straightened her shoulders. "I'd like to think I do. I was called in for the interview."

"Ah," the woman said as she glanced behind her to the clipboard. "You must be Lilliana Ross."

"Lily, please," she said and held out her hand.

The woman took it and smiled. "I'm Cassie. Why don't we go to the back and talk?"

Sammi watched the two Americans interact and recognized by Cassie's mannerisms that she liked Lily. If Sammi was a betting person, she'd wager a hefty sum that Lily walked out with the job.

"Of course," Lily said.

Cassie's dark eyes lifted to Sammi. "Can I help you with anything?"

"Actually, I hope you can. I'm looking for Jane."

"Jane?" Cassie repeated, some of the spark gone from her eyes.

Sammi wasn't offended. Jane had mentioned how close everyone was at Dreagan, and now that she thought of it, she recalled Jane mentioning a Cassie.

"I'm Sammi Miller, Ja—"

"Jane's half-sister," Cassie finished for her with a kind nod. "Let me call the house and get her over here. She'll be so pleased to see you."

Sammi wasn't so sure of that, but she needed at least a day of rest and to see to her wound again. It felt as if it were becoming infected.

She could barely move her arm now. Dressing and

showering was becoming a chore with only one arm, not to mention trying to wash her hair.

Before Cassie made the phone call, she stuck her head around the corner and said something to whoever was there. While she called the house, a tall man with faded jeans riding low on trim hips and a burgundy tee with a dragon design mimicking a tribal tattoo came walking into the shop.

It was hard to tell how long his dark hair was because he had it pulled back in a queue, but his aqua eyes glanced at Sammi before they landed on Lily. After a hesitation, in which he took in every inch of the petite woman, he looked away and walked around the counter to a case of whisky waiting to be stocked on the shelves.

Sammi's gaze turned to Lily to find she was staring at the man as if he were the pot of gold at the end of a rainbow. Granted, he was drool-worthy, but Sammi had seen many men like him during her days at the pub. They were gorgeous, and most of them knew it. To those men, females were meant for entertainment and nothing more.

But by the way Lily couldn't look away from him, Sammi was going to have to caution her. Then she realized that maybe she shouldn't. Everyone needed to fall in love at least once, and everyone needed to have their heart broken once. That way, when love came again, it was all the sweeter.

At least that's what her mum had always said. Sammi hadn't given that piece of advice a try. Oh, she'd had her heart broken when she was a teenager, but she hadn't fallen in love.

And she never would.

Cassie hung up the phone and met Sammi's eyes. "Jane is on her way. Lily, why don't we go in the back?"

Sammi gave Lily a wink of encouragement, and then found herself alone with the man.

"So you're Samantha," he said without looking at her. She turned toward him fully and glared, not that he saw it. He kept stocking the whisky as if he hadn't just spoken to her. "I prefer Sammi."

"You prefer a male name?"

"Do you prefer to walk around holding your twig and berries after I kick you?"

He paused. Then he looked at her over his shoulder, a wide smile upon his lips. "I thought you'd be more like Jane."

"Quiet and demure, or klutzy?"

"Either. Both."

"Leave her alone, Rhys," Jane said as she let the door close behind her, though there was no censure in her tone. "Sammi manages to stay upright. As for demure, I think she's brilliant just as she is."

Sammi hated when Jane said things like that because it always made her eyes prick with tears. She looked into Jane's amber eyes and knew everything would be all right.

"I'm so glad you're here," Jane said and rushed to her.

Sammi tried not to grimace when Jane hugged her, but she didn't hide it quickly enough. Jane pulled back at the same time Rhys faced her.

Jane's gaze silently probed her for several minutes before she asked, "What happened?"

"Nothing. Why? Can't I come see my half-sister?"

"Absolutely," Jane said, her gaze still searching. "It's just . . . well, to put it bluntly, you haven't."

Sammi cringed. "I know. I'm sorry. I wanted to take a few days and see you. If you aren't busy, that is."

"Not at all. I'm beyond happy that you're here. Are you sure everything is all right?" she asked again.

Sammi forced a laugh. "Of course it is. Why would you keep asking that?"

"You've lost weight, not that you had a lot to lose to begin with. You've got dark circles under your eyes too, and you're holding your left arm oddly. And is that blood coming through your shirt near your shoulder?"

Suddenly, the past four weeks slammed into Sammi. Or maybe it was because she was finally on Dreagan—Jane had let it slip that it was one of the most heavily guarded areas in Scotland—and felt safe enough to let down her guard.

Either way, it was as though her body had simply reached its limit. Sammi could barely hold her eyes open she was so exhausted. She grabbed the counter to keep on her feet and her fatigue at bay while she searched her mind to come up with some lie.

But she didn't want to lie anymore, not to Jane. She couldn't tell them the truth, but she could give them something. "It's a small wound, and it's better if you don't know anything. I just need a place to stay for the night."

"You'll stay longer," Jane stated with a nod.

But Sammi was already shaking her head. "No."

"Banan, tell her," Jane said.

Banan's tall form walked around the counter to Jane. Sammi hadn't even known he had entered the shop. He stood behind Jane, his hands on her shoulders as his gray eyes met Sammi's. Whereas Rhys's hair was long, Banan kept his dark brown locks cut short.

"Jane is right. You need to stay," Banan said.

Sammi knew it was useless to argue now. She would be up early and gone before they knew it. Now that she knew she was at Dreagan and could stay, she could barely keep upright. Her stomach growled, her wound ached, and her eyes fought to stay open.

"Let's get you to the house," Jane said as she turned Sammi and guided her to the door. "Banan will get your things. Once you're fed and rested, I want you to tell me what's going on. I can help."

Sammi kept her gaze straight ahead and put one foot in front of the other by sheer will alone. She refused to collapse. There was nothing Jane could say that would convince Sammi to tell her any of her troubles. The less Jane and Banan knew, the better.

At least that's what she prayed for.

CHAPTER
TWO

Tristan strode angrily from the mountain. For weeks, he had been hounded by Phelan who repeatedly asked whether he remembered anything before he had become a Dragon King.

No matter how many questions Phelan asked, no matter how many stories Phelan told of him and his twin, Ian, Tristan remembered nothing of it.

There was no denying he was an exact replica of Ian Kerr based on the photos he'd been shown, but whatever connection Ian and Duncan shared hadn't been passed on to him. Duncan had been killed, but Phelan said Ian had heard Duncan's voice in his head afterward.

Maybe Duncan had died, his soul at least. Tristan had his body, but a new soul. He didn't know, and he was tired of everyone pestering him about it.

"Tristan, wait," Laith said as he hurried to catch up. "We're all just trying to help."

Tristan came to an abrupt halt and turned to Laith to look into the Dragon King's eyes that were the color of

gunmetal. "Why is it difficult for everyone to comprehend that there is nothing in here," he said and punched
a finger against the side of his head, "about Duncan
Kerr? My memories began when I woke up in the snow,
naked and holding a sword two years ago."

"Because there's no denying you are Ian's twin,
mate. We just want to help."

Tristan put his hands on his hips and let out an exasperated sigh. He looked around him, at the stark,
rugged beauty of Scotland and felt some of the tension
ease from him. There had never been any doubt he
was a Scot. He had the brogue, but it was more than
that. Scotland was in his soul, in the very fiber of his
being.

"What if there are no memories of Duncan?"

Laith shrugged. "Then there's no'. We move on."

"And if there are memories, and they're just buried?"
he asked hesitantly, almost afraid to voice what had
plagued him since he'd learned who Ian was.

"If the memories are there, it's up to you whether
you want them to come forth, Tristan. They may stay
hidden because you are no' ready. Or, like you've said,
they may no' even be there."

"I doona want to see Ian."

"You can no' run from him forever."

Tristan rubbed the back of his neck. "I just doona
want to see the discouraged look in his eyes. I know
what he wants, but I can no' give it to him."

Laith's next words were stopped when they spotted
Banan and Jane leading a woman to the manor. The
woman wasn't quite as tall as Jane, and her wavy, sandy-
colored hair lifted off her shoulders in the breeze.

The woman pushed her bangs out of her eyes, which caused her not to see Duke come bounding around the house.

The Great Dane stopped next to her, but his sheer size caused her to have to quickly regain her balance when the dog leaned against her. That's when Tristan saw her wince and protect her left arm by holding it tightly against her.

"Who is that?" Tristan asked.

Laith watched them a few more seconds before he said, "I gather by the way Jane is fussing that she's Sammi, Jane's half-sister."

While Banan took Duke's collar, Jane ushered Sammi into the house. Just before Sammi walked in, her head turned and she looked right at Tristan with her powder-blue eyes. It was like a punch in the gut.

Startling, disconcerting.

Amazing.

The surprising connection that seemed to zip between them left him pitching, tumbling. Plunging.

And he wanted more. So very much more.

"Tristan?"

He pulled his gaze away from the now-empty doorway and looked at Laith. "What?"

"Whatever you're thinking involving Sammi, I wouldna advise it."

Tristan frowned and glanced at the house, wondering what kind of injury Sammi had. "What do you mean?"

"Forget it." Laith gave a shake of his head, a wry smile upon his lips. "I've got to see what happens next. Come on. Let's go meet Sammi."

The fact that Tristan wanted a closer look at the

woman should have been enough to make him walk the other way. He was just getting ensconced in his life at Dreagan. Phelan and the other Warriors were complicating things enough. Tristan certainly didn't need a woman added to the mix.

Yet he followed Laith into the manor. The sound of voices came from the kitchen. As they stopped at the doorway of the kitchen they saw Elena pouring some tea and Jane fixing a sandwich while Sammi sat at the table desperately trying to stay awake.

He found his gaze drawn to her no matter how hard he tried to look away. Even in profile, she was beautiful with her long, graceful neck and her fall of sandy-colored hair about her. She sat tall and straight in the chair, as if it was as natural as breathing.

Tristan saw her fall asleep twice and jerk awake both times. The third time, she listed to the right. He rushed to her, grabbing her just before she hit the floor. Jane, Elena, and Banan turned as one from whatever they were doing to gawk at him.

He gazed down at the woman who slept in his arms, completely taken unawares as he looked into her oval face. Her cheekbones were incredibly high, her nose small, and her lips as decadent as sin.

Even in sleep, she made his body hunger to know her, his lips crave to taste her, and his hands ache to caress her. Desire shot through him like lightning, making him burn.

Making him yearn.

Tristan moved a strand of her hair out of her lashes and wished she would open her eyes so he could look into their cool color once more.

Then he remembered where he was, and just who he was holding. "I think the food is going to have to wait."

"I knew she looked tired," Jane said, a frown marring her forehead.

Tristan easily shifted Sammi's body into his arms and stood. "She's too skinny."

"I knew she had lost weight too," Jane said with a shake of her head. Then she looked at Banan. "I think she's in some real trouble."

"We'll get it out of her," Banan promised.

Tristan was careful not to touch Sammi's left arm as more blood seeped through her shirt. "What about her injury?"

Banan let out a string of curses as he walked from the kitchen. "She said it was nothing. Bring her, Tristan."

Jane was at his heels, tripping twice, as he followed Banan up the stairs. Despite both of them watching him like hawks, Tristan found his gaze drawn again and again to the woman in his arms.

Her hair, a unique mixture of blond and light brown, hung over his arm, the waves teasing him to touch them. Her exhaustion and injury worried him that someone had pushed her to her limits, and he wanted to know who had done that to her. And why.

Her jeans hung too loosely on her already small frame. The lime green collared pullover looked as if it had once fit her to perfection but now was just a little baggy.

Banan threw open a door to one of the rooms on the second floor and pulled back the covers on the bed as Tristan walked inside. Gently he laid Sammi down, and not once did she even stir.

"What's happened to her?" Jane asked in a soft, worry-filled voice. "That's not the Sammi we saw four months ago."

Across the bed Banan caught Tristan's gaze and gave a slight nod. Tristan leaned down and gently lifted her sleeve and saw the ugly, puss-filled wound.

"We need her shirt off," Tristan said as he looked at Jane and Banan.

Jane was quick to find scissors and cut the shirt off her sister. That's when they got their first good view of the wound.

"That's from a gunshot." Banan's voice was laced with fury and retribution.

Jane walked until she stood beside Tristan and gently touched Sammi's wound. Jane's eyes lifted to Banan. "I think it's infected."

"The stitching isna professional," Tristan remarked. Then he frowned as he studied the uneven sutures. "It almost looks as if Sammi did them herself."

Banan clenched his jaw. "She's exhausted, starving, driving a car that isna hers, and she's injured. Whatever secret she has, she willna give it up easily."

"And I'm not going to give up until my sister is safe," Jane said, straightening and daring her husband to argue.

Banan quickly lifted his hands. "I'm just stating a fact, my love. We'll make sure that no matter what, she is taken care of."

"We need Con to heal her," Jane stated.

Before Banan could argue, Tristan said, "If Sammi doesna know who we are, it might be better if we clean this as best we can and only use Con as a last resort.

After the fiasco with Denae and Kellan, the less Sammi knows, the better."

"I agree," Banan said.

Jane rolled her eyes, but her concern was palpable. "Let's just get the wound seen to immediately."

Tristan pulled the chair from the corner closer to the bed. "Get me some scissors, hot water, bandages, and I'll need thread and a needle to stitch it again."

"That's it?" Jane cried. "She needs medicine. It's infected."

Banan took Jane's hand and dragged her to the door. "We willna know the extent of the infection until we remove the stitches that are already there."

"Right, right," Jane said. She turned and only missed running into the door because Banan guided her the other way.

It wasn't long before Jane returned with an armload of supplies. She took two steps into the room and tripped on the corner of the rug, landing hard on her knee, but she didn't drop a single thing.

Tristan took the scalpel, rubbing alcohol, cotton balls, bandages, and needle and thread and laid them out on the bed. Banan then walked in with a pitcher of hot water that he poured into a bowl and set on the table next to Tristan.

Tristan tried not to look at the white satin bra cradling Sammi's breasts, but he couldn't help but notice the firm mounds—or ignore the hunger that arose in his body.

Instead, he concentrated on what he was about to do. Her breathing was even, even if the wound looked as if it were causing her an extreme amount of discomfort.

He cleared his throat when Banan caught him staring at her breasts once more. Tristan took the scalpel and carefully cut the crude stitches. Sammi had managed to stop the bleeding, but that didn't mean she had gotten the bullet out.

That thought caused Tristan to gently turn her onto her right side to make sure there wasn't a second wound, and just as he suspected, there wasn't.

"The bullet may still be inside her," he told Jane.

Banan stalked to the doorway and gave a loud whistle. Within seconds Darius, Laith, and Ryder came into the room. Tristan was intent on removing the stitches while Ryder lifted a light over him and held it there so he could see.

With the stitches removed, Tristan carefully prodded the abrasion. Sammi shifted away from him. Darius grabbed her ankles while Banan knelt on the other side of the bed prepared to hold down her right side while Laith grabbed her left arm.

Tristan looked to Jane. "I've never dug out a bullet."

"None of us have," Banan said. "You doona have a choice since Kellan isna here. Get to it."

Tristan took a deep breath and probed farther into the wound. Sammi once more tried to pull away, but she was held down. Moving as quickly as he could, Tristan prodded for the slug with tweezers while Jane wiped away the blood.

Sweat beaded his forehead the longer it took and the more pain he was causing Sammi. Then the tweezers hit something metallic. It didn't take long for him to realize the bullet was imbedded in her shoulder bone.

Tristan wiped his forehead with his arm and glanced at Sammi's face. She was pale, but at least she hadn't woken. Who had done this to her? Who would want to hurt someone so beautiful?

He rotated his shoulder to stretch it and focused on the slug. It seemed to take eons before he finally got it to loosen. With one final tug, he felt it give.

"Got it," Tristan said as he pulled the bullet out and held it up for everyone to see.

He looked at Sammi to find her powder blue eyes open and watching him. Time halted, froze as they stared at each other. Then her lids closed, breaking whatever hold she had over him.

There was no moment to consider his reaction as Tristan handed the bullet to Laith and set about cleaning the wound and draining away the puss so he could stitch it again.

With the last thread in place, Tristan tied it in a knot and cut it. Ryder clapped him on the shoulder and moved away after he set aside the light.

Tristan sat back and saw the blood on his hands. Suddenly, an image of those same hands covered in blood flashed in his mind, but his skin had been pale blue with long blue claws extending from his fingers.

As quickly as the image appeared, it vanished, leaving Tristan with an odd feeling in his gut. He tried to forget it, but he didn't think he would ever be able to. Was it a vision from his past, the past everyone claimed was of Duncan Kerr?

"Good job," Banan said.

Laith held out the bullet after he had cleaned and dried it. "I think you all need to see this."

Ryder took the mangled slug and looked at it. "There's something etched on it."

"What is it?" Tristan asked.

Banan took it next and after looking at it a moment walked out of the room only to return with a magnifying glass. He held it over the bullet for a minute.

"This can no' be," he mumbled.

Jane wiped Sammi's brow with a damp cloth. "What is it?"

The bullet and magnifying glass were passed to each of them until Tristan finally got to see. He saw what was obviously a dragon etched into the metal.

"What does this mean?" he asked.

Laith snorted. "It means we're fucked."

"It means Ulrik. It means that he has revenge in mind," Darius said.

CHAPTER
THREE

Sammi stared at the tray across her lap and tried to ignore her sister's determined glare. Sammi awoke feeling rested and without her body aching as it had for the past month.

That's when Jane explained she had fallen unconscious at the kitchen table. They had brought her upstairs and found the wound. Apparently she had someone named Tristan to thank for removing the bullet.

It wasn't like she had left it in on purpose. She hadn't even known it was a bullet. She'd thought it had been something from the blast.

They had blown up her pub. They had killed Daniel. And they had tried to kill her.

She didn't feel the need to push these bad men to see how far they would go, because she knew firsthand how malicious and cruel they were. That kind of fear, that kind of terror was now a part of her. Everything she looked at was a potential threat, as was everyone.

It had changed her, and not for the better.

"Sammi, please," Jane begged.

Jane had been pressing her for answers for the past thirty minutes. Maybe Sammi should have pretended not to feel well. It might have put Jane off for a little while. Enough so that she could leave Dreagan while they slept.

"I know you mean well, and that you want to help. Please trust me when I say it's better if you don't know," Sammi finally said as she stirred the sugar in her tea.

Jane shook her head, her short auburn hair swaying against her cheeks. "Screw that," she said, her American accent taking on a hard note. "I'm your sister. I can help."

"Half-sister," Sammi corrected and then immediately regretted it when she saw the hurt look in Jane's eyes.

"Half, whole. It doesn't matter. We're family. You came here for help."

Sammi let the hot tea slide down her throat. Her mother had always said tea could help anything. How Sammi wished that were true. Nothing could help her now. It was only a matter of time before the Mob caught up with her.

If she hadn't been wounded, if she had been rested, the last place she would have brought her troubles was to Jane's door. She'd put her sister and everyone at Dreagan in the path of a madman who had no problems killing anyone who got in his way.

"I shouldn't have come," Sammi said as she set her cup down.

Jane tucked her hair behind an ear. "But you did. You knew you would be safe here."

It was on the tip of Sammi's tongue to tell Jane

everything. She was so tired of carrying such a burden alone, but if Jane and the others knew, it would only put them in danger. No matter how tired Sammi was, she couldn't do that to them.

Jane had been so kind and giving, even when Sammi had tried to keep her distance. Jane hadn't given up though. She had taken her time and slowly gotten to know Sammi with phone calls, e-mails, texts, and even visits to the pub.

There was kindness and acceptance in Jane's amber eyes and it took everything Sammi had to keep her secret buried deep. She had come to Dreagan because she knew Jane would help. It had been selfish and stupid, and Sammi bemoaned her weakness.

She had just been so tired of being alone, of dealing with everything alone.

However, she knew Jane well enough to know she was like a dog with a bone. Jane wouldn't let it go until she got some kind of explanation. So, Sammi decided to give her one.

"There was an accident at the pub. I was hurt, and I thought I could take care of it myself," she said with a shrug. "It was stupid not to get it seen to properly. I'm much better now, so I'll return to the pub this afternoon."

"That might be difficult," came a deep, sexy voice from the doorway.

Sammi's head swung around to the doorway to see Banan and another man. Her stomach plummeted to her feet, because Sammi had been sure those shrewd, intoxicating, dark, velvet brown eyes had been nothing more than a dream.

But as she found herself sinking, falling, drowning into them, Sammi was elated to discover the eyes—and the man—hadn't been a figment of her imagination.

She drank in the very masculine, very virile man before her. Without knowing anything about him, she instinctively knew he was dangerous and seductive, wild and alluring.

Even as she silently cautioned herself, she was inexplicably drawn to him. The attraction was immediate and alarming the same time it was captivating and enticing.

She wanted to run her fingers through his light brown hair streaked with gold that hung thick and glossy just past his shoulders. Brows the same pale brown slashed over his eyes. He was clean-shaven, giving notice to his strong jaw and chin.

He wore a shirt that molded to his broad shoulders. His arms were crossed, causing his muscles to bulge against skin kissed by the sun.

Her eyes drifted lower to his jeans hanging low on his narrow hips and encasing his long legs close enough she could sense they were as corded with muscle as the rest of him.

He was a walking fantasy. In all her life, Sammi had never seen anyone as drop-dead gorgeous as the man staring at her now. She had wanted to know him when her fever-induced mind had thought he was a dream, but now . . . now she knew to get close to him, to know him might put the heart she had guarded so well into peril.

"Sammi?"

She jerked at Banan's voice but couldn't pull her gaze away from his companion. For long seconds his dark eyes held hers until she looked away. Only to find Jane watching her peculiarly.

"What?" she asked Jane.

Banan walked into the room and came to stand beside Jane's chair. "Did you no' hear Tristan?"

Tristan. The name fit the man to perfection, just as his clothes did. Had he spoken? Oh, yes, he had. That's what had drawn her attention. His amazing, captivating voice that made her stomach flutter with exhilaration.

But what had he said?

Then she remembered. Sammi idly turned her teacup around on the tray. She was being cornered in her lie, a lie she'd constructed to protect her sister.

"Sammi, please," Jane urged. "Why would it be impossible for you to return to the pub?"

"I told you there was an accident." Sammi prayed they left it at that and didn't probe further.

Jane blew out a harsh breath. "What kind of accident? What happened?"

Finally, she looked at her sister. "Leave it, Jane."

"You don't trust me." Jane's words were said in a whisper, the hurt in them slamming into Sammi like fists.

Banan pulled Jane up and walked her to the door whispering something in her ear. After a minute she nodded and walked away. Banan then closed the door, leaving Sammi alone with him and Tristan.

By the look on Banan's face when he turned back to her, Sammi knew the interrogation was about to begin.

"Don't even try," she said before he could open his

mouth. "There's nothing to tell other than what I've already said."

"You're no' a verra good liar," Banan said.

"I'm actually very good." Why it offended her that he said she wasn't, Sammi didn't know. All she needed was a little more time to rest, and then she would be gone.

Tristan drew in a deep breath. "The pub is gone. There's nothing left."

As if she didn't know that. She had been there. Felt the heat of the fire, suffered the impact of the blast.

Experienced the hate of it all.

When she didn't reply, Banan briefly squeezed his eyes shut. "Your pub is gone. You were shot. That piece of shite you drove up in isna your car, Sammi. It doesna take a genius to figure out something is going on."

Damn but she'd thought she could pull something over on them. It had been naïve and foolish to think they would believe her lies. They left her little choice though. "I'm not telling you anything to keep you all safe. It was wrong of me to come—"

"But you did," Banan interrupted angrily.

Sammi deserved his ire, but she wasn't going to give in. "I knew my wound was getting worse. I needed to rest, and I knew Jane would help."

A muscle ticked dangerously along Banan's jaw. "Aye. You're her family."

"Why no' go to the hospital?" Tristan asked.

Sammi felt his dark gaze on her and shivered. His voice, just like his gaze, was electric, charged. Thrilling. She would definitely have to keep her distance from him.

"I couldn't chance it," she admitted.

Banan took the seat Jane had vacated and leaned his forearms upon his thighs. The frown he wore no longer held anger, but concern. "Who is after you, Sammi?"

"Bad people. Very bad people." God, why had she let that slip? It wasn't too much, at least, and as Banan had mentioned, an idiot could've figured that out. Still, she shouldn't have told him.

Tristan walked to the foot of the bed and braced his hands on the iron footboard. "How long have you been running from them?"

They were asking such simple questions, but if she wasn't careful, they would get it all out of her piece by piece. "A while."

Banan exchanged a look with Tristan. "Vague answers again."

"It took verra little to discover what happened to your pub," Tristan said. "Why did you no' want Jane to know that it was blown up and that your business partner is missing?"

Sammi squeezed her eyes shut. Poor Daniel. She'd known he was dead, but hearing it brought a fresh wave of pain. Even though Daniel had brought it on himself by being involved with such people.

"Where is Daniel?" Banan asked. "You doona seem the type of woman to blow up your own pub because your ex-lover pissed you off."

Sammi's eyes flew open as she glared at Banan. "Daniel was my friend and had a good head for business. He made me money."

"Did you know he had spent some time in jail for petty crimes?" Tristan asked.

She glanced at him but couldn't look in his eyes. "Not at first. Only once we realized we made better friends than lovers. He told me about his past, but he said he had changed."

Banan sat back, causing the chair to creak. "Daniel lied, did he no'?"

"Yes." And that's all she would tell them. Let them dig into Daniel's past or hers. She wasn't going to say any more, and the first chance she got, she was leaving. The more distance she put between her and Jane, the better.

"You should eat," Tristan said into the silence.

Sammi looked at the tray loaded with fruit, meats, bread, and fried eggs that were now cold. She had been famished when Jane brought in the food, but then the questions had begun.

"When was the last time you had a good meal?" Banan asked.

Sammi scrunched up her face and looked at him. "What's that supposed to mean?"

"You're skin and bones. No' the way Jane and I last saw you."

"Maybe I'm on a diet," she said with a shrug, hoping he bought it and had forgotten how much she loved junk food.

Banan gave a loud snort, telling her he knew she lied.

"Fine," she said. "It's only been a day since my last meal."

"You've been here three," Tristan said.

No. That couldn't be. The last time she had remained at one place for longer than two days, the Mob had come close to catching her. She had learned the hard way to stay on the move and talk to as few people as she could.

It was always the tingle at the back of her neck that alerted her she needed to move on. That tingle was back, something she hadn't expected while at Dreagan.

Then again, she hadn't intended to stay but one night. What had she done? What had she brought to Jane?

The dread, the anxiety was like acid churning in her stomach, making her sick.

"Sammi?" Banan said as he jumped up and came to stand beside her, his hand on her arm. "What is it?"

"I have to go," she said and tried to lift the tray off her. Her shoulder twinged, the stitches pulling at her effort.

Tristan was immediately at her other side. "Easy," he said and took the tray. "You'll bust the stitches."

Even with the tray gone, she couldn't leave the bed because Banan kept ahold of her arm. Then Tristan was back, boxing her in.

"You don't understand," she cried. "If they come, they'll destroy it as they've destroyed my life!"

She was panting from the exertion, sweat dotting her skin. Something warm and wet ran down her arm, but she was too upset to worry about it.

Sammi shoved the covers aside and swung her legs over the side, barely noting that she was in a Victoria's Secret cotton T-shirt gown that must belong to Jane.

Tristan's hands came down on her shoulders and held her steady as he knelt beside the bed. "You're bleeding."

"I have to leave."

"Why?"

Sammi shook her head. It was as if her thoughts were muddled, as if sleep once more weighed her down. "They'll come for me. They always come for me."

"Who?" he persisted.

Sammi's already weak body was fast losing what little energy she had. Tears stung her eyes as frustration filled her. She was so tired, and they kept asking questions. She couldn't remember what she had told them and what she hadn't. The burden of it all pressed down on her, sinking her further and further into a place she knew she'd never come back from.

She shoved him aside and got to her feet. He was standing before her once more, blocking her way and forcing her to look at him. His hands were large and held her carefully but securely in front of him.

He watched her cautiously, as if studying her. In his eyes she saw truth and understanding. If anyone could help her, it just might be Tristan.

If she dared to tell him.

He smoothed a lock of hair away from her face, his large hand gentle and reassuring. It would be so good to let someone else carry her burdens for a while. She was just so . . . tired.

"Sammi, who is after you?" he urged, his voice going deeper, smoother.

It was almost as if his voice was inside her head. "I don't know who they are exactly."

He gave a nod, a slight lift to the corner of his lips. "Tell me what you do know. Let me help."

She shook her head. Sammi didn't know how she kept from telling him everything. In her mind she recounted the entire incident.

It was a relief actually. To share her burden within her mind helped more than she had realized. She should have done it sooner.

"It's all right." Tristan's thumbs were slowly rubbing her arms in circles. It was such a small movement, but it was comforting. His touch soothed her, calmed her.

Reassured her.

How could she fight something that felt so good? Her dream man was touching her, talking to her in his sexy voice. If only she was brave enough to tell them all she knew. If only she had the strength to stay on her feet for more than two seconds.

She didn't resist when he pushed her back onto the bed. His hands were quick and concise as he pulled up her sleeve and wiped away the blood before replacing the bandage.

Then she was once more beneath the covers. As soon as she was able, she would leave, she told herself as her eyes grew heavy. It was the only option left to her.

"I doona think she even knows she told you," Banan said.

Tristan gazed at Sammi. The panic and fear he had seen in her eyes left him cold. "Nay, she didna."

"How did you do it?"

He had no idea. Something inside him urged him to push Sammi, but even as he did it, he could feel his magic probe into her mind. Now he knew the magic he had as a Dragon King—he could make people tell him whatever he wanted.

Sammi wouldn't appreciate it. If she ever found out.

Tristan shrugged. "It just happened."

"Ah," Banan said with a nod of understanding.

Tristan rubbed a strand of her hair between his fingers. He wanted to pull her into his arms and hold her. He wanted to shelter her from the people who dared to go after her.

He looked up to find Banan watching him. Tristan released Sammi's hair but didn't step away from the bed.

"Sammi is Jane's sister," Banan said. "Doona trifle with her."

"In other words, stay away?"

Banan walked around the bed to stand beside him. "I'm just asking that you no' mess with her if you need to ease your cock. Find another woman for that."

Tristan made himself look away from her and into Banan's face as he calmly changed the subject. "Our initial check showed she hasna used her credit cards, mobile, or accessed her bank in a month."

"The pub was destroyed a month ago. That means she's been out there on her own this entire time."

"What has she been living off of?"

"By how skinny she is, I'm betting she missed quite a few meals." The longer Tristan thought of all Sammi had told him, the angrier he got. "I'd like to meet the assholes who blew up her pub and shot at her."

"Me as well. Want to help me look for them?" Banan asked with a cheeky grin.

"I'd like nothing better. Then I'll show them they should pick on someone their own size."

"And if it's Ulrik?"

"We'll put him in his place once and for all."

CHAPTER
FOUR

Sammi's eyes snapped open. For a minute she simply stared at the wall. She couldn't remember the last time she had felt so rested. It wasn't just her mind either. Her body was better as well. Her shoulder still ached, but it wasn't the constant pain of before.

She rolled onto her other side to see the clock read 5:03 a.m. in soft green light. Sammi jumped out of bed and shoved aside the curtains to see the sky already lightening.

It would be dawn soon. She could easily slip out of the manor to her car and leave before anyone woke. It wasn't exactly the nice thing to do, but she wasn't trying to be nice.

She was trying to keep her sister and those at Dreagan safe.

Sammi jerked off the nightshirt as she strode into the bathroom and turned on the shower. A quick dig in her purse produced a clip that she used to secure her hair before she stepped into the spray of the hot water.

Careful not to get her stitches too wet, Sammi hurriedly showered. She dried off just as quickly and only then wondered where her clothes were.

She walked out of the bathroom and let out a sigh when she spotted her jeans and several shirts stacked neatly on a chair. Not wasting another minute, she dressed and ran her fingers through her hair.

It didn't really matter what she looked like while running for her life. Sammi stared at her reflection in the mirror and hated the person she had become.

At least she had managed to keep the truth from spilling out and involving Jane and the others more than they already were.

Her life hadn't exactly been perfect, but she'd had the pub and a decent living. She might have been lonely and actually contemplating Internet dating, but it was a far cry from where she was now.

How had she not known Daniel had been involved with such people? Was the idea of making money so appealing that anything that might have caught her attention had been pushed to the back of her mind?

If only she'd seen who he really was. Maybe then she would have fired him instead of getting involved in such a fiasco.

With Daniel's lie of her being out of town when the Mob had paid a visit to her pub, they knew she was alive. So there was no rest for her. The Mob would continue searching, waiting for her to screw up somehow so they could find her.

In all the time she had known Daniel, she'd never seen him so scared. He hadn't been the wisest when it

came to getting involved with the wrong people, but
he had always managed to talk his way out of any situation.

Until this last time.

Sammi could still hear the leader's voice in her head.
And it gave her chills of dread every time.

With a shake of her head, she turned away from the
mirror and walked to the door. Slowly, she turned the
knob without making a sound and inched it open.

When she didn't see anyone standing across from
her door, she looked to the left and then the right. There
wasn't a soul in sight, just as she'd hoped.

Getting out of the massive house, however, was going to be another matter entirely. Sammi kept to one
side of the long corridor and half-ran, half-walked to
the left, only to come to a wall.

With no other choice, she turned and started back
the other way. It didn't take her long to find the stairs.
By the time she reached the bottom floor, her breath
was coming in great gasps.

Sammi paused as she tried to remember how Jane
had brought her into the manor. It wasn't from the front
door. Cautiously, she moved from room to room until
she finally located the kitchen.

Just as she was about to walk into the room, she spotted a man pouring two mugs of coffee. Sammi hastily
plastered herself against the wall and prayed he didn't
see her.

She ducked behind a tall plant seconds before the
man walked out whistling some nameless tune. Sammi
released the breath she'd been holding.

After counting to five, she stood and ran into the kitchen. The smell of the coffee was tempting, but she ignored it as she slipped out of the manor.

A quick look around showed she was alone. She wanted to run to her car, but that would only cause suspicion. So, with great effort, she kept her pace to a fast walk until she passed a row of tall, thick hedges and she saw the distillery and guest parking.

Sammi ran the last bit to the stolen car, sliding on the gravel when she grabbed the door handle. She managed to stay on her feet and yanked the door open. Once she was behind the wheel she cast another glance around.

In the fields off to her right she could see men releasing sheared sheep loose from their pens. Her luck was holding because other than that, there was no one else about.

She didn't give it another thought as she started the car and put it in reverse. In no time she was driving down the long drive and she let Dreagan grow smaller in her rearview mirror.

"Are you sure this is the way to handle this?" Jane asked Banan for the third time that morning.

"Aye, love."

Tristan didn't take his eyes off the faded red of the car as Sammi drove away. "She wanted to leave last night. Had I not forced her to sleep, she would have. Now at least we're prepared to follow her."

Jane blew out a frustrated breath. "She'll never forgive us."

"Would you rather have her forgiveness or have her

alive?" Banan asked. "Because that's what it's going to come to. The Mob is after her, love."

Tristan rubbed his jaw. "I find it verra concerning that there is another woman on Dreagan running from someone."

"That does seem odd," Jane replied with a frown. "You don't think the Dark Fae have anything to do with this, do you?"

Tristan and Banan exchanged a look.

Banan took Jane's hand in his. "At this point, anything is possible. We willna know until we see if anyone is following her."

"Just be careful. Both of you," Jane added. She gave Banan a kiss and wrapped her arms around his neck as she held him to her. They stayed like that for several minutes.

Then, to Tristan's surprise, Jane hugged him. "Keep my sister alive."

"I will." He stepped away and walked to the waiting BMW 640i Coupe.

A moment later Banan slid behind the wheel and started the car. He gave Jane a wave as they pulled away. "She'll never forgive me if anything happens to Sammi."

"We willna let anything happen to her." Tristan felt Banan's gaze on him.

It wasn't just that Sammi was in trouble that made Tristan jump to protect her. She was Jane and Banan's family, which meant that even though Sammi had no idea they were Dragon Kings, she was also a part of their family.

Unbidden, the image of hands the color of pale blue

and long claws covered in blood flashed in his head. Tristan hadn't allowed himself to consider why that image suddenly appeared or the meaning behind it.

He knew the Warriors' skin changed the color of the primeval god within them when they called the god forth. Tristan also knew they had claws.

Had it been a flash from his past? Were there memories there as Laith had suggested, and they were just repressed? If so, what had he done to let one out?

More importantly, did he want more?

In some ways, it was easier to continue on as he was, without the memories of a past life as Duncan Kerr, an immortal Warrior with a god locked inside him.

Then there was Ian. Duncan's identical twin brother.

So far, Ian hadn't come to Dreagan or attempted to contact him, but Tristan knew it was only a matter of time until he did. Then what?

"That's a deep frown you're wearing," Banan said.

Tristan relaxed his features and shrugged. "There's a lot to think about."

"Why do I have the feeling you are no' referring to Sammi and her troubles, but instead to a certain Warrior named Ian?"

"Is it that obvious?"

Banan shook his head as he glanced at the screen on the dash where a red light was flashing, showing them where Sammi was, thanks to their putting a tracking device on her car obtained from Banan's friend and contact in MI5, Henry North. "I know Phelan has been pushing you. Doona be angry with him. He's doing it for Ian. And for you."

"He doesna know me."

"He may no' have known you as Duncan, but he knows you as Tristan. The Warriors have as tight a bond as we do. They look out for their own. Ian nearly didna remain in control of his god he was so devastated by your—I mean Duncan's—death."

Tristan shifted in his seat and plucked at the seat belt he hated wearing. "Did you know who I was when I first came to Dreagan? Did you know I was once a Warrior?"

"Nay. No' at first."

"When did you realize it?"

Banan's lips flatted. "The first time we fought alongside the Warriors. I think Con knew before that, but he kept it to himself."

"Has anyone wondered that there might be a verra good reason I doona remember that other life?"

"It has occurred to us."

"But everyone still thinks I should meet with Ian." Tristan had expected the rest of the Kings to stand beside whatever decision he made about the matter. Instead, they, like Phelan, thought he should meet Ian.

Banan slowed the car to go around a sharp turn before he pressed the accelerator and the engine roared as it sped down the road. "Because you have what we do no'. Family. All of our family either died in the war with the humans or they were sent away."

"You have Jane," Tristan reminded him.

A crooked smile appeared on Banan's face at the mention of his mate. "Aye. I do. Sammi is a part of that new family."

The rest—but it wasn't the same—was left unspoken. Tristan didn't mind that the Kings were his only family. He didn't mind that he had no memories before two years earlier when he fell from the sky. Perhaps that was something to be worried about.

"If you really doona want to see Ian, then we'll stand behind you," Banan said.

Tristan looked at the King of the Blues. "What would you do?"

"That's no' easy to say. I remember my family so I would do all I could to find them if given the opportunity. I think you're right though. I think the memories of when you were Duncan are gone because you couldna be a Dragon King and want to be with your twin."

Tristan thought again of the pale blue skin and claws he had seen in his mind. Though he hadn't asked, somehow he knew that when he had been a Warrior, his skin had changed to the pale blue.

"She's stopping," Banan said suddenly, pulling Tristan from his thoughts.

Tristan stared at the screen and the red dot, which was no longer moving. "It could be traffic. She is twenty minutes ahead of us."

"Aye, and that is the village. She stopped there. I know it."

"Why would she chance it?"

Banan chuckled. "Because Sammi loves to eat. She was starved for so long, but her body now has food in it again. She'll be hard-pressed to skip a meal so soon."

"I'd hate to think anyone was watching Dreagan without us knowing, but I'm almost hoping the bastards try to take her soon. I'd like to meet them."

Banan's eyes gleamed with excitement and vengeance. "Me too."

Tristan smiled, recognizing the same need to defend, to protect. Except this felt different with Sammi—almost as if she were his to guard.

His.

The thought sent a bolt of lust straight to his cock.

CHAPTER
FIVE

Sammi turned off the car but remained inside as she casually let her gaze roam over the small village. There were four pubs, one restaurant, a co-op, and a gas station along with a bank and post office.

The size of the village should have put her at ease. Instead, the tingle returned full force. She rubbed the back of her neck and looked around for what had put her on edge.

Her stomach rumbled loudly, reminding her of one reason why she'd stopped. She needed food and the P.O.S. needed petrol.

"A quick bite for both of us," she mumbled as she opened the door and stepped out.

There wasn't a cloud in sight. The sky was so bright blue that it hurt her eyes to look at it. However, it was perfect for wearing sunglasses so no one would know who she was looking at.

Sammi slid on her shades and adjusted her purse on her shoulder before she walked into the restaurant and found a table that gave her a view of the door, but was close enough she could dart out if needed.

It was early enough that she was able to get her order in almost as soon as she sat down. The waitress was quick to bring her some coffee, and Sammi was thankful for the dose of caffeine it offered.

Since she was sitting by a window bathed in sunlight, she was able to have a reason to keep her sunglasses on. Sammi gazed out the window and found her thoughts turning to soulful, deep eyes and brown hair streaked with gold, of a muscular body that her hands itched to touch.

Tristan. She didn't want to think of him but there was something compelling and captivating about him. It wasn't just his sublime body or mouthwatering good looks. It was the way he looked at her—as if he wanted to see her soul.

And then there was his voice. Sammi closed her eyes, a smile beginning, as she thought about the rich baritone. The way he said her name made chills run over her skin.

Sammi rubbed her arms as her body reacted just thinking about Tristan's voice. She still didn't understand how she had been so intent on leaving before, but he had managed to calm her.

She stirred more sugar into her coffee, puzzled at how her fears had seemed to just melt away from her when he had focused his gaze upon her. His touch had been nonchalant as he gripped her arms, and yet that was all it had taken to soothe her.

Was her body telling her what her mind hadn't caught

up to yet? That she desperately needed a man? Surely not. She had gone longer than a year without a date before. Hadn't she?

She thought back to her last date, which had been after Daniel. Her food was placed in front of her as she counted up the months. It wasn't a year. It was nearly three.

"Oh, God," she mumbled.

"Is something wrong with the food?" the waitress asked.

Sammi jerked her gaze up and forced a smile through her embarrassment. "Not at all. It looks delicious."

She dug into her eggs and sausage as the waitress walked away, looking at Sammi as if she had grown another head. Sammi soon forgot her as she devoured the food.

It had been good seeing Jane again, but all the visit did was reaffirm why she had to stay away from any friends or family. It would be so easy to let them close, but she knew the devastation when they left her.

Nothing was worth that kind of pain.

Sammi wanted to linger over another cup of coffee, but it was time to fill up the P.O.S. and get on the road again. She rose and tossed down some bills as she heard the door to the restaurant open.

She glanced up through her sunglasses and saw a man with coal black hair and thick streaks of silver walk in. The silver in his hair wouldn't have been noticeable except for the fact he wasn't an old man. He looked to be in his thirties and drop-dead gorgeous as he stood in full motorcycle leathers and dark shades.

His head turned as he surveyed the restaurant as if

looking for someone. And then his gaze came to rest on her. She didn't know how she knew since she couldn't see his eyes, but there was no doubt he was looking at her. Sammi's skin felt flushed, her body tingling with a need that hadn't been there a second before.

If she hadn't been on guard, she might have fallen for the hunky guy, but there was no time for attachments—of any kind. No matter how much she might want them.

Sammi gave him a moment to move away from the door so she could leave, but he remained where he was. With clenched teeth, she grabbed her purse and walked purposefully to the door.

Just as she neared him, the man removed his sunglasses and stepped close to her, causing their bodies to collide. Another flush consumed her but was drowned out by the fear that swarmed her.

Sammi lifted her gaze and found herself staring into red eyes. She blinked and shook her head. It had to be a trick of the sun.

Instead of checking to see if it was the sun, she slid past him when the door opened and two elderly couples wandered in. It gave her the time she needed to get outside.

Once on the sidewalk, she didn't slow. She was being watched. The tingle was back, but so was the fear and the anxiety. She had felt it all too frequently since running from Oban.

Sammi climbed inside her car and started it up. A check of the gas said she had a fourth of a tank. She hoped it was enough to get her to the next town, because she wasn't going to linger in this one any longer.

She pulled out of her parking spot and drove away. As she did, she looked in the rearview mirror to find the hunky guy from the restaurant standing on the sidewalk staring after her.

"Damn!" she shouted as she slammed her hand on the steering wheel.

She was going to have to ditch P.O.S and find another car now. If the hunk was working for the Mob, they would know what she drove and could easily track her. If he wasn't, then she was just being cautious.

Sammi was nearing the edge of the village when her car began to sputter and then just died. She pulled the car over and turned off the ignition even though the car was lifeless. With her heart pounding, she was trying to convince herself it was just a coincidence that the stolen car had finally died.

"There are no coincidences," she said, repeating the words her mother had spoken so often when she had been alive.

Her hands shook as she put her purse over her head and looped one arm through. Behind her lay the village. The post office was on one side of her and a housing division on the other.

The only way out lay before her in the wild, open expanse of the countryside. She swallowed past the growing lump of dread in her throat. What choice did she have? She couldn't call Jane and ask for help. The point in leaving Dreagan was to take the evil away from her half-sister.

Returning to the village also wasn't an option. The organization after her didn't care if they took out innocents in their effort to capture her.

Her gaze returned to the mountains around her. She could live off the land for a while and really disappear. An image of the time her mother had tried to take her camping when she had been ten came to mind, causing Sammi to smile at the catastrophe that had occurred.

Then her eyes began to tear up thinking of her mother. How she missed her. There had been an emptiness inside her ever since the day her mother's spirit left her body.

Out of the corner of her eye, Sammi saw a Lexus SUV pull to the side of the road behind a parked car. That's all it took for her to know she had to make a decision.

She leaned over the passenger side to look for any kind of weapon that might be tucked underneath the seat. A knock on her window had her whirling around, a scream on her lips.

The guy immediately held up his hands. "I was just going to see if you needed help pushing the car into the station. I'm a mechanic."

Sammi rolled down the manual window a couple of inches, her heart still in her throat from her scare. "Um . . . I think it might have finally, officially died."

The man laughed, and that's when she noticed the grease on his hands and clothes. "You'd be surprised what I can bring back to life."

He had kind blue eyes and weathered skin that probably aged him more than he actually was. Sammi glanced at the gas station and saw that there was nothing behind it. A look in her rearview mirror showed the Lexus was still parked and there were men inside it.

"Thanks. I'll take you up on that offer," she said.

The man looked behind him with a frown. "Is someone bothering you, miss? My brother-in-law is a constable here. Should I get him?"

"No need. Once I'm back on the road, I'll be fine."

He didn't seem convinced, but he walked to the rear of the car. "Put it in neutral."

"She looks on edge," Banan stated tightly.

Tristan nodded. "That Dark Fae is still back there. I'd like a little time with him."

"No' here. No' now." Banan ran a hand down his face. "You've already called the others and let them know. They'll be on alert. I still can no' believe one of those evil shites is this close to Dreagan. They know better."

"He isna after us." Tristan swung his head to look at Banan. "He's after Sammi."

Banan's forehead furrowed deeply. "How did she get away from him? He had his sights set on her. I've seen women strip bare after just a look from a Dark One."

"I doona care. I'm just glad she did." Tristan had been getting out of the vehicle as soon as he saw the Dark Fae, but Banan had held him back. "We are no' seriously going to let that Dark Fae go, are we?"

Banan let out a deep breath. "If we do, it'll make Ulrik think we've no' yet figured out his role in this."

"There's no doubt this is somehow connected to the Dark Fae and whoever is trying to expose us."

"There's no one else but Ulrik. The bullet you pulled out of Sammi proved that."

Tristan heard the note of sadness in Banan's voice. He didn't know Ulrik, but he couldn't imagine the betrayal felt by Banan and the other Kings who did know him. "I'm sorry."

"We all knew this day would come. It would've been easier had Con just killed him instead of leaving him without his magic or the ability to shift."

"We'll put an end to this. Right now our focus needs to be on Sammi and how the Mob figure into it. Do you think they targeted her because she's Jane's sister?"

Banan shrugged. "I asked myself that and didna come up with an answer. I think it's something we should keep in mind until we get more pieces to this ever-increasing puzzle."

"Agreed."

Tristan watched as Sammi and the mechanic stopped the car in the garage. She got out and said a few words to the man before she went into the station.

He lost sight of her behind the high shelves, but it wasn't like she could go anywhere but back out the door she had come in.

Banan's mobile flashed a text. "Ryder, Rhys, and Laith just arrived."

"Good. I'm no' liking that Lexus SUV. It hasna moved nor has anyone gotten out since it pulled over."

"It couldna possibly be Ulrik or his men. How would they know where Sammi was?"

Tristan slammed his fist on his thigh. "How could we be so fucking stupid? She's Jane's sister, Banan. Where else would she go if she was in trouble?"

"Son of a bitch," Banan said as he dropped his chin to his chest. "They led her to believe she was being followed."

"And we assumed that's what they were doing."

"That assumption could get Sammi killed or taken."

Tristan unbuckled his seat belt as he leaned forward to stare into the store. "That means they targeted her from the beginning to get to us."

"Kellan and Denae were taken by the Dark Fae, Tristan. What do they have planned for Sammi?"

"Whatever it is, it can no' be good." Tristan barely got the last word out when he saw something in the field behind the gas station. "I doona believe it. Sammi is on the run!"

CHAPTER
SIX

The shrill ringing of the phone interrupted his thoughts. He set down his pen and reached for the mobile atop his desk. He brought the phone to his ear and leaned back, propping his feet on the large desk and readied his English accent. "Yes?"

"We've found her. She was at Dreagan just as you said she would be."

"Good, good. Do you have her?"

"Not yet, sir. We've got her cornered. We should have her within the hour."

He dropped his feet back to the ground and squeezed the phone. "Don't muck this up, Stevens. I've waited a long time for Samantha Miller. Take her quietly. Those at Dreagan will know soon enough that we have her."

"There's one more thing, sir," Stevens said hesitantly.

He ground his teeth together in frustration. "Spit it out."

"There's a Dark One here."

He sat up straighter. A Dark Fae? So near Dreagan? He certainly hadn't contacted them to join in the hunt for Sammi. He planned on bringing them in once he had Sammi, but not before. The girl was meant for something other than the pleasure of a Dark. "Where is he?"

"Gone now."

Through all the centuries he'd had total control over everyone and everything. The only factor that proved volatile was his alliance with the Dark Fae. As was being proven now.

"If he or any of the other Dark return, call me immediately. They took Denae last time and look how that turned out. I'll no' . . ." He paused and cleared his throat, hating the Scots brogue that came out when he was upset. "I'll not have them interfere again. Now, is there anything else, or are you going to earn the money I'm paying you?"

"That's all, sir."

He hung up and set the mobile alongside four others. Thanks to one screwup after Kellan and Denae had been kidnapped, he'd had to get new numbers.

It wouldn't take the Dragon Kings long to focus their efforts on their enemy. And he was more than prepared for it. They had no idea what was going to come at them.

Or from how many sides they would be attacked.

It was almost too fun to watch.

He rose from the chair and walked around the desk to the double glass doors open to the garden. It was just another ordinary day for the humans. But it wouldn't remain that way for long.

Dragons would once more rule the realm as they had

been born to do. No more would they hide and cower. The dragons would put the humans back in their place.

It would mean a war between him and the Dragon Kings, but he wasn't worried. He had an ace up his sleeve, one the Kings would never see coming. He could hardly contain his excitement as each day passed and it brought him closer to his goal he'd been planning for thousands upon thousands of years.

"The first one to be taken out is Con," he said as he leaned a shoulder against a column and gazed at the area of color in the garden. "Kellan will be second."

After that it didn't really matter the order. The Kings would either side with him or die. There would be no taking away of their power, no preventing them from shifting. They would simply die.

That wasn't to say he would make it an easy, painless death. After all, he had suffered. They would as well.

He thought of the Dark Fae. Their reason for being so near Dreagan must have something to do with Tara-eth losing his arm to a mortal and losing their captured Dragon King.

His intention to bring them in later might not have been such a good idea. He reevaluated the scenario and how pesky it had been to capture Samantha Miller.

He smiled as he turned on his heel and began to form a new plan.

Sammi ran as fast as her legs would carry her. She stumbled and floundered her way to a copse of trees to give herself a few seconds to gain her breath before she took a quick turn to the right and headed to the mountains.

She wanted to look behind her to see if anyone followed, but she couldn't chance it. The terrain was uneven and dangerous to someone who didn't know what they were doing—which meant her.

Her purse banged against her outer thigh roughly enough to leave a bruise. It was nothing compared to the ache in her shoulder. Her boots worked well as she hit the base of the mountains and started her climb. The landscape sloped gently for a ways, and the trees would easily cover her.

Sammi began to smile. This was how she was going to get them off her trail for good. Or so she thought until fifteen minutes later when the climb went nearly vertical and her thighs burned so badly she could barely go another step.

Tristan let Banan have the man who remained behind in the Lexus as he took the two who raced after Sammi. He didn't bother following them, because he knew they would take the same path Sammi had taken. Instead, he waited in the trees.

He glanced over his shoulder to see Sammi make her way higher onto the mountain even if her ascent had slowed to a snail's pace.

But it was the men who had driven her to it. Anger coursed hotly, vibrantly . . . dangerously through him as he turned back to the approaching men. They wore jeans and plain dark-colored shirts, but there was no denying the glimpse of guns he saw tucked into the waist of their pants.

Tristan flattened his back against a pine and waited

until the two reached the trees and passed him. He took two steps after them.

He lifted his arms and place a palm on each of their chests as he came up between them. They halted in surprise, giving him enough time to elbow one in the nose before he turned and punched the other in the face.

Both men fell soundlessly to the ground.

"You didna leave me one to play with," Banan said as he rushed up, though there was no smile on his face.

"They didna give me much sport either."

As one they turned to the mountain.

"We could follow her," Banan suggested.

Tristan shook his head. "She'll keep fighting us and try to sneak out again. She believes she'll lead them to us."

"Aye," Banan said with a loud sigh. "We can no' tell her who we really are."

"She's no' stupid. She'll figure it out when Jane doesna age."

Banan kicked a fallen log. "I know. Jane was trying to use that argument last night with me. The fact remains she can no' be alone."

"I'll follow her."

Banan eyed him with his gray gaze. "If she knows she's being followed she's likely to do something foolish."

"I'll be in the sky. She'll never know I'm there."

Banan nodded. "See to her then. I'll take these two along with the one in the SUV and see if we can get anything out of them."

"Whoever is masterminding this can no' know we've stopped them."

A sly smile pulled at Banan's lips. "Oh, he willna. How easily you forget that Guy can wipe memories, my friend."

Tristan chuckled. He almost wanted to be there and be a part of hearing Ulrik's name declared their leader. Then he thought of Sammi.

"Keep her safe," Banan said.

He clapped Banan on the shoulder and rushed to the base of the mountain so he could get a better view of Sammi. He would wait until the cover of darkness before he took to the skies. Until then, he would have to follow her at a distance, but close enough to help if the Dark Fae decided to show themselves again.

It didn't take long for Banan and the others to get the men to a secluded location. They had the three in chairs but didn't bother with tying their hands or feet.

"Wakey, wakey," Laith said as he slapped the first man viciously.

The man shook his head and blinked several times before he rubbed his jaw and looked around him. "Where am I?"

Banan remained leaning against the wall. "Give me your name."

"Fuck you," the man snarled.

Rhys landed a hard punch in his kidney, leaving the man gasping for breath. "Let's try that again."

"Name," Banan repeated louder.

"Stevens."

Banan didn't press him for his whole name immediately. That would come later. There were more important issues at hand. "Who do you work for?"

Stevens's eyes grew large. "I can't tell you."

Ryder rubbed his hands together as he walked around the three men. "I'll tell you what we know. You're English, you and your comrades apparently can no' dress without talking to the others first, and you're working for a man who has sent you after Samantha Miller."

"You left out that they couldna fight," Laith said.

Ryder nodded. "That's right. Now, Stevens, your other two friends are still deep in dreamland. If you tell us what we want to know, they never have to know you were the one who told us."

Banan watched as Stevens considered Ryder's words. Even before the man shook his head, Banan knew Stevens wouldn't take the deal. Stevens and his team were highly trained military men. It was going to take a lot to break him.

Now Banan wished he had kept Tristan with him so Tristan could use his mind tricks on the men and get the information they needed.

"I can get the info from him," Laith said.

Banan flattened his lips. He could well imagine what Con would say if he knew what they were doing. At least it wasn't on Dreagan land. "It may come to that."

Rhys stood in front of Stevens. "You know who and what the Dark Fae are, do you no'?"

Reluctantly, Stevens nodded.

"Do you know who we are?"

"Aye. You're from Dreagan."

Rhys exchanged a look with Banan before he asked, "Do you know what we are?"

"*What* you are?" Stevens repeated as his gaze grew worried.

Rhys seized the opportunity that presented itself. "So your master hasna told you about us."

"He has. We know everyone at Dreagan is dangerous."

"He got the dangerous part right," Laith stated in a cold voice.

Banan came to stand beside Rhys and looked at the men on either side of Stevens. "What else did your master tell you about us?"

"It was need-to-know, and I didn't need to know."

Just like a military man, used to taking orders. Banan grabbed the man by the throat and squeezed. "You've got one opportunity to tell me what your plan was for Sammi or I rip your throat out. I doona expect all three of you to walk out of here. The question is, will you be the smart one?"

Stevens grabbed Banan's hand and pushed back in his chair as he tried to get away. "We were to grab her," he croaked out.

He immediately released Stevens. "And take her where?"

"We don't get those orders until I call in and confirm we have her," Stevens wheezed.

Rhys crossed his arms over his chest. "Tell us who gives the orders."

"He'll kill me," Stevens said.

"I'd be more afraid of us," Con said as he casually strolled into the house.

Banan eyed Con, whose gaze was directed at Stevens. As usual, Con was impeccably dressed. This time he wore a navy dress shirt and dove gray slacks.

As if sensing he was fast losing ground, Stevens shook his head. "It doesn't matter what you do to me. He'll do worse."

"Then he obviously hasna told you who we really are," Con said tightly. He then turned his head to Laith. "Show him."

"Gladly," Laith said as he stripped off his shirt and walked outside.

Con grabbed Stevens by the back of the neck and dragged him to the window. "Watch," he ordered through clenched teeth.

This was a side to Con Banan hadn't seen in . . . ages. And Banan wasn't so sure it was for the better. It was a mystery how Con knew where they had been.

Banan knew the moment Laith shifted into a dragon, because Stevens's face went white as death.

Stevens stumbled backward and mumbled, "Jesus."

"Be more afraid of us," Con told him, still holding the man in a firm grip. "Now tell us who your master is."

Stevens opened his mouth, but before he could get any words out, Dark Fae appeared around them.

CHAPTER
SEVEN

Somewhere in a small cottage . . .

Rhi wiggled her toes as she gazed at her toenails after another delightful pedicure along with a manicure. This time she chose a bright orange titled A Good Man-darin is Hard to Find, and as usual, her technician had come up with a new design that looked like a feather slanting diagonally along her nails in black and silver.

"I think Jessie has outdone herself," Rhi said with a smile.

Her mani/pedi times were something she did as often as she liked. There was nothing like having those few precious hours being pampered.

She set her new polish on the shelf with the others, making sure to put it with the other oranges she had. Her collection was never complete. At least not as long as they kept coming out with such great colors.

Rhi stepped back and surveyed her shelf. Some people collected movies, CDs, or figurines. She collected nail polish. Excitement coursed through her as she realized it was just days away before OPI announced their new summer colors.

"Hmm. I may have to get another shelf," she said with a twist of her lips.

Not that it mattered. She was Fae, a Light Fae to be perfectly clear, and she could acquire anything she wanted. The accord with the Dragon Kings stated that no Fae—Light or Dark—could remain on the realm of Earth for long periods of time. She tended to ignore that fact.

Besides, she wasn't the only Fae who was breaking the rules. The Dark were infesting Ireland.

Rhi fell back on the mattress of her four-poster bed. The Kings had claimed Scotland while the Fae had chosen Ireland. Frankly, Rhi would have chosen somewhere like Bora Bora or Saint Lucia.

Her smile faded as she thought of the matter at hand—the Dark. They had always been a nuisance to the Light, but they had done the unthinkable by kidnapping a Dragon King.

Kellan couldn't technically be called a friend, but he was the closest thing she had within the Dragon Kings. It was for him and his mate—Denae—that she had gone into the den of the Dark Fae to help them.

In the process she'd learned the man that had been mentor, friend, and family hadn't died in the Fae Wars as she had thought. He had turned Dark.

Seeing Balladyn had brought back so many memories, including ones of her Dragon King lover. Though if she were honest, the memories of him were never far from her mind.

Rhi winced as she heard her queen's shout in her head telling her the Dark were attacking the Dragon Kings.

"Do the idiots have a death wish?" she mumbled as she rose and looked for her new black combat boots. "Didn't the war with the Kings tell the Dark dumbasses they couldn't win?"

Rhi finished tying the second shoe as she looked inward, into her mind's eye to search for Dark Fae in Scotland. As soon as she located them, she used her magic to teleport to the house.

She remained veiled to everyone for a heartbeat as she took in the situation. The Dark outnumbered the Kings three to one, and there were three mortals who joined in with the Dark. By the way Rhys glared at one of the mortals, Rhi suspected the Kings had been . . . speaking . . . to the humans before the Dark arrived.

Rhi dropped her veil and materialized, her sword in hand. She spun and ducked beneath Laith's fist to swing her sword up at the second Dark One fighting Laith.

The blade, forged by the Light in the Fires of Erwar, was a death strike to a Dark. The evil bastard screamed as the metal poisoned his blood and he died a slow, painful death.

She looked up to find Laith staring, his gunmetal eyes holding hers for a second before the battle drew them away.

Rhi moved to her second victim, the feel of battle settling over her quickly and effortlessly. She might have to think on that later after she kicked some Dark Fae ass.

Faces blurred and the yells from battle faded as she focused on one enemy after another while she moved about the room.

She was just about to plunge her sword into the chest of a Dark when she was knocked from the side. She tucked her shoulder and landed so that she rolled to her back and then returned to her feet without jarring anything too harshly.

When she stood once more, her gaze landed on none other than Balladyn. Just as the first time she'd seen him as a Dark Fae, it was like a kick in her stomach, leaving her wheezing for air.

Balladyn's red eyes gleamed as he wrapped his big hands around one of the three humans' head, stopping the man in his tracks. With barely a twist of his hands, Balladyn broke the mortal's neck.

As if it was a signal, the two remaining humans were quickly dispatched, leaving only the Dark, the Kings, and Rhi.

She twisted her wrist in a circle as she swung her sword around her. The man who had helped her grieve through her family's death and the loss of her lover was gone. In his place stood a monster filled with only evil and malice.

It was just her luck that Con zeroed in on Balladyn as well. Rhi teleported between the two before Con could attack Balladyn.

"Rhi," Con said with a grimace.

She ignored the derision in his voice. "This one is mine."

Con's black eyes narrowed as he looked over her shoulder to Balladyn. "Why?"

Rhi gave Con a shove and whirled to face her ex-friend with her sword raised and ready.

"Hello, pet," Balladyn said in his Irish accent, using the nickname he'd given her when she was just a young Fae. "I should've known you'd do anything to spend time with this lot."

"I warned you to pick a side. I warned you that I would kill you."

"Dangerous times, remember, pet?" His red eyes blazed for a moment.

Rhi hated the lump in her throat full of emotion for the man who had been a rock for her, a rock that had faltered and crumbled. Now she was going to have to kill him.

She took a deep breath and swung her sword.

In the space of a second, the Dark vanished. Rhi had used so much momentum in her attack that she couldn't stop her sword. It clanged against the tiled floor.

For long minutes she remained in that position while she tried to get her emotions under control after encountering Balladyn again so soon.

"Who was that?" Con asked softly from beside her.

Rhi hated that she hadn't heard him approach. She lifted her sword and slid it into the scabbard she wore along her back. Of course Con would want to know the very thing she didn't want to tell him.

"Rhi," Rhys said from across the room. "How did you know?"

Ah. Something she could—and would—answer. "My queen told me. What was going on to bring the Dark to you?"

Con stepped in front of her. "A situation. You're no' going to tell me who that was, are you?"

"No," she replied simply and walked around him. He could push her, especially since she couldn't lie without experiencing great pain. Something Con knew all too well. "Dark Fae so close to Dreagan. That's not a good sign."

Laith nudged one of the dead mortals with his foot. "And neither is the fact they killed these men."

She considered that for a moment. "They killed instead of rescued the mortals? That's someone who doesn't care who is lost. That sounds like Taraeth for sure."

"Have you seen him?" Con asked.

He was being too nice, his voice too soft. It grated on her nerves. She saw Laith staring at her again. "No. Is Denae still safe?"

"She's with Kellan."

Which meant that of course she was. Rhi rolled her eyes. The conceit of the Dragon Kings. It didn't help that they had every reason to be so arrogant. "Good."

She was about to teleport out of the house when Con's hand latched onto her arm. Rhi turned her angry gaze to him. "What?" she demanded.

"That Dark Fae knew you."

Rhi shrugged, noticing out of the corner of her eye that the other Kings were watching and listening intently. "If you'll remember your history, the Dark were once Light who turned to the spells that would eat away at our souls."

"He knew you. You can no' lie, and you can only evade the question for so long. Who is he?"

Damn him, but she hated Con. Thanks to her mother she had gotten the unenviable dilemma of feeling intense pain every time she tried to lie.

"He used to be a friend," she reluctantly answered.

Ryder rubbed his jaw. "A close one by the use of the endearment."

"He's my concern," Rhi said. "I've answered your question. Let me go."

The fact that Con still had ahold of her only set her teeth on edge. Of course, he always rubbed her the wrong way. Their hatred was mutual, so it wasn't as if she was hurt by his words.

With deliberate slowness, Con released her and stepped back. "So you have."

"Rhi, wait," Banan said before she could teleport away. "What have the Light discovered about the Dark's intentions?"

She shook her head and fisted her hands so she wouldn't rub the spot Con had touched. "No more than what we've always known. They like to cause chaos and wreak havoc. I don't know what any of you were thinking sending Kiril to Ireland to spy, but I wouldn't leave him there for long. Already there are rumors circulating that a Dragon King is in Cork."

"Do they know it's Kiril?" Con asked.

"Not yet. He's putting himself right in the middle of things. That can be disastrous."

"He's a Dragon King."

Rhi bent and dusted off her combat boots. "Yeah. And if another one of your Kings is taken by the Dark again? What then?"

"I willna be calling on you, if that's what you're wondering."

Now this was the Con she knew and hated. Rhi laughed as she straightened. "You didn't the first time. I went in because it was Kellan, and I actually like him."

"And we appreciate that," Banan said before Con could respond.

Rhi pulled her gaze away from Con to look at Rhys, Laith, Ryder, and Banan. "I can't show my face in Cork. Get word to Kiril that he's probably going to be discovered soon."

"We need what he can get from the Dark," Laith said.

"So you put a King with a Scots accent in the middle of Fae territory? That's smart," she said sarcastically.

Rhys cleared his throat. "We couldna wait on your spies."

Rhi didn't take offense at his comment. It was the truth that none of the Light Fae had learned anything of consequence. "The Dark notoriously keep their plans within their own ranks. They don't trust anyone, especially the Light. It's not like we can use a human as a spy. They would spill everything at the first look of a Dark Fae their way."

"Speaking of," Banan said. "Is it normal for a human to not be affected by a Dark?"

Rhi glanced at each of the Kings around her. There was something going on, and by Con's dangerous look, it was doubtful she was going to discover what it was any time soon.

"No," she said. "Denae was the first I'd ever seen. As I told Kellan, the only thing I can come up with is that Denae and Kellan had made love before the Dark kidnapped them."

"What if a human has had little to no contact with a King?" Banan pressed.

Rhi thought back over the centuries. "Humans might try to withstand a Fae's seduction, whether it be a Light or a Dark. Some have even managed it for a few seconds, but the humans always give in to the pleasure they know they'll get."

Banan reached down and picked up one of the chairs that had fallen over and leaned his hands on the back of it. "What would you think if I told you I saw a Dark look at a human woman today, and she was able to walk away?"

"I'd say he was probably not very interested in her if he let her walk away."

Banan shook his head. "Nay. He was interested. She walked away."

Rhi looked down at the dead mortals and noticed their clothes for the first time. It was similar to what MI5 had worn while they had been after Denae.

More humans in military dress. Dark Fae daring to come close to Dreagan. Dragon Kings interrogating the mortals. It all meant only one thing—war was getting closer.

She met Banan's gray eyes. "Watch whoever that female is, because that Dark Fae won't give up so easily if he truly wants her."

"Damn," Ryder mumbled and walked out of the house.

Banan's mouth tightened. "As I thought."

"You're dismissed," Con said from directly behind her.

Rhi whirled around and raised a brow at him. "Do you think there will ever come a time you'll stop being such a prick? Wait. I know the answer. No."

She teleported out before she let her fist connect with his smug face.

CHAPTER
EIGHT

Sammi didn't stop walking until the sun began to set. With the growing darkness she remembered all too vividly why she wasn't an outdoorsy kind of girl.

She absolutely hated bugs and all the creepy-crawly things that seemed to come out in the night. Then there were the unknown sounds that kept her wondering what was going to jump out at her the minute she closed her eyes.

"If only you could see me now, Mum," she whispered and lowered herself to sit against a tree.

She might prefer a nice, warm bed, running water, and toilets, but she was prepared to live without them in order to stay alive.

Not even as a child had she been afraid of the dark, but that was quickly changing. The snap of a twig behind her had her jerking around and peering into the growing shadows.

The only sounds she did recognize were the hoot of an owl and the screech of a fox, and even then it seemed much scarier out in the wild alone in the dark.

Sammi opened her purse and took out a bottle of water and a bag of pretzels. It wasn't exactly a fine dining experience, but it was food.

The crackle of the cellophane seemed abnormally loud and caused the creatures of the night to be silent for a few moments. If she thought the sounds were scary, the silence was terrifying.

Sammi didn't breathe a sigh of a relief until the sounds returned once more. She finished her pretzels and drank half the bottle of water before her eyes began to grow heavy.

Knowing she wasn't going to get much in the way of sleep, she settled more comfortably against the tree and tried to rest.

Cork, Ireland

Kiril stood in his back garden and looked at the night sky. He desperately wanted to take flight, but he was being watched by the Dark Fae. They suspected he was a Dragon King.

Most Dark Fae had no clue what a King looked like in human form, which played to his advantage. On the other hand, many of the Dark knew certain Kings in dragon form after the Fae Wars.

Kiril had killed his share of Dark, and he was prepared to do it again. The recent skirmish had only whetted his appetite to take out more of the vile beings.

There was nothing good about a Dark Fae. They preyed upon everything and everyone and expected no repercussions. He was going to be the one to bring down fire upon the lot of them.

He swirled the amber liquid in his glass and inhaled the fragrant aroma of Dreagan scotch. At the pub he managed to get down some Irish scotch, but it lacked the artistry and love that went into making Dreagan.

Kiril went still as he sensed movement off to his right. The Dark drew closer to his house every day while he was gone. They had gotten as close as the pool today. He could smell their stench. Whatever they looked for, they wouldn't find it.

There was nothing they would find. It was one of the main reasons he made sure not to have anything even resembling a dragon in his home. He wasn't sure how long he would have to go without shifting, but he prayed it wasn't too long.

Already he itched to take to the skies and soar upon the currents. His friends were counting on him as well. The union between humans and the Dark was enough that he would risk being captured by the Dark Ones.

To make matters worse, Banan had notified him by their mental link that Sammi was in trouble. Kiril had never met Jane's sister but that didn't mean he wouldn't do all he could to help Banan.

Kiril took a drink of the whisky and sank into one of the wicker chairs on the patio. He straightened his legs out in front of him and crossed them at the ankles.

If he could figure out what the Dark Fae were getting out of an alliance with the humans and the Kings' enemy, then he could determine who it was.

Kiril hoped it wasn't Ulrik, because if it was the banished King, there was only death in Ulrik's future.

* * *

Tristan was surprised Sammi fell asleep so quickly after watching her nearly come out of her skin from the sounds of nature around her.

He moved closer and situated himself so he could see her and anyone who might try to follow the track she had taken. After she stopped, he made a wide circle around her, scouting the area and found nothing that would cause him alarm. For the moment.

Tristan watched her as long as he dared before he stood and stripped out of his clothes. He folded them neatly and hid them among a cluster of ferns before he took off running and leapt into the sky as he shifted into dragon form.

He'd had no choice. If he remained near her he would do something foolish like try and get closer to her so he could touch her again. He still didn't understand the growing—and overwhelming—need he had to feel her silky skin.

In two flaps of his humongous wings he was high above the mountains. Tristan circled back the way Sammi had walked and let his dragon eyes survey the area. He was both relieved no one followed her, and irritated because he really wanted to ease the ever-increasing frustration within him.

And he knew that frustration lay with a gorgeous, sandy-haired, blue-eyed temptation that had walked into his life. She was an enticing lure, an inviting compulsion.

A tantalizing invitation.

One he had been warned against.

A quick glide over the village showed nothing unusual either. With that, he turned, dipped one wing to turn around, and flew back to Sammi.

It wasn't as if Tristan blamed Banan for cautioning him to keep his distance. Tristan might well do the same if he'd had a sister. How could he stay away from someone so beguiling, so fascinating as Sammi?

She had been in his mind since he first saw her. His body had responded swiftly, rapidly. As if it recognized Sammi.

He gave a mental shake of his head. There wasn't time to think about all the ways he wanted to make love to Sammi when she was in such danger.

To his annoyance, he immediately thought of Ian. From one problem to another. Tristan forced his mind away from thinking of the twin he was supposed to have and focused on the issues at hand.

He had hoped to hear from Banan by now regarding what information they had gotten from the three men. Tristan wasn't going to wait any longer. He used the mental link connecting all Dragon Kings and zeroed in on Banan's.

"What have you found out?" he asked.

Banan's sigh was loud, even over the mental link. *"It's no' good."*

"Just tell me."

"We learned nothing more than we already knew."

"I find that hard to believe. Are you still questioning them?"

The silence was deafening. When Banan finally did answer, there was an undercurrent of anger and impatience Tristan knew all too well. *"We were about to get the name of the mastermind, but just as the human was telling us, Dark Fae arrived."*

Tristan was so shocked he almost didn't tilt to the

side in time to fly between two of the mountains. *"How did they know?"*

"A verra good question. They knew exactly where we were."

Tristan flew higher, his gaze never leaving the area where Sammi was. *"I had a bad feeling ever since I saw that Dark One. We now know this so-called Mob after Sammi is the same group who caused the stir with Denae at MI5."*

"Doona forget they got the Dark Ones and humans to join together."

"Do you still think its Ulrik?"

Banan grunted. *"Who else would etch a dragon into a bullet? It was a sign to us."*

"I know I'm still new as a Dragon King, but are you telling me we doona have any other enemies who would want to expose us?"

"You have a point, but there are too many instances where only Ulrik would know things."

Tristan wasn't quite ready to lay responsibility at Ulrik's door. For one, he hadn't met the King. For another, it was only stories he was hearing. Perhaps when Kellan and Denae returned to Dreagan after their holiday he could have Kellan find him the history of what happened since Kellan wrote it all down without taking sides.

"There's something else," Banan said.

Tristan instantly knew he wasn't going to like whatever Banan had to say. *"What is it?"*

"Rhi was here. I asked her about Sammi's reaction to the Dark One in the village. Rhi said that she hadn't heard of a human walking away from a Fae, but if a

*Dark had taken notice of her and she didna react, he
would likely find her again until she did succumb."*

"No' what I wanted to hear, Banan."

"Me either. How is Sammi?"

Tristan glided atop the trees and scared away a fox
that was headed straight for her. *"Sleeping now. She
thinks she's alone, and I want to keep it that way.
She was smart enough to buy food and water while in
the store, but I doona know how long it'll last."*

"Whoever is after us knows we're onto them."

"Which means they'll be coming for her."

"And know you're protecting her. The Dark Ones
will probably come with them. You shouldna be alone
out there."

Tristan wholeheartedly agreed. He wanted to be the
one to watch over Sammi, but the truth was, the Dark
Fae could easily outnumber him and capture her.

He had seen exactly what the Dark could do to a female. Denae had been lucky since she was somehow immune to the Dark, but Sammi wouldn't be so fortunate.

*"It's for the best until I can somehow persuade her
to return to Dreagan."*

"If you do that, you'll have the eternal gratitude of
my mate."

"It'll be tricky, if I can do it at all. I've got to convince her that I just happened to stumble upon her."

Banan chuckled wryly. *"Good luck with that."* Then
all humor left his voice as he said, *"Stay on guard, because they will come for her."*

"They can try."

The communication was severed, but it gave him a
lot to think about. Tristan remained in dragon form for

another hour before he needed to be closer to Sammi. The idea of a Dark Fae finding her left him on edge.

He glided low to the ground and shifted back into human form. Tristan dropped the few feet from the sky with his legs bent. He remained still, his gaze raking the area for any signs of danger.

Only when he was satisfied there was none did he straighten and look at Sammi. Her head was tilted to the side and her lips were parted as she slept sitting up.

Tristan silently made his way to her. He told himself he wasn't going to get too close, but the next thing he knew, he was beside her.

He couldn't stop looking at her. Her glorious waves of sandy blond hair were too tempting not to touch. Even as he knew he shouldn't, Tristan lifted a thick strand in his fingers. This was as near as he could get to her. Not only was she Banan's sister-in-law, but Tristan somehow knew that Sammi was different from any woman he had met before.

Suddenly he was transported to a dark, dank prison as he sat against the stones with his hands clenched. There was another voice in his head, a deep, resonating voice demanding he kill, demanding he cover the earth with blood.

"Easy, brother."

He looked up into a face that mirrored his own.

"All will be well."

The words reverberated in his head when Tristan blinked and found himself once more beside Sammi with her hair in his hand. That was the second time he had touched Sammi and the second time some memory decided to reveal itself.

Or was it as simple as that? Was there more to his repressed memories?

Tristan shook his head and dropped his arm as he stepped back. There wasn't time to think of such things. Sammi was in danger, and not just from the Mob. The Dark Fae were most likely after her as well.

He could have gone the rest of eternity without ever encountering the Dark again. They were nefarious, unpleasant beings that stopped at nothing to get what they wanted.

The fact no one knew what they wanted is what made everyone nervous and irritated. The Dark could attack anywhere, at any time.

Then there was the Kings' unknown enemy. That's what made Tristan anxious. Not knowing an enemy meant you couldn't prepare. And that usually caused someone to get hurt. Or worse—dead.

His gaze shifted to Sammi. Banan was so sure it was Ulrik, but that almost seemed too easy. Then again, as a Dragon King, Ulrik would know every move they would make.

Tristan stood before he pulled Sammi into his arms and took her lips as he hungered to do, to learn her taste, to know what her curves felt like against him.

She had a sensual way about her that seemed second nature and caused a very carnal, very physical reaction within him.

He had to move, had to release some of the energy, the coiling need to battle. With long strides he patrolled the area, always keeping Sammi within sight.

CHAPTER
NINE

Sammi woke with a start, alarmed to find that she had slept for six hours without so much as moving a finger. Luck must be on her side, otherwise anyone could have crept up on her and killed her.

She grabbed her neck as pain exploded when she tried to move it. A crick in her neck. Just what she needed. Sammi got to her feet and began to stretch out her kinked body.

As she worked out the stiffness, she stood near the edge of the mountain and looked out over the vast beauty surrounding her. She had been so intent on getting as far away from the village as possible that she hadn't realized just how high up the mountain she had come until then.

She was lucky that the mountain she was on had a forest, but that would only last for so long. Sammi didn't think about what would happen then. She was going to take things one day at a time.

A glance at her watch told her it was five in the morning, but at least the sunlight made the shadows disappear. Sammi's mouth watered as she thought of the breakfast Jane had brought to her while she had been at Dreagan.

But it wasn't just the food that made her wish she could return. There was Tristan. The way he watched her with his dark eyes, the way his deep voice made her stomach tremble.

For a moment in time, she had felt safe with Tristan. He had cast her worries aside. It was as if his mere presence had taken the weight off her shoulders.

She knew how silly that sounded. Tristan had done what anyone else would do. He had seen to her wound and tried to calm her.

Here she was thinking how handsome he was, and he most likely thought she was insane. Sammi briefly squeezed her eyes closed at the thought. It wasn't like she should be thinking of Tristan anyway. He was back at Dreagan.

And she was on her own.

Again.

Sammi shut off her mind when she reached that dark place, or at least she tried to. It had only ever been her mother and her all her life. She had been fiercely independent, but she had taken for granted the times her mother was there. Then she wasn't.

The pain of losing her mother had blindsided her. It's what made her keep her distance from Jane and everyone else. Sammi came up with reasons why none of her relationships worked out, but the truth was that she didn't trust herself to get close to anyone again.

Death was a part of life, and she had always thought herself a strong person. Until she had to bury her mother.

The late-night phone calls crying about a guy or laughing with her mother about first date fiascos would never happen again.

No more shopping trips, Sunday brunches, or her mother's famous scones.

Sammi wrapped her arms around her stomach and doubled over. It had been years, but still the pain of losing her mother was as fresh as the day it happened.

She remained in that pose until the grief subsided enough that she could take a deep breath. As she straightened, she reached for her purse and grabbed the bottle of water. Her gaze moved upward to the incline of the mountain where she needed to travel. It was blanketed by mist that prevented her from seeing much of anything.

After drinking the remaining half of her water, Sammi put the empty bottle back in her purse and started to climb. Her leg protested loudly, but she kept moving because what other choice did she have?

Sammi had gone only about fifty feet when she reached the mist. It was thick and hung about her like a cloak. It stirred of its own volition, as if it were alive.

"That's utter nonsense," she said aloud.

But she wasn't sure if it was nonsense. The mist moved, breathed as if it were a being. Sammi's skin was covered in chills that had nothing to do with the dampness of the morning and everything to do with the eeriness of the mist.

She let out a shaky breath. In her heart she knew that there was something in the mist with her. Still, her blood turned to ice and her heart thudded like a bass drum.

Sammi fisted her hands to stop them from shaking

and slowly turned around to return the way she had
come, but the mist had swallowed the trail. The mist
was so thick she couldn't even see the tree she had
just passed.

It coiled around her legs until she jumped back and
got her legs tangled in the long leaves of a fern. Sammi
hit the ground with a groan, her backside bruised. She
rolled to her side, the mist scooting away so that she
was able to see the thick layer of pine needles upon
the ground.

She inwardly berated herself and took several deep
breaths to calm her racing heart. Then she climbed to
her feet. It took her a minute to figure out which way
she needed to go by the slant of the mountain.

Then, she marched onward, determined not to be
scared of something as trivial as the mist. Mist came
down from the mountains every day. It wasn't alive.

Yeah, right.

She ignored her conscience and kept walking. Without knowing what was ahead of her, she focused on
what was immediately around her. She walked slower,
and she didn't trip nearly as much as she had the day
before.

After three hours, Sammi stopped to rest atop a
small rock. The mist hadn't cleared, and she was beginning to doubt it would. It was too thick, too dense, even
in the growing sunlight, which normally pushed it away.

Sammi ate a granola bar, the sound as loud as a gunshot in the unnerving silence of the mist. The moment
she was finished eating, she stuffed the wrapper in her
pocket and was on her feet again. She had to get out of
the mist.

The farther up the mountain she walked, however, the fewer the trees until there were no more. Huge rocks and boulders took the place of the trees, and strangely enough, Sammi was happy the mist was there to hide her. She would feel exposed without the trees.

The smaller rocks were loose and moved under her feet whenever she walked. Twice she twisted her ankle as her foot slipped off a softball-sized rock.

It didn't take long for the rocks on the ground to become a major problem. Suddenly there were boulders all around her so that she had to squeeze through them in order to continue. The path became more and more narrow until she had no choice but to go around a boulder.

Sammi didn't think anything of it until the mist pulled back and she saw the four-inch ledge she was standing on. Fear stopped her cold before she tried to turn and retrace her steps. Inch by agonizing inch, Sammi tried to get off the ledge.

Even going slowly, she only succeeded in slipping. She grabbed the boulder and decided she'd have to shuffle around it. Moving slower than a snail, Sammi moved around the boulder.

The more ground she covered, the more confident she became. But that didn't halt the terror. She knew what was behind her—absolutely nothing.

If she fell, she was dead.

Sammi was halfway around the boulder when one of her hands, sweaty from fear, slipped. Instead of stopping and wiping her hands, she decided to keep moving. She was so close to getting off the ledge that she thought she could make it.

It was a fatal mistake, as her foot slipped off the ledge and her hands couldn't get ahold of the boulder.

A scream lodged in her throat as she felt herself falling backward, her arms cartwheeling as she looked for anything to hold onto. Air whooshed around her as the boulder grew smaller and smaller.

Sammi knew she was going to die a horrible death, but she couldn't manage to release the scream. Instead, she squeezed her eyes closed, her mind drifting from Jane to the regret she had for not kissing Tristan as she'd wanted to.

Suddenly, something slammed into her, halting her fall. There was no pain, no bright white light calling her to Heaven. Yet it felt as if she were being lifted.

Hesitantly, Sammi opened her eyes to see a gigantic appendage covered in amber scales wrapped around her. Amber scales?

She lifted her head and spotted the colossal wings. She closed her eyes again and pinched her arm as her blood hammered in her ears. It hurt, which meant she wasn't dead or dreaming.

Sammi gripped the claw as she opened her eyes and looked up again. To find herself gazing at the underside of a dragon's head. She looked from the dragon's head all the way to the tip of its tail.

Dragons weren't real. She must have hit her head or something, because there was no way a dragon had saved her from certain death.

She couldn't take her eyes off the wings and how the sun glinted off the amber scales to make them look as if they were polished and gleaming. That's when she noticed the scales beneath her hands were warm but hard.

Sammi bit her lip when the dragon suddenly stopped atop a mountain covered in mist and gently set her down upon the ground. Not once did its substantial talons graze her skin when the claw released her.

She stumbled backward as she looked up at it. Should she be terrified of such a creature, the same creature that had just saved her life? Sammi wasn't sure what to feel for the dragon. Was she supposed to thank it?

The dragon's apple-green eyes briefly looked at her before it leaned to the side and fell.

Sammi rushed to the edge of the mountain and saw the dragon spread its wings and soar up from the valley to disappear into the clouds.

When she was finally able to swallow, she found the mist once more around her. Her knees buckled and she collapsed into a heap upon the ground.

"What the hell just happened?"

She pinched herself repeatedly to make sure she was really awake. "This can't be. Dragons don't exist."

Tristan let out a sigh when he was once more in the clouds. Terror and pure, complete dread had made his heart miss a beat when he saw Sammi fall. He had been afraid he wouldn't reach her in time. He had already been on his way to her when he saw her try to get around the boulder, but then she had slipped.

The dread that had seized him had been awful. She hadn't even screamed. She had simply fallen with her eyes shut. Even now he could feel his own heart pounding erratically against his ribs.

If he hadn't been so concerned with the mist, he might

have seen what she was about to do and prevented her from attempting to go around the boulder.

At least she was safe now. It hadn't been the smartest move in letting her see him, but he hadn't had much of a choice. There had been no time to do anything other than snatch her out of the air.

The way she had looked at him with a mixture of surprise, fear, and curiosity made him want to reassure her he wouldn't harm her. In order to do that, he'd have to shift into human form, thereby showing her exactly what he was.

That wasn't an option.

He circled above her now and moved inside a cloud so he could see her. It was easy enough to keep the clouds moving at whatever pace he wanted, and he did just that while he watched the mist grow thicker around Sammi again.

Something had called to the mist, and it hadn't been him. If he wasn't mistaken, it was shielding Sammi much like the forest had done. But it could also be the Dark Fae tricking her into trusting it.

Tristan wanted to roar his anger, but he didn't dare. That was only allowed with a thunderstorm. It made him wish he had been a Dragon King when they ruled the land. To fly whenever they wanted, to roar when they chose.

He felt confined, trapped. Much as he had in the mountain. He didn't know what mountain. All he knew was that he had been held prisoner deep inside a mountain by something evil.

Tristan growled as he pushed those thoughts aside. He could think of it later. Right now Sammi needed him.

How he wished he could talk to her and tell her to think more carefully. She didn't think at all, just reacted to a problem.

In her defense, she had narrowly escaped being shot at and blown up. Her stitches had pulled, and her wound was bleeding again.

He wouldn't be able to approach her at all now. She had seen him, in his dragon form no less. There was no way he could explain that.

All he could do now was watch her from above and let Banan know where she was to come get her. He would remain in the clouds and out of sight at all costs.

By the end of the ordeal she would believe she had imagined the entire thing. At least he hoped she would.

The way she had looked up at him with her powder blue eyes had pierced him to his very soul. Desire had been instant and urgent.

He groaned as he remembered the way she had stroked his scales. It was like she had been caressing his cock because the need had gone straight through his body to his rod. He had desired her before.

Now he craved her with a ferocity that set his blood afire.

CHAPTER
TEN

Sammi looked to the sky often, searching for any sign of the dragon. For the next two hours there was nothing, and she was beginning to think she'd imagined the entire thing.

Except for the scrape on her palm where she had tried to hang onto the boulder.

It had happened. She had fallen and been saved by a dragon. She refused to even think she might be going crazy. If she allowed herself to travel along that path, she just might end up insane.

Instead, she recalled the feel of the wind as it had sped around her, whipping her hair into her face. She remembered being stopped midair as if cradled. And she had been—in the palm of a dragon's hand.

His fingers—all five of them—had gently closed around her. How had she forgotten that? She wouldn't ever forget the warmth of him, or the hardness of his scales. And his color.

Amber.

She couldn't say how she knew it was a male, only

that she did. His green eyes, as bright as apples, had looked at her with concern.

Sammi stopped walking. There was something about the dragon's eyes, something she recognized, almost as if she had seen him before.

Which was impossible. She would definitely remember seeing a dragon. Yet she couldn't shake the feeling that she knew him. Was that why the fear she had first felt was fading—rapidly?

Just before she was about to continue her trek, she heard the booming beat that she recognized as that of the dragon's wing as he flew.

She looked to the sky, but could see nothing but thick clouds for miles. The clouds were moving swiftly but showed no signs of thinning anytime soon.

Sammi adjusted her purse and started walking. The dragon was near. She knew it as surely as she knew her mother was in Heaven. Just as she knew that she would get another glimpse of the magnificent creature if she was patient.

The rest of the afternoon went by without another sound from the dragon. She decided to call it a day when she found some rocks protruding from the mountain. They'd shelter her in case it rained during the night, as it was wont to do in the mountains.

She ate the lone apple in her bag, and then discovered that she had managed to drink her last bottle of water throughout the day.

Sammi sighed and got to her feet. She had heard water as she walked. It couldn't be that far. If the mist would clear she would probably be able to find it easily enough.

Not wanting to get turned around again, she dug into her large bag and pulled out the colored chalk she used to write on her board at the pub and made a big X on the rocks so she could find her way back.

She followed the sound of the water and surprisingly found it easy enough.

"If only everything was this easy," she mumbled as she knelt beside the water.

Above her, cascading over dozens of rocks, was a waterfall that fell ten feet into the stream that then meandered down the mountain.

Sammi pulled out both of her empty bottles and filled them. She was putting the cap on the second when she glanced at the water and saw an image of a man as if he stood over her.

He had black hair shot with silver, but it was his red eyes that took her aback. She instantly recognized him as the man from the restaurant.

She whirled around, but no one was there. A glance in the water showed only her reflection.

"Maybe I am going crazy. Dragons and guys with red eyes. That's just no possible."

After going in two different directions and not finding the marks on the trees, Sammi began to get anxious. She let out a loud sigh when, on the third attempt, she found her marks that led her back to her camp.

Sammi settled back against the rocks and looked out over the mountains. It was hours before dark would descend in the Highlands, but her eyes were already getting heavy.

She was getting weaker, her shoulder ached, and the meager food she had bought wasn't going to last her another two days, especially when she could eat it all right then.

After wiping away the blood from her stitches, Sammi settled on her side and used her purse as a pillow after taking out the water bottles.

In that place between waking and sleep, Sammi found herself thinking about Tristan and the dragon, until they became one and the same.

Tristan with his mysterious air about him, and the dragon, a creature of myth and legend come to life.

She thought of Tristan's soulful dark eyes and the dragon's alarm and concern—that same look had been in Tristan's gaze when she had tried to leave Dreagan and he'd stopped her.

Sammi's eyes flew open as realization hit her. She knew why the dragon's gaze had looked so familiar. It reminded her of Tristan.

Out of the corner of her eye, she thought she saw a flash of amber through the clouds. The sun had set behind a mountain peak casting the side of her mountain in shadows. She kept still as if asleep, and closed her eyes until they were slits but she could still see.

And then she waited.

Between dozing, she would wake, thinking she heard the dragon getting closer and closer. This last time was different. She cracked open her eyes to see the dragon glide effortlessly down from the clouds heading straight for her.

Her breath locked in her lungs as she watched the dragon tuck his head and roll as the amber scales changed into sun-kissed bronze skin.

The man rolled as he hit the ground and came up on

bent knees with his hands on the ground and his head still tucked, his long, light brown hair falling to hide his face. Slowly, almost warily, he lifted his head and his hair fell around his shoulders in disarray.

Sammi recognized him before he stood. She knew that hair, had longed to run her fingers through it. Then he straightened.

She drank in the sight of him, from his wide shoulders corded with muscles to his narrow waist to his tight butt and long, muscular legs.

Her eyes jerked up to his lower back where she saw what had to be a tattoo, but it was so long and narrow that she couldn't make out what it was

Then he turned to face her. Sammi had seen gorgeous men before, but not one of them compared to Tristan in all his glory. He stood as imposing as a vengeful spirit and as commanding as a god. He was startlingly handsome, dazzlingly strong.

Mind-bogglingly virile.

The wind whistled about him, as if caressing his body as she longed to do. It pushed his hair away from his face. Sammi bit her lip as he closed his eyes and lifted his face to the sky as if being in human form pained him.

Her gaze lowered from his face to his chest and his impressive body, but it wasn't just the thick sinew that caught her attention—it was the tattoo that covered his entire chest.

The tat was done in an amazing mixture of red and black ink, making it neither red nor black, but a beautiful mix of both.

The tat itself was of a dragon. It stood on its hind

legs with its wings spread wide. The tail wrapped from his waist around to his back. Her eyes drifted lower to his flaccid rod and long legs.

His eyes opened and looked at her before his narrowed gaze shifted to the mist. A muscle ticked in his jaw as if he were deciding what to do.

The decision had already been made for Sammi. He had disappeared once. She didn't want him to leave again. When he took a step into the mist, she jumped to her feet.

His head whirled to face her, and all emotion fled from his face. He hesitated as if trying to decide to remain or go into the mist.

"I saw you," Sammi said, hoping it would keep him near. She wasn't sure why. She was both relieved she wasn't going insane, and a little scared knowing Tristan was a dragon.

A dragon!

Where she might have run from him earlier, she recalled all too well how he had calmed her where others never could. He had reached a place inside her that only her mother had ever been able to touch.

The fact he could do that is what kept her from being frightened. She did, however, have a healthy dose of anxiety for just what he might be able to do.

"You're dreaming."

A shiver raced over her skin at the sound of his voice. How she loved his voice. Sammi shook her head. "I'm not."

"You hit your head when you fell earlier. You're dreaming now, Sammi. Your shoulder hurts, and you have a concussion."

She smiled as she realized to what lengths he would go in order to make her believe she hadn't seen him shift from a dragon to a human. "I did fall, but I didn't hit my head. I was saved by a magnificent amber dragon. You."

His chest expanded as he took a deep breath, causing the dragon tattoo to puff out. "With your injuries, I can see how dreaming this would help you cope."

Irritation filled her. She knew she wasn't dreaming, just as she knew she hadn't hit her head. "Shift back into a dragon. Let me see you again."

"I can no'."

She took a step toward him. "I'm not supposed to know, am I?"

Tristan glanced away.

That was answer enough. "You've been with me this whole time, haven't you? And don't you dare say I'm dreaming," she said before he could try that tactic again.

"Dammit, Sammi," he grumbled and ran a hand through his hair.

She let out a long breath. A kernel of doubt had begun to fester until then. "Your secret is safe with me."

"That's just it," he said. "It's no'. They're after you because of your connection to Dreagan."

"Dreagan?" she repeated, grasping that he meant her sister. "Jane."

"Aye. Jane."

"They want Jane?" she asked, more confused than ever.

"They want us."

Us, as in other dragons. Sammi's eyes widened. "Banan's a dragon, too?"

"We're Dragon Kings, actually," Tristan said and then frowned as he stiffened. "Shite!"

She opened her mouth to ask what was wrong when he closed the distance between them in two strides and grabbed her uninjured arm as he dragged her after him.

He wedged them both between two boulders, his body pressed against hers from shoulder to thigh. Sammi looked into his dark eyes and found him staring at her.

"What is it?"

He tucked a lock of hair behind her ear. "They've found you."

She tried to run, but he held her steady.

"Nay, Sammi. Trust me."

But she couldn't listen. She had seen exactly what they could do. They killed indiscriminately, brutally. Viciously.

"Listen. Listen!" he repeated when she continued to struggle.

Sammi paused and heard the unmistakable sound of a helicopter. She glanced around his shoulder before sliding her gaze back to him. "Oh, my God."

"They shouldna be on our land. No one flies over Dreagan but us," he ground out.

She blinked. "We're on Dreagan?"

"Aye. You left it to go to the village, but you returned when you ran to the mountains."

Sammi leaned her head back and winced as the sound of the 'copter grew closer and closer. "What do we do?"

"Nothing. They willna find you here."

She felt his hand alongside her face as his fingers slid into her hair. She forgot all about running with Tristan around. Her lips parted as she longed to kiss him, to run her hands over his sculpted body.

He was gorgeous, imposing. Irresistible, captivating. Seductive.

With a look or a word, she was putty in his hands. The world seemed to be at his beck and call just waiting for him to tell it what to do.

Sammi was completely and utterly enthralled with the man who was also a dragon. A dragon who had saved her life.

A dragon who made her heart race and her stomach flutter with anticipation and excitement.

"If they do find you, they willna live to hurt you," he vowed in that seductive timbre of his.

She calmed, because there was no way they could hurt Tristan—her dragon.

CHAPTER
ELEVEN

The chopper was loud as it hovered near them, and it was all Tristan could do not to lean down and kiss Sammi. He struggled to rein in his desire without succeeding.

Sammi's hair was like cool silk against his hand. She gazed up at him with passion-filled eyes that made his cock twitch with need.

The mist cocooned them, blocking out everything but the sound. A flash of color had Tristan glancing up to see Rhi smile and point to the sky where she used magic to make it appear as if he was in dragon form and flying away.

The helicopter took the bait and flew away the same instant Rhi disappeared.

Leaving Tristan alone with a woman he couldn't seem to stop touching. She was an enchantress, luring him in with her charismatic eyes, tempting body, and sinfully full lips.

He knew he should pull away even as he stared into her powder blue eyes and wound her sandy waves around his fingers. Tristan didn't lie to himself for just one kiss, because he knew one taste of her would never be enough.

Since he first saw her on Dreagan he hadn't been able to get her out of his mind. Her gaze had ensnared him, her delicate touch had mesmerized him, and her courage had fascinated him.

It was too dangerous to give into his desire out in the open. They might be on Dreagan land, but Sammi was still a target.

Tristan dropped his hand and moved away from her. He closed his eyes and fought to contain his raging body. His cock was hard and aching, his body heated and eager.

"What now?" she asked.

Tristan swallowed and kept his back to her. The safest place for her was back at the manor, but that would mean giving her up to Jane to take care of.

He wasn't ready for that yet. But neither should she remain where she was.

"Isn't this where you tell me I belong with my sister?" Sammi asked. "How she and everyone will keep me safe?"

Tristan fisted his hands. "That's what Jane and Banan want me to do."

"And you don't?" she asked, a note of surprise raising her voice.

He rubbed a hand on the back of his neck. "There is much you doona understand."

"I'm getting the picture now," she said as her voice grew nearer. She walked around him and stopped when she stood before him. "The dragon on the label of Dreagan scotch. You changing from a dragon to human form. And what did you call yourself? Oh, yes, a Dragon King. And this," she said as she traced his tattoo with her finger.

Tristan stopped breathing at her touch. The dragon part of him, the primal, beastly part of him rumbled with excitement at her touch.

He swallowed past the desire and need to focus on her eyes. "So you believe we can protect you."

"Without a doubt."

He narrowed his gaze. "Why then do I no' believe that you'll return to the manor?"

Her hand dropped away, leaving him aching to have her touch once more.

"Because of Jane. Because of Banan. Because of you. I was wrong to have brought all of this to your door. These people are dangerous. I've seen what they can do without hesitation. I don't want Jane's world shattered as mine has been."

Tristan looked over her head and took a deep breath before slowly releasing it. He debated whether to tell her about Rhi and the Dark Fae, and was about to think better of it when he remembered the Dark One in the village.

"There is more in the world than just us Dragon Kings," he said as he looked back at her.

She shivered and rubbed her hands along her arms. "Does this have anything to do with guys that have red eyes?"

"Shite," Tristan said and gave a shake of his head in regret. "Aye, it does. I wasna sure you saw him."

"In the village and here."

"Here?" Tristan grabbed her and pulled her against him as he looked around them. All desire vanished as the threat to her took precedence. "Where? When?"

She bit her bottom lip and jerked her chin to the left. "At the stream. I was filling my water bottles and saw his reflection in the water as if he were standing over me, but when I turned around no one was there."

"What you saw is a Dark Fae."

"I gather the red eyes aren't a sign of goodness."

"Nay. They are evil. The males like to take women and pull out all the hope and laughter from their souls until they are just shells. Some then use the women for sex."

"And the female Dark Fae?" she asked after a moment's hesitation.

"They take men for sex. The more sex they have with them, the more the men are bound to the Dark Ones. Either way, once they have you, you've lost your soul."

"Why do they want me?"

Tristan walked to where her purse was and picked it up to hand to her. "They're working with the men who are after you."

"Just great," she said with an exasperated sigh. "Anyone else want to join in?"

"Doona ask that," he told her.

She pulled out of his grip. "Okay, so the Mob is scary, and what you've told me about the Dark Fae is downright terrifying. But why do I get the feeling you're more worried about the Dark Fae?"

"Because you walked away from one."

She shrugged, her brow puckering in confusion. "So?"

"So," he said as he tilted her chin up. "Their allure stops women in their tracks. No one walks away from a Dark."

"Oh."

"Exactly. That Dark wants you now that you were no' falling all over him."

She visibly swallowed. "Can the Dark Fae get inside the manor?"

"They're no' supposed to be on Dreagan land at all."

"I lost my mother a few years ago. Jane is all the family I have. I don't want her getting hurt."

"It's why you willna return to the manor," he guessed.

She gave a slow nod. "I don't want to die either. What do I do?"

"Do you trust me?"

"Oddly enough, I do."

"There is somewhere I can take you."

She slid her purse over her head and looped the strap through one arm so that it rested across her body. "Then what are we waiting for?"

"I'll have to take you while in my dragon form."

"I wanted a better look at you anyway."

Tristan must be going crazy to agree to shift in front of her again, but with the helicopter full of mercenaries after her, there wasn't time for anything else.

He walked past her until he was far enough away to shift. Her quick inhale when he stood before her in his true form made his gut clench.

There was wonder in her eyes as she looked him over. Tristan wanted to remain still and allow her that time, but it would have to wait.

He held out a palm and waited for her to walk to

him. Once he had her in his grasp, he leaped into the air and spread his wings.

In two flaps of his wings he was in cloud cover. Normally he wouldn't have cared, but with the chopper about, he didn't want to take any chances with Sammi's life.

Shifting into dragon form didn't stop the hunger for her. In fact, it only increased. He imagined stripping her clothes off one by one and laying her down before covering her body with his.

He thought about sinking into her slick heat, of hearing her cries of pleasure, and he flew faster. The unrelenting yearning had a grip on him that refused to abate.

Ten minutes later he spotted the cottage they used during patrols and tipped his wings so that he flew to the ground. Tristan landed and gently set her down, already missing the way she stroked his scales.

Before he shifted back into human form, he contacted Banan over their link and let him know he had Sammi. Tristan ended the connection before Banan could ask where they were or what had happened.

They were deep in Dreagan territory, and Tristan doubted any Dark would dare to venture there. If Sammi wouldn't return to the manor, that left only one option— having the others come to them.

Banan opened the door to the antiques shop called The Silver Dragon. The entire drive to Perth he'd been listening to Jane, over his mobile, beg him to let someone else go, but Banan couldn't do that. Jane didn't realize that when it involved her, he couldn't sit by and do nothing.

And this time there was nothing his friend in MI5, Henry North, could do to help. This was Dragon King business.

A glance around the shop showed a large front area with the antiques displayed by time periods and arranged in a manner most would find appealing.

Banan let his gaze wander from the Victorian section, past the Regency, Georgian, and Jacobean to the Elizabethan and Renaissance, and finally to the Middle Ages.

The shop was larger than he expected with a second floor housing an impressive array of books on one side and weapons on the other.

Banan lowered his gaze and found who he had come to see. Ulrik. The banished Dragon King stood as still as a statue. He wore dark jeans and a thin cream sweater with the sleeves pushed up past his elbows.

Ulrik's black hair was in a queue at the base of his neck. The only emotion was the fury that burned in his gold eyes.

They stared at each other silently until Banan said, "It's an impressive shop."

"Say whatever you came to say and get out."

Banan had been prepared for a sarcastic comment or even a dig at the fact none of the Kings had visited Ulrik in all the thousands of centuries since he had been banished.

What Banan hadn't expected was to be ordered to leave.

"If you want revenge on us, then take it, but leave everyone else out of it."

Was it Banan's imagination or had a flash of confusion flitted through Ulrik's gaze? Banan couldn't be sure.

"Revenge," Ulrik repeated. "Aye, I'll have it."

"I'm here to ask what I need to do for you to leave Sammi out of it."

Ulrik lifted a black brow. "Am I supposed to know a Sammi?"

"You've sent men after her," Banan said tightly. He should have expected Ulrik to play innocent, but it infuriated him. "She doesna know anything. Leave her out of it and take your revenge on me."

"Why would I want to make things easy on you?"

"Because you were once honorable."

At those words, Ulrik's mask of indifference fell and rage filled him. "Before those I called brothers betrayed me, you mean?"

"Mortals shouldn't be involved in our fight. Why you want to expose us we've no' figured out yet, but we will. If you think by alerting the world to us that Con will grant you your magic back, then you doona know him at all."

"Oh, I know Con better than any of you. You think he's some hero, but there is more to Constantine than any of you realize. He keeps it hidden well, I'll give him that."

Banan cut his hand through the air. "I doona care about your grievance with Con. I'm here to offer myself in whatever capacity you want to stop this nonsense about hunting Sammi. What kind of man have you become to use ex-MI5 and Dark Fae?"

"How about you live for hundreds of millennia without the ability to shift into dragon form and tell me what kind of monster you turn into," Ulrik said tightly, his lips pulled back in a harsh line.

"You willna call off your men, will you?"

Ulrik simply stared at him.

Banan ran a hand down his face. Ulrik had had his woman killed. Banan wasn't going to use Jane as an excuse and have Ulrik take her from him. That was something he couldn't bear.

He had come here to beg, which was the hardest thing he had ever done. But he was willing to do anything for Jane. Now he realized it had been a waste of time.

Banan turned on his heel and strode to the door. His hand was on the knob when Ulrik's voice rang out.

"Doona ever return. Tell Con he can stop having me watched and followed as well."

Banan shoved open the door and walked out into the rain to his car parked down the street.

CHAPTER
TWELVE

Sammie couldn't stop smiling. She had been flying. Strange how she had always been afraid of flying in an airplane, but felt completely at ease with Tristan.

She backed away as Tristan folded his enormous wings against him, and in a blink, he was in human form. With her blood burning through her veins, Sammi watched him walk toward her.

He walked like a predator, a conqueror. A king who ruled and commanded all. He was sex and sin, decadence and sensuality.

He was, simply put, spectacular.

She forgot to breathe as his dark eyes pinned her. His strides lengthened, his purpose plain. Sammi's lips parted as he drew near.

And when he pulled her into his arms, she wrapped hers around his neck and lifted her face. The kiss was consuming, captivating. Overwhelming.

She slid her fingers into his thick hair and melted while he kissed her as if there were no tomorrow. He tempted, he seduced, he enticed.

And she willingly followed.

Sammi moaned in frustration when he ended the kiss and pulled back. She forced open her eyes to see the blatant need shining in his dark gaze.

Their breaths were ragged, their chests rising and falling rapidly. Standing before her was a man that wasn't supposed to exist. She knew nothing about Tristan other than that Jane and Banan relied on him and he could turn into a dragon.

She trusted him. Her heart knew him.

And her body wanted him.

Sammi unwound her fingers from the cool strands of his hair and let her hands slip over his shoulders to his chest.

Beneath her hands she could have sworn the dragon tattoo heated. Tristan watched her as she traced the dragon and learned the feel of his skin.

Thick muscle as hard as steel beneath warm skin. She caressed over the ridges and valleys of the sinew. His stomach clenched when she traced the tail of the dragon to his side.

His hand covered hers before pulling it up to his mouth where he spread her fingers and kissed her palm. "That tickles."

"I've never felt such . . . need . . . before. I don't know what's happening between us, but I want to see where it leads."

"It's no' wise."

"I don't care. This," she motioned between the two of them, "is amazing. I don't even care if it's one-sided."

"It's no'," he said, his voice deepening.

She licked her lips, still tasting him upon her tongue. "Then why did you stop kissing me?"

"I told myself I just wanted a taste of you, to know if it would be as good as I thought it might."

"Was it?"

He kissed her palm again, this time flicking his tongue against her skin. His gaze held her captive. "Better."

Anticipation raced along her spine. Sammi rose up on her tiptoes and took his bottom lip between hers. A moan rumbled from his chest as she sucked on his lip.

In a blink, he had her backed against the cottage, his hands on either side of her head as he gazed at her. "You doona know what you're doing."

"Don't try to tell me it's because I'm scared, because the truth is the only time I'm not terrified is when I'm with you."

Sammi was getting ready to beg when he took her hand and tugged her after him as he entered the cottage. He whirled around and slammed the door as he drew her against him.

Just as his lips met hers, a woman's voice said, "Hey, handsome. Am I interrupting?"

Sammi turned her head to find a drop-dead gorgeous woman sitting on the kitchen table idly swinging her legs. Her long black hair was pulled to one side in a fishtail braid that hung over her shoulder. Silver eyes that were crinkled in the corners with a smile watched them.

Tristan let out a long sigh. "Rhi," he mumbled.

Sammi wanted to scream in frustration when Tristan stepped away from her to hurry down a hallway and return wearing a pair of jeans. She looked from Tristan to the beautiful woman at the table, unsure of what to make of what was going on.

The woman slid sensuously from the table, a wide smile on her perfect face. "Nice to finally meet you, Sammi. I'm Rhi."

"Rhi," Sammi repeated. "How do you know—"

"We have something in common," Rhi spoke over her. "Neither of us likes to go by our full name. I think Sammi is wonderful. Lucky you. I could only shorten mine to Rhi. I guess I could've gone with something completely different like Charlie or something."

"Rhi," Tristan said as he crossed his arms over his chest.

Rhi rolled her silver eyes. "After all I did for you two."

"I'm feeling a little lost," Sammi said. "Someone please explain."

Tristan dropped his arms and walked to the couch to sit. "Do you remember how we spoke about the Dark Fae?"

Sammi nodded. "Yes."

"There are also Light Fae. Rhi is a Light Fae."

She whipped her head around to Rhi to find the Fae smiling brightly. "I don't normally help the Dragon Kings, but Tristan proved himself when we got Kellan and Denae away from the Dark last month. I didn't expect to find Tristan jumping in to help Jane's sister, but then again, it doesn't surprise me."

Sammi held up her hands, palms out. "Wait. Just hold on." She rubbed her eyes as she took in what Rhi had just said. "I feel like I'm in a hall of mirrors where I'm getting a part of the story but so much is left out."

"That would be Con's doing," Rhi said, the hatred dripping from her voice.

Sammi glanced at Tristan to see him wince. She didn't know anyone by the name of Con, so how could he have something against her?

Rhi guided Sammi to the couch and plunked her down next to Tristan. "I'll condense the story for you. The Dragon Kings and Fae don't like each other because of the Fae Wars long ago. There is a truce, but the Dark broke it. The Dark are after a Dragon King and anyone else connected to them."

"Keeping up so far," Sammi said. "So how do you factor in?"

Rhi waved away her words. "Not important. I saw Tristan helping you and decided to give some assistance as well."

"The mist?" Sammie guessed.

Rhi winked. "Perfect cover."

"A Dark found her," Tristan said.

Rhi's smile faded quickly. She jerked her head to Sammi. "Tell me everything."

Sammi explained about seeing the Dark in the water for a second time. When she finished Rhi's forehead was furrowed as she paced back and forth.

"Can you describe the Dark One?"

"Handsome," Sammi said.

Rhi grunted. "All Fae, Dark and Light, are good-looking. I need something specific."

"He had long hair with silver running through it."

"They all do," Tristan said.

Rhi sank down on the stuffed chair next to the couch and frowned. "I was hoping I might know which one had been sent. Few keep their hair long now. Most cut it, so that will help narrow things down a bit."

"No' enough," Tristan grumbled.

Rhi sat back and crossed one leg over the other. She ran her thumb over her silver nails with a striped design on each forefinger and ring finger. "They won't be stupid enough to come this far onto Dreagan land."

"They killed the men Banan and the others were interrogating," Tristan pointed out.

"I was there. The Dark killed them because they were humans. Humans don't know how to keep alliances or pacts," Rhi stated. Then she looked at Sammi. "No offense meant."

Sammi scooted back on the sofa. "None taken."

"Let's no' forget the mercs who came onto our land in a chopper," Tristan said.

Rhi folded her hands in her lap. "Ex-MI5. They were testing you to see if you would attack."

"Ex-MI5? It's the Mob after me," Sammi said.

Rhi and Tristan exchanged a look, which only angered Sammi. There was still more of the story she wasn't getting.

Tristan cleared his throat. "We think the Mob targeted your pub to get to Jane and thereby Banan."

"Not possible," Sammi said. "Daniel was laundering money for a couple of years. Why would they wait that long? Besides, it was Daniel skimming money that brought the Mob to my door."

Rhi scrunched her face. "That could be the truth. The Mob isn't known for being forgiving. If they thought someone cheated them, they would keep after them until they got what they wanted."

"They think I wasn't at the pub the night they blew it up," she said. "Daniel told them I was away. I tried to stay hidden after that, but I still felt as if they were following me."

Rhi looked to Tristan. "Has Banan called Henry North yet?"

"No' that I know of."

"Maybe I'll pay him a visit," Rhi said with a grin.

"Nay, Rhi," Tristan stated. "Doona trifle with Henry. He's a good man."

Rhi sighed dramatically and rolled her eyes. "Fine."

"Who is Henry North?" Sammi asked.

Tristan braced his forearms on his thighs. "He works for MI5 and is a friend. The fact is, Sammi, when the Dark Fae showed up we began to suspect there was a connection between you and our enemy. We stopped the mercenaries who were after you, and while I followed you to keep you safe, Banan and the others took the men for questioning."

"Where the Dark killed them before they could tell you anything," Sammi finished. "I understand all of that, but I'm telling you, there's no way the Mob is in with the Dark Fae and MI5."

"There has to be a connection," Tristan insisted. "That is you and Jane. Jane, as mate to Banan, is a link to the Dragon Kings."

Rhi added, "And you are Jane's only sister. It makes sense."

It seemed like too much of a leap for Sammi, but then again, she didn't have any knowledge of fighting evil things, and apparently Tristan and Rhi did.

Suddenly Sammi had a thought. She looked from Rhi to Tristan. "What if we're looking at this all wrong?"

"How?" Tristan asked.

"What if it isn't the Mob, the Dark Fae, and these mercenaries? What if it's just one group?"

Rhi was shaking her head before she finished. "The Dark Fae are separate. They did strike a deal with the Kings' enemy, whoever that may be."

"So what if the Mob and the unknown enemy are one and the same?"

Tristan ran a hand down his face, his expression full of unease.

Sammi shrugged. "I'm probably wrong. I don't know who this enemy of the Dragon Kings' is anyway. Hell, I don't even know what a Dragon King really is."

"A Dragon King is as old as time," Rhi said. "They're immortal and powerful. They shift, as you've seen, and they can only be killed by another Dragon King. The rest of their history I'll let Tristan tell you. As for the evil . . ." She paused and drew in a deep breath. "He wants to expose the Kings. No one knows why."

"Has anyone seen him?" she asked.

Rhi gave a slow shake of her head. "Only his voice. They say he has a cultured English accent."

Sammi felt as if the floor came out from beneath her. Tristan wrapped an arm around her and she clung to him. "The man who killed Daniel. He had a cultured English accent."

"You're safe here," Tristan vowed.

Rhi raised a brow at Tristan. "Your enemy has managed to get MI5 and the Dark to ally with him. It makes sense he would use the Mob as well. Sammi was right. We found our connection."

Sammi wished she had kept her mouth shut. She had thought she stood a chance against the Mob. Now she knew she had no chance at all.

CHAPTER
THIRTEEN

Somewhere in Ireland . . .

Taraeth stared at his missing arm and could still feel his fingers moving. Humans had always been used as entertainment. He had neither hated nor cared about them. Now, he loathed one mortal with all the viciousness in his black heart.

Denae.

She had not just been immune to his seduction, but she had dared to use a blade forged by the Light Fae that had taken his arm.

But the punches didn't stop there. He had used a blast of magic with enough force to kill two humans, and somehow Denae had survived.

He had yet to figure out how she had managed to do what no other mortal had been able to. None of his spies had been successful in learning her new location either. Kellan, damn his dragon heart, was being cautious with his mate.

"As well he should be," Taraeth muttered to himself.

Because when he found Denae, there was going to be nothing left of her for Kellan to mourn.

Taraeth looked up when he heard someone outside his chamber. The twenty-foot iron double doors slowly opened as Balladyn strode toward him.

Balladyn was once a high-ranking warrior in the Light Fae army. He had been good of heart and pure of soul. His exploits as the Queen's Guard were legendary, even among the Fae.

Taraeth had wanted him on his side from the very beginning. It had taken a great amount of bribery at first, and when that hadn't worked, Taraeth had tried another tactic. During one of the battles in the Fae Wars Taraeth had sent an entire battalion to find and wound Balladyn.

After that, Balladyn was in his clutches. It hadn't taken nearly as long to break him as Taraeth had expected, but then again, the pure of soul rarely were, because somewhere deep down inside was a grain of evil waiting to take root.

"What have you learned?" Taraeth demanded.

Balladyn stopped before him and lowered his head in a bow. "Samantha Miller has evaded me once more."

"Humans aren't that adept, Balladyn," Taraeth growled. "She had to have had help."

"I suspect she did. There was a mist about her that was anything but normal."

Taraeth tried to scratch his face only to realize it was with his missing hand. "The Light don't yet know what we're about. They couldn't have helped her. Do the Kings have an ally in the Light?"

"They have a truce with the Light just as they did with us," Balladyn said. "The Kings hate all Fae."

"That might be the case, but I saw a Light while Kellan attacked with the other Dragon Kings. The Light Fae stood near Denae. She looked familiar."

Balladyn clasped his hands behind his back, his glossy black and silver hair hanging straight down his back. "As you say, my lord."

"I doubt the Kings would sully themselves to align with a Light, but let's be sure anyway," Taraeth said. "Find out who the female was who helped them. I'd like to have a word with her."

"Is this before or after I capture Samantha Miller?"

Taraeth stared at Balladyn, wondering if that was sarcasm he'd heard or a simple question. "After. We need the human to get to Banan."

"Samantha is related to Banan only by marriage. The Dragon King won't put Dreagan in danger for her."

"You know so little of humans," Taraeth said as he stood and walked around his spacious king's chamber with its vaulted ceiling. "Banan wants his mate happy. Samantha is Jane's sister, so Jane will do anything for her sister. Thereby, Banan will give himself up in exchange for Samantha."

"We couldn't hold Kellan, and he was not yet mated. Banan will be even more difficult to hold."

Taraeth chuckled as he walked around his lieutenant. "Banan will be even *easier* to hold. As long as he believes we will leave Jane alone, he'll do whatever we want."

"A brilliant plan."

"It's why I'm leading and you aren't." Taraeth glanced at the door. "You're dismissed. Don't come back until you have Samantha Miller."

He waited until the doors closed behind Balladyn before he grasped the shoulder of his missing arm. Whispers moved through the corridors of his kingdom. He felt their eyes on him when he walked among them.

They questioned his leadership since being maimed by a human, but he would show each and every one of them why he was the only one fit to lead.

The alliance with MI5 served its purpose. It was the union with Maitland that he had yet to figure out. He and the Dark got a great deal, but Maitland wasn't stupid. Maitland claimed to want nothing more than to expose the Dragon Kings and take them down.

Taraeth knew there was much more to it. It might take him awhile, but he would learn just what it was Maitland was keeping from him, just as he would eventually learn Maitland's real name.

It would take patience. That he had in spades. After all, he had waited thousands of years to have Balladyn as one of his own.

The sky was clear but for a few clouds drifting lazily by. The half moon shed only meager light upon the ground, but Tristan didn't need it to see as he scoured the area from the air.

He circled back around the cottage and made a wider arc as he thought of Sammi and her kisses. They had rocked him to his very foundation and created a craving for her he knew would never lessen.

That was why he was in dragon form patrolling. It

was a coward's way out, but he wasn't strong enough to resist Sammi and her appeal.

He had left her after their silent meal to take a shower. The mere thought of her naked beneath the water had sent him running into the night not even bothering to shed his jeans before he shifted.

Tristan glanced at the cottage to see the last light turn off. Had she gone to bed? He groaned as he imagined her lying back with her sandy waves around her.

A black blur whizzed past, knocking into him. Tristan roared his irritation, only to hear Laith's laugh in his head through their mental link.

"Your mind was elsewhere. Or should I say it's on Sammi," Laith said.

"Sod off."

Laith laughed louder. *"I'm no' sure why you're up here when you obviously want to be with her."*

Tristan swung around and went the other direction, hoping it would let Laith know he didn't want to be in the conversation.

Laith wasn't deterred however. *"Tristan. Why are you no' with her?"*

"Leave it."

"Nay. No' when I know something is wrong."

Tristan swung around when he saw Laith flying toward him. *"How can you know anything about me? I doona even know myself!"*

Laith was silent for a moment before he said, *"I wondered when this would come up. For two years you settled into your role as Dragon King as if it had been yours for thousands of years."*

It was true. Tristan had done exactly that. Not even

when he learned he had a twin who was an immortal Warrior did it bother him.

Then he met Sammi.

He touched her and saw flashes of his past, a past when he had been Duncan Kerr.

It was those memories that showed Tristan he had been deluding himself when he thought his life was just how it should be. He had a past he wasn't sure he wanted to know because he didn't know how it would affect his future.

"I'm a Dragon King," he stated.

Laith moved next to him and looked at him with vivid purple eyes. *"No one disputes that. The fact you are in dragon form is enough for me."*

"Is it? Why was I made into a King? Why was I brought here now? What am I meant to do?"

"None of us have those answers, mate. I doona care why you were brought to us. Frankly, I'm just glad to have another Dragon King. We lost so verra many in the wars with both humans and Fae."

"I need to know why I was chosen to be a King."

Laith hit his wing against Tristan's. *"Is that what's stopping you from going to Sammi?"*

"She's no' just some woman, Laith. She's Jane's sister."

"Aye. Sammi shouldna be trifled with, and if you were anyone else I'd be telling you to stay away."

Tristan blew out a breath and saw flames erupt from his nostrils. *"Why am I different?"*

"Because of the way you look at her, jackass. Doona think we didna all see it."

He glanced at the cottage to see the glass doors

leading from the bedroom to the garden were thrown wide. Sammi reclined on one of the lounge chairs in a white robe with the edges falling open to reveal her lean legs with one slightly bent and the other stretched in front of her.

"Tell me you doona crave her, hunger for her," Laith urged. *"Tell me she isna in your thoughts every hour of every day."*

"Aye, I want her. After kissing her, I doona know how I can keep my hands from her."

Laith circled away. *"For once, Tristan, do something that you want to do. Forget about what's expected of you. And for God's sake, stop thinking!"*

Tristan couldn't take his eyes off Sammi. The glimpse of her legs was enough to make his blood heat. Maybe Laith was right. Maybe he did overthink things.

He certainly always tried to do what was expected of him. It seemed the natural thing to do when he'd arrived and learned just who he was.

The others had been around for hundreds of thousands of millennia. He was still trying to learn the history of the Dragon Kings.

Why he had become a King and hadn't just died began to plague him when Phelan had told him he had a twin—Ian. Tristan hadn't wanted to believe it. He had all but pushed it from his mind until the images began to flash in his head.

They came at the oddest times, but always when he was touching Sammi somehow. There was no magic in her bloodline of ancestors, so she wasn't a Druid.

He stopped thinking as he circled tighter over the cottage and found Sammi watching him. There was a small smile on her face, and even from a distance he smelled the clean scent of her soap.

With Laith and the others patrolling, there was no reason for him to stay away. He did as Laith suggested and didn't just stop thinking, he forgot everything but what he wanted—Sammi.

He landed and immediately shifted into human form. Sammi's smile grew as she cocked her head to the side. "That never gets old."

Tristan slowly began to close the distance between them. The night was suddenly full of sounds as the scent of flowers from the garden filled the air.

"I was beginning to wonder if you would ever come down," she said as she swung her legs over the side of the chaise and sat up. "I love watching you, but I'm glad you're here."

"Where else would I be?"

She lifted a shoulder casually and slowly blinked. "Where do you want to be?"

"With you," he answered without hesitation. It was the one thing he did know, the one certainty that hadn't faded since he first saw her.

She rose and walked around the chaise to the bedroom. Just as she reached the doorway, the robe opened before it slid down her arms and floated to the floor.

He drank in the sight of her naked backside as his cock hardened.

"Then what are you waiting for?" she asked as she looked at him over her shoulder, her powder blue eyes passion filled.

CHAPTER
FOURTEEN

Sammi had never done anything so impulsive in her life, but it had felt . . . right. There had been no second-guessing herself, no wondering if she was making a mistake. There was just a certainty she had never experienced before.

She turned when she reached the bed and found Tristan already inside the room. Earlier she'd lit four candles and set them about the room to give it a golden glow. This was a night of magic, a night of dreams.

A night where she put aside all her fears and insecurities and let herself go.

Tristan's gaze gradually raked down her body and back up again. Her skin heated from the fire in his eyes, and desire pooled low in her belly.

"Beautifully perfect," he said in his deep voice. "I've wanted to tear your clothes off for a while."

"All you had to do was ask."

He stepped to her and lifted her hand until their palms were against each other. "I'll remember that next time."

"There's going to be a next time?" she asked as her stomach fluttered in excitement.

"Oh, aye. I suspect many more next times."

His fingers spread and then laced with hers. Only then did he tug her against him until they stood flesh to flesh. She had felt his wonderful body before, but just like watching him shift into a dragon, she wanted more.

She set her hand at his narrow waist and once more felt his dragon tattoo heat beneath her palm. "Does every Dragon King have such a tat?"

"Aye. Each one is different, just as we are different dragons." He used his free hand to push her hair away from her throat before he bent his head and nuzzled her.

"Why the tattoo though?" she asked as her eyes slid shut from the exquisite pleasure of his lips.

"It represents who we are. We are dragons," he murmured, "who can shift to human form."

She clung to him as his mouth kissed and licked to her ear. "It warms beneath my hand."

"Hmm. That's no' all that's hot for you."

Sammi shivered as he took her mouth in a possessive, dominating kiss. His hand slid sensuously down her back to cup her butt and bring her against his thick arousal.

He then brought both of her arms above her head as he leaned back, their eyes locking. Sammi couldn't pull in a breath because her body ached for him. With one kiss he had her trembling, needy.

Utterly infatuated.

His hands caressed down her arms leisurely, leaving a path of heat in his wake. Dark eyes, fathomless and full of promise, held her pinned, daring her to give in.

As if she had any choice. They had been on this road since she imagined she dreamed him. Now he was standing before her, his lips wet with their kisses.

"So damned beautiful," he whispered.

Sammi sucked in a breath when his hands traveled to her breasts and lightly stroked the underside before cupping them, as if testing their weight.

Her nipples hardened, an ache settling low in her belly. He continued teasing her while he learned her by following her sides to her waist and then her hips.

For several seconds they simply looked at each other. Sammi had never felt such desire, such overwhelming hunger for another before. She reached for him the same instant he grabbed her.

They came together in a tangle of limbs and lips as they kissed frantically, madly. Senselessly.

Desire, fierce and savage, consumed them. Nothing mattered, nothing existed but the two of them and the ever-growing attraction.

The kiss deepened, pulling her further and further down into his seduction, into the passion. Into the pleasure that awaited them.

The back of her legs hit the bed, but before she could fall back, Tristan tightened his arms and lifted her off her feet as he kneeled on the bed. Then, slowly, all the while kissing her senselessly, he lay her down.

His weight atop her was a heady thing. She barely had time to enjoy it before he shifted down her body and closed his lips around her nipples.

Sammi gasped, her hands flying to his head to hold him as he teased and tantalized until her breasts were swollen and her nipples aching points.

Only then did he lift his head and kiss her. She rocked her hips against him, needing the contact to ease the need pushing her.

He slid a hand between them and spread her legs to expose her sex. The cool air washed over her. She fisted the covers in her hand when his fingers delved between her legs and parted her curls.

Her back arched when he dipped a finger inside her. Desire tightened, coiling with each touch, and bringing her closer to the edge.

Then he touched her clit. Sammi let out a low moan when he circled the swollen nub. The pleasure was unlike anything she'd ever felt. No one touched her like Tristan.

She whispered his name when his tongue flicked over her clitoris. Time stood still as he brought her higher and higher as his tongue licked and laved.

When the climax struck, Sammi wasn't prepared. She screamed at the intense impact as it swept her, seized her, taking her to a place she had only dreamed existed.

Tristan watched the flush cover her skin as the orgasm claimed her. He had never seen anything so stunning, nor had he ever held anyone so amazing in his arms before.

With her body still trembling from her climax, Tristan wrapped her legs around him and gathered her against him as he sat up.

Her powder blue eyes were glossy, her lips parted as her chest heaved. But she looked at him as if he was everything she could ever want.

The worries of his past, of his future, and what he

was meant to do were forgotten as he sank into her gaze. She erased all his doubt, all his burdens.

And in their place was her.

Sammi.

She filled every empty space inside him, spaces he hadn't known existed until she had come along and pierced him with her beautiful eyes.

"Tristan," she said in a voice husky with passion.

He pulled her onto her knees as she hovered over his throbbing cock. Tristan hissed in a breath when she rubbed her sex across the tip of his arousal. Electric currents of need and desire sparked through him, setting his already heated blood to blaze.

His hold tightened and he claimed her lips in another kiss. He couldn't stop touching or kissing her. She was like a drug, and once he'd had a taste, he needed more.

All thought halted when she gradually slid her tight, wet sheath down his cock. He didn't release his breath until she was fully seated.

Then the only thing that filled his mind was imprinting himself fully and unconditionally upon her. He wanted her mind wiped of any other man that had come before him—and any who dared to come after.

Tristan held her hips as he shifted his body. They stared wordlessly into each other's eyes as he rocked his hips slowly. Her hard nipples grazed his chest, causing him to moan. Unable to hold off, he pinched a nipple and heard her suck in a breath before she groaned and rotated her hips.

That's all it took to push him past the point of no return. He flipped her onto her back and set his hands on either side of her head. He pulled out of her, and then gave a hard thrust as he sank deep.

She whimpered, her nails digging into his arms. Again and again he filled her, taking them higher, pushing them further. A sheen of sweat covered them, desire consumed them.

Her body was pliant, giving, eager. He tried to hold back a wildness that rose up in him for the first time, and each time he pulled back, she held tighter.

The rhythm increased as he plunged inside her tight body again and again, going deeper, driving harder. The wildness, a madness that seemed to be centered around her, took him again.

He wanted to pound into her, marking her as his for everyone to see. The ferocity of it caught him off guard, and he once more pulled back.

"No," she begged as she held him in place.

She couldn't understand the part of him that wanted to break free, a part he had never encountered before—a part that could hurt her.

Her hips rose to meet his thrusts, her soft moans turning to cries as she called his name over and over.

Tristan was powerless to deny her or his body. He gripped her hip with one hand and plunged mercilessly. The harder and deeper he thrust, the more she took.

The first convulsion of her body around his cock as she climaxed sent him spiraling into his own orgasm. He filled her once more as his seed poured inside her and her tight walls milked him.

A bubble of peace, of pure bliss surrounded them as they fell in a tangle of limbs, content to be in each other's arms.

* * *

Banan strode wearily into the manor. He hadn't taken two steps inside when a form blocked his way. He looked up into Con's enraged face.

"You went to see Ulrik."

It wasn't a question, and Banan didn't treat it as such. "I did."

He walked around Con into the parlor and poured himself a serving of whisky. Before he put the stopper in the crystal decanter, he poured himself more.

Then he lifted the glass and drained the entire thing.

"I take it things didna go well," Con said from the doorway.

Banan glanced at him to see his arms crossed, his face set in a neutral mask of indifference. Banan knew better. He knew the efforts Con had gone to in order that no Dragon King had contact with Ulrik.

And frankly he didn't care how pissed off the King of Kings was.

"I forbade any of you from seeing Ulrik."

Con might be the King of Kings, but he didn't make decisions for individual Dragon Kings. He tried, and some even listened to Con most of the time.

Other times, the Kings did as they wanted.

The only exception was when it came to protecting Dreagan and their secret. In that, all Dragon Kings were united.

"Con, I say this with the deepest sincerity. Fuck off."

Banan didn't wait for a reply as he poured more whisky.

"What did he tell you?" Con asked.

Banan wasn't distracted by the soft tone. That's

usually when Con was the angriest. He looked up at Constantine and raised his glass in salute. "He refused to help."

"I could've told you that."

"You could've, but I had to try. I know you can no' possibly understand that."

Con dropped his arms and pushed away from the doorway. "I understand perfectly."

"Do you? I doubt it. And it doesna matter. Sammi is still in danger, which means so is Jane, and I'll do anything to protect what's mine."

Con's black eyes grew cold. "As will I."

"Have you seen Ulrik?" Banan asked as Con started to walk away.

Con jerked as he halted and then faced Banan. "Of course."

"Nay. Have you really seen him?"

"If you mean have I spoken with him, that would be nay. I doona bother to get close enough to exchange words."

"He's no' the same man," Banan said as he set down his empty glass and walked to the doorway next to Con. "He's . . . hard, cruel. Fierce."

Con lifted a blond brow. "Your point?"

"He wants revenge. And I think he's going to get it."

CHAPTER
FIFTEEN

Tristan was laughing as he sat next to his brother. Ian made another joke that had everyone at the table in the great hall doubled over in laughter.

"See? I told you I'm funnier than you, Duncan," Ian said as he elbowed him.

Tristan's eyes snapped open. He stared at the ceiling as he pulled reality to him. He lay on his back with Sammi snuggled against him. Sweat beaded his skin as the memory floated through his mind like a leaf on the wind.

And it was a memory.

It hadn't been a dream. He could still feel the wood of the table beneath his hands and how it was scraped and scratched from centuries of use.

He could still hear everyone's laughter. Tristan touched his side where Ian's elbow had connected with his rib. It tingled, as if it had just happened.

Tristan pulled his arm from beneath Sammi and sat up. He sat on the edge of the bed and ran his hands through his hair. It had seemed as real as the room around him.

The lights from the many candelabras and torches, the heat from the fire from the huge fireplace, the ale upon his lips.

What was going on? Why were these memories plaguing him now after two years? What did they want with him? And what was he going to do about it?

He stood and silently opened a drawer from the bureau and took out another pair of jeans. At the door he paused and looked at the bed. Sammi was sprawled out, a hand lying palm up as if she were reaching for him.

But who was she reaching for? Was he Tristan? Was he Duncan? Or was he someone else? His head began to pound as he tried to unravel the knots of his past.

Then he began to wonder if he should. Perhaps his past was knotted to keep him from learning something he'd rather not know.

Tristan briefly closed his eyes as he realized he couldn't figure any of it out with Sammi around. She confused him even more, clouding his mind to anything but lust and complicating his decisions.

He'd known it was better to stay away from her. After having her in his arms, after marking her, he wouldn't be able to keep from touching her. And right now with his past seeming to blur with lines of the present, he might just put her in danger.

Tristan walked out of the bedroom and then out of the house. He stopped once he was outside, his face lifted to the sky.

Life had been relatively uncomplicated a few days ago. He might have been dealing with Ian wanting to meet him, but there had been no memories of his past life, no confusion over what he was supposed to do or why he had become a Dragon King.

"Hey, handsome."

He cringed when he heard Rhi's voice. The Fae had a way of always being at the wrong place at the wrong time. Well, that wasn't entirely true. She had helped save Kellan and Denae as well as Sammi.

Tristan shoved his hands into the front pockets of his jeans. "Hi, yourself."

"I expected you to look . . . content, happy even after your *alone time* with Sammi, not all mopey and depressed. You didn't screw up, did you? Don't all Kings make love perfectly?"

He heard the teasing in her voice, but he couldn't manage to even crack a smile. "It was as near to perfect with her as I suspect it can get."

Rhi came to stand in front of him, a deep frown marring her forehead when she looked at his face. "Damn, handsome. You look like hell."

"At least I look how I feel." He shook his head.

Every fiber of his being wanted him to return to Sammi, to crawl back in that bed and take her body again. To forget who he was or whatever he was supposed to be.

But protecting her required his mind be clear of everything. It was so muddied now he wasn't sure which way was up. "What are you doing here?"

Rhi shrugged and walked back to her seat on the stone wall. "Thinking."

"At Dreagan? I thought this would be the last place you wanted to be."

There was a faint smile as she shifted her gaze to look at the mountains. "It is, and yet at one time it was my favorite place to be. You think you finally find something worth keeping, something that could never be taken from you, something that will keep your world steady. And then it's yanked away, snatched right from your hands. The rightness, the completeness you felt seems like a distant memory as you drift through time."

"You loved him deeply."

There was a beat of silence, a sadness so profound that it weighted the air. "Yes. Yes, I did."

Tristan knew it was a rare event for Rhi to talk about her Dragon King lover. He wanted to know who it was, but he knew better than to ask. Not now, at least. "How long ago did you lose him?"

"Hundreds of lifetimes ago. Sometimes it feels like yesterday."

"Is that why you're here? You want to be close to the memories you have?"

Her silver eyes caught the light of the moon, making them look metallic. "No. I'm here because I need quiet to think. And because it never hurts to have someone else help keep watch other than him," she said and pointed to the sky as Laith flew overhead, the black of his dragon blending effortlessly with the night.

"What are you thinking about?"

Her smile was too wide, too bright as she focused on him. "Tell me what has driven you from your lover's bed."

Tristan withdrew into himself as he recalled the newest memory. She'd changed the subject, but he let it slide since he had a question of his own. "Do you know how Dragon Kings are made?"

"I don't think anyone does. When we came to this realm the Dragon Kings were already here."

"You never asked your lover how he came to be?"

She let out a soft sigh. "He was a dragon, Tristan. He was chosen to be a King because of his strength and the power of his magic. He was a natural born leader."

"I fell from the sky," Tristan said and looked to a distant mountain. "One minute there was nothing, and then there was the cold and snow and the howling wind."

"You remember nothing before then?"

Tristan closed his eyes and thought back. It was a place he hadn't bothered to look closer at because it hadn't mattered. Until now. "Blackness. I was . . . floating."

"You could have been in that space between life and death. I heard one Fae describe it after we healed him. He had been far gone, and at one point he stopped breathing."

Tristan opened his eyes and looked at her. "Where was this place?"

"It exists all around us," she said with a wave of her hand. "It's not a place you can find on a map, and I don't know how some go there and some don't."

He faced her and asked, "What did the Fae describe it as?"

"He said it was as if he could see everything from the past to the present and even the future. He saw everyone, heard everything. He witnessed cities rise and cities fall. He beheld civilizations crumble into dust as new ones were born."

"And he remembered all of it?"

Rhi flicked her long hair over a shoulder. "For all of a few minutes after we healed him. After he slept, he recalled nothing of the event."

"So he could've made it up."

"He could have, but he didn't. I especially remember him talking about floating and the darkness before a timeline of life was displayed for him to see."

Tristan snorted as he turned away. "I want to know why I was made into a Dragon King."

"Isn't it enough you came back, handsome? And so close to your twin?"

He speared her with a glacial look. "What do you know of my past?"

"Nothing more than anyone else, but there's no doubt Ian is your brother right down to the way a vein ticks on the side of your forehead when you get angry."

"I do no'," he said even as he reached up and rubbed his left temple.

She twisted her mouth in a wry frown. "Is lying to yourself helping? Is that what's keeping you from Sammi's bed?"

"Nay. It's the memories." He wasn't sure why he told Rhi. It could be because she didn't have ties to Dreagan or MacLeod Castle.

For long minutes Rhi was quiet, the night broken only by the sound of Laith's wings beating as he flew around them. "Memories of when you died?"

"Memories of a life when I was . . . Duncan."

"I didn't think you had those memories," she said in confusion.

"I didn't. Until I met Sammi."

Rhi put her hands on either side of her hips and tapped her nails on the stones. "How?"

"When I touch her the memories come."

"Every time you touch her?"

He gave a shake of his head. "Nay. It's random. I doona know when they'll come. I had one tonight. It woke me."

"And you're sure you were Duncan in this memory?"

"I was in a castle surrounded by men who I knew to be close friends. Ian was beside me, teasing me."

Rhi listened raptly. "The men. Can you describe any of them to me?"

"Three wore gold torcs around their necks. They were brothers, I'm sure of it."

"Any other memories?" she asked in a soft voice.

Tristan hesitated before he swallowed and said, "I saw my hands except my skin was pale blue and there were long blue claws extended from my fingers. My hands were covered in blood that I somehow know was from a battle."

"Is that all so far?"

"There is a third."

Rhi slid from the wall to her feet. "I've heard enough already."

"I'm in a mountain," he said over her. "I'm being held prisoner with Ian. It's a bad place we're in, Rhi."

Her silver eyes met his. "Yes, it was. It still holds evil."

"These really are memories then?"

"Yes."

He let his chin drop to his chest. "So I really was Duncan Kerr?"

"Is that so bad?"

"I doona know. I've no' remembered everything."

Rhi came to stand beside him as they looked out over the valley below them. "Ian Kerr is a good man, and his wife, Danielle, is a powerful Druid. Ian, along with the other Warriors from MacLeod Castle have fought to keep evil Druids from harming the world."

"Is that how I died? By fighting against evil?"

She was silent too long. Tristan knew whatever had happened to end his life hadn't been good.

"Never mind," he said. "I doona want to know."

Rhi placed a hand on his arm. "I don't know why you couldn't remember your past life, or why you are here now. I also don't know why you became a Dragon King, but I can say with all honesty that you are one of only a few Kings that I like. They are better because you are now one of them. You embraced your life as King just as all Dragon Kings from the beginning of time have welcomed their role. Your past doesn't define you, Tristan. Your actions in the present do."

With a smile of encouragement, she was gone.

Tristan liked Rhi. She had a way of livening up any situation with her constantly changing nail color, her sarcastic comments, and her beauty.

The fact Con couldn't stand to have her around only made her needle him mercilessly when she did help them, which was more often than she should with the way Con treated her.

Tristan wondered if it had anything to do with her Dragon King lover.

He inhaled deeply and called out to Laith via their link. *"I need to leave. Watch over Sammi."*

"Tristan? What's wrong? You sound . . . strange."

"It's nothing. I just need to see about something."

He removed his jeans and ran to the edge of the mountain where he jumped off and shifted into dragon form. It was time he paid MacLeod Castle a visit.

CHAPTER
SIXTEEN

Sammi stretched languidly before she rolled over, expecting to find Tristan—and found cool sheets instead. Her smile faded as she opened her eyes to discover she was alone.

She sat up, the sheet held against her nakedness as she looked around the brightly lit room. The panic she first felt dissipated when she comprehended how late she had slept.

Shoving her wild hair out of her face, she scooted to the edge of the bed and yawned. There hadn't been much talking between her and Tristan the night before, but she imagined he would try and talk her into returning to the manor.

Which she was still against.

He would argue with her, but she wasn't going to budge. It didn't matter that everyone at Dreagan thought she was being used to get to Jane. They could very well be right. In which case, she was going to make sure no one could harm Jane, and the only way to do that was to stay as far from the manor as she could.

"That'll be easy on sixty thousand acres," she said with a chuckle.

Sammi rose and padded into the bathroom where she took a quick shower. She couldn't remember the last time she had felt so relaxed and . . . sated.

The smile she couldn't stop wearing grew larger when she thought of Tristan's wonderful mouth, hands, and body. She had never had someone touch her so deeply, nor had she ever responded so completely to someone.

Her smile slipped when she realized just how much she was thinking of him. Hadn't she learned her lesson when she lost her mother?

"Immortal," she said as she reached for the soap. "He's immortal."

That meant he couldn't die. She wouldn't suffer that same devastating, destroying grief she had endured with her mother's death.

"We had one night together. It was just one night. That isn't serious," she said as she washed and rinsed her hair and then her body.

By the time she was drying off she found the smile wider than ever. She was really going to have to get herself under control before Jane or someone else took one look at her and knew she and Tristan had been together.

Sammi found herself chuckling while dressing. She was starving. A quick run of the brush through her wet hair and she hurried into the main living area expecting to find Tristan.

When he wasn't in sight, she went into the kitchen only to come up empty again. Her heart thumped dully against her rib cage.

Then she remembered that he was most likely patrolling the skies as he had done the day before. Their talk would wait, and it gave her time to come up with more arguments about why she couldn't return to the manor.

She opened the fridge and rummaged until she found some ingredients to make a sandwich. With her hands full of meat, lettuce, a tomato, and cheese, she kicked the refrigerator door shut with her foot and turned to set the contents on the counter.

"Oh!" she screamed, jumping back when she saw a man with shoulder-length wavy, dark blond hair and gunmetal gray eyes.

He hastily lifted his hands and wrinkled his nose. "Sorry, lass. I thought you heard me come in. I'm Laith. I'll be your guard for the day," he said with a warm smile.

Sammi put her hand to her chest to calm her racing heart and couldn't help but notice how handsome Laith was, if women liked the wickedly gorgeous type. She much preferred the quiet, commanding men herself.

Then his words registered. "You're guarding me?"

"That I am," he said and leaned his hands on the bar separating them.

She looked down at his faded red tee with the distinctive white script of Coca-Cola across the front.

"Sammi," he called as he came around the bar. "Is everything all right?"

"Where is Tristan?"

"He had a few errands to run. He'll be back. He asked me to watch over you until then."

It was a plausible explanation, one she might have believed if she hadn't seen the worry on Tristan's and Rhi's faces when they let her know a Dark Fae was tracking her.

The smile that she hadn't been able to stop wearing couldn't be found now. The dull thud against her rib cage was her heart telling her something was wrong.

She grabbed the counter to keep steady. "Is it true only a Dragon King can kill another Dragon King?"

"It is," Laith grudgingly told her.

"How old are you?"

A muscle ticked in his jaw. "Sammi, you are no' supposed to know about us."

"I get that, but I do. So get over it." She licked her lips and softened her voice. "Please tell me."

"Billions of years old. We've been around since the beginning of time."

This was worse than she expected. They were *billions* of years old and only a few were married? Would Banan just find someone else when Jane grew old and died? Didn't he care at all? And how was Jane all right with all of it?

"So," she started, her voice cracking. She cleared her throat and tried again. "So, most of you don't tie yourself down to anyone."

Laith's forehead furrowed for a split second before he smiled. "Tristan is different, Sammi. He's the newest Dragon King, so he hasna been around as long."

That news didn't make things any better. "But most of you don't tie yourselves to a woman," she said again.

"Aye," Laith said with a loud sigh. "Most of us doona,

but there is a reason for that, lass. There is much about our history you doona know, so you can no' comprehend why we're alone and choose to remain that way."

"I think I get it."

"You doona," he said and took hold of her arms. "Banan, Guy, and Hal found their mates and married them. So did Kellan. It happens for some of us."

"And the years they remain married is a blink in time?"

Laith drew in a deep breath. "It should be Jane telling you what it is to be a mate to a Dragon King, no' me. Banan and Jane are mated for eternity. Jane will remain alive as long as Banan does."

"What?" Sammi hadn't known what Laith might tell her, but she hadn't been prepared for that. "You mean Jane will live forever?"

"Aye, lass. None of the Kings takes a mate lightly. It's why many of us doona remain with one woman for too long."

Sammi backed up and rubbed her temple as her head began to ache. "Where is Tristan really?"

Laith dropped his hands and walked back around the bar. "He'll have to be the one to tell you that. All I know is that he had somewhere to go."

She wanted to call Laith back when he walked out of the house, but she couldn't think of anything else to ask. Instead, she walked into the living room and sank onto the couch.

Last night she hadn't thought about the days to come or what she might want. All she had on her mind was Tristan and following her heart. It had been so very long since she had done something for the sheer pleasure of doing it, but that's exactly what the night with Tristan had been about.

Their passion had been explosive, their desire overwhelming. For the first time in months she forgot her life was in danger. She had let him consume her. It had been freeing, liberating.

And she had foolishly let the connection between them strengthen while she slept in his arms.

Sammi snorted. It hadn't happened when she slept. It hadn't even happened when they had made love.

It happened when she realized what he was and how he had been protecting her. That was the moment he had taken her breath away.

Their night together had simply destroyed the barriers around her heart without her even knowing it. She woke thinking she would have Tristan to herself to explore more of what was between them.

Fate once more gave her a slap in the face to remind her just who was in charge of things.

She thought about her sister mated to a King. Jane was now immortal. The thought left her reeling. It also bothered her that Jane hadn't said anything, but why would she? Sammi hadn't been there for the ceremony. Hell, she hadn't even known there was a ceremony.

There had been a celebration that she hadn't attended. Would things be different had she gone to the party? Would she have seen Tristan then and let herself give in to the desire?

Sammi knew she wouldn't have. She had a tight rein on her feelings, especially when it came to the opposite sex. It was only the predicament she was in now that had weakened those protective walls around her.

Tristan, being the amazing man—Dragon King—that he was had shattered those walls.

If he could do that without even trying, what could he do to her if he really tried? That thought chilled Sammi. She refused to be put in a situation where she could lose herself to someone.

Which is exactly where she was headed with Tristan. She didn't need to see into the future to know that she craved him as if he were the other half of her. It was dangerous ground she found herself on.

It was better that he was gone. It gave her time to collect her thoughts and erect a stronger barrier around herself, one that he could never touch.

Her body wanted him, and she knew she would give in to that temptation again, but she would never allow him close. He might not die on her, but he could still leave in other ways.

She wasn't strong enough to endure that again. Everyone thought she was made of steel, but it was an act she put on to protect her delicate heart.

Tristan had almost led her to make a fatal mistake, a mistake she would have made had she woken up with him beside her. She had been angry when Laith told her he was gone for the day, but now she was glad.

She would be strong when he returned—strong enough to sever that glorious, wonderful link between them before she did something disastrous like fall in love.

Tristan knew all about the shield over the land and MacLeod Castle that prevented mortals from seeing what was being hidden in plain sight.

He flew through the shield, the magic sizzling startlingly over his scales. As soon as he passed through it, he caught sight of the castle and the homes dotting the vast land.

With barely one circle around the castle, men came running out of the castle into the bailey. To his left he spotted a man with indigo skin and wings flying beside him.

"You can land in the bailey," he said and dove toward the castle, spreading his wings at the last minute and coming to land atop the battlements before jumping to the bailey.

Tristan tucked his wings and repeated the move by the Warrior, except when he spread his wings and landed in the bailey, the blast of air had the men bracing themselves.

One of the Warriors with a torc stepped forward. He had light brown hair and soft green eyes. Tristan eyed him, recognition just out of reach. It was as if he knew this man, as if he had been a close friend. The gold torc around his neck brought back the memory he'd had while holding Sammi.

"Do you know who I am?" he asked.

Tristan shook his head, not bothering to shift into human form. He wasn't completely sure coming to the castle was a wise move.

"I'm Quinn MacLeod. I had hoped . . . I thought you might remember since you came back."

Tristan looked at the others around the bailey, all Warriors. But the one he had come to see was missing.

"Ian isna here," Quinn said. "He and Dani live in Ferness near Charon, Phelan, and Malcolm."

"I can bring him here," said a man who had the same features as Quinn, as well as a torc.

Tristan guessed he was a MacLeod, but he couldn't place a name or the face.

"I'm Fallon, Quinn's eldest brother," he said. "I can jump—teleport that is—and bring Ian here if you'd like."

This was a mistake. All this proved was that he didn't know these people. Tristan spread his wings to fly when Quinn shouted his name.

"Tristan! Wait! Please. We've been hoping to see you. Phelan told us you doona have the memories of when you were Duncan." Quinn glanced at another brother who came up beside him and nodded. "This is Lucan, the middle MacLeod. I can introduce everyone to you."

He shook his head and took a step back. What had he been thinking would happen when he arrived? A part of him had believed he would take one look at the castle and all the memories would come flooding back.

The other part had prayed he wouldn't recollect anything else.

"Do you recall anything?" Lucan asked. "Do you remember Deirdre?"

The name made Tristan jerk back. He hated the name with a viciousness he couldn't explain, but he didn't know the woman.

Quinn took another step to him. "Do you remember Cairn Toul Mountain?"

The mountain. That's where he had been kept prisoner with Ian. There had been others there, he was sure of it, but the faces were too blurred in his memories to make out.

"It doesn't matter," said a feminine voice from atop the castle steps.

She had long dark hair with dozens of tiny braids atop the crown of her head with gold bands at the ends. The woman, just like Quinn, looked familiar, but Tristan couldn't place her.

"We survived Cairn Toul together," she said as she walked down the steps to stand beside Quinn. "We'll get through this as well, Tristan."

CHAPTER
SEVENTEEN

Tristan wasn't sure if he was sorry he went to MacLeod Castle or not. They had tried in vain to keep him there, but he had taken to the sky not long after the woman—Marcail—appeared.

The way Quinn had wrapped his arm around her stated the woman was his. But who was she? She acted as though she knew him, as if Tristan should know her.

He shook his head as he quickly—and briefly—checked in with Laith to make sure all was well with Sammi. She was going to want to know why he had left. He wondered if she thought he had run away from what happened between them.

He had, but he wouldn't tell her that. Tristan had known whatever was between him and Sammi was explosive. He hadn't counted on being rocked to his very foundation just by having her in his arms.

Life had been as close to ideal as he ever expected. Right up until he saw Sammi. That's when everything went spinning into utter chaos.

But it was a passion-filled, ecstasy-ridden chaos that he craved more of.

It was Sammi—touching her, kissing her—that had somehow triggered his memories. He was sure of it. Explaining it was difficult, but it was a certainty he felt in his gut.

The memories of his past life alarmed him, startled him. They were as clear and real as the world around him. So far the memories had been fleeting, but the emotions were high. What would happen if the memories lasted longer? Would he find himself living in that world instead of the one he was in?

It was a vicious circle he could find himself in if he wasn't careful.

He glided upon an air current as he grew closer to Dreagan. His thoughts turned back to Sammi. Whether or not he wanted to face Ian and the fact he'd had a past life, she had somehow forced him to confront it.

Tristan dropped a shoulder and altered his course as he flapped his wings to fly back to Sammi. He would convince her to return to the manor so he could watch over her as well as find Kellan to talk about the Kings and learn more of their history.

He had barely finished the thought when there was a push on his mind. It never entered his mind that it would be anyone other than a Dragon King. Tristan opened his thoughts, and immediately realized he didn't know who was contacting him.

"Hello, Tristan. Or is it Duncan?"

It was just a little farther to Dreagan land. Tristan flew faster, unsure of who this was or why he wanted to talk. *"It's Tristan."*

"Hmm. You doona sound so sure."

The Scots brogue was thick and heavy, the confidence stifling. *"Who are you?"*

A burst of laughter met his question. *"Oh, you know who I am."*

Ulrik. It had to be. Tristan crossed into Dreagan land and dove down to land atop the first mountain he reached. *"What do you want?"*

"I doona want anything. I simply want to warn you."

"About?"

"Samantha. She isna safe. Even on Dreagan. The Dark will come for her."

"You have an alliance with the Dark. You can stop them."

A low chuckle sounded through his head. *"You're a good Dragon King, Tristan, but you've much to learn yet about us. I suppose Con told you I was the one masterminding everything to expose you. Tell me. Why would I do that if I can no' shift into a dragon anymore? Why would I do that without my magic? What would I gain?"*

"You could force Con to return your magic."

"If it were that simple, I'd have done it centuries ago."

"Your revenge then."

There was a beat of silence. *"Never fear, young Tristan, I will have my vengeance."*

"If it isna you, then who is Dreagan's enemy?"

"I never said I wasna Dreagan's enemy."

Tristan stamped a foot and rocks rained down the mountain. *"Enough of the games. What do you want?"*

"I want the dragons back in control. I want to erase every human on this planet."

With his dragon eyes, Tristan could see Dreagan Manor in the distance. *"That's obvious. What do you want with me?"*

"Join me and I'll stop the Dark Ones from taking Samantha."

It was a tempting offer only because it would keep Sammi safe, but for how long? If Ulrik got what he wanted, all humans would be gone. That included Sammi. *"Why me?"*

"Why no' you?"

"I'm going to need more than that before I make a decision."

"Nice," he said, a smile in his voice. *"I expected you to jump at the chance to save your woman, but perhaps I was wrong. The Kings have made a habit lately of falling for humans so easily."*

"The way you did?" Tristan knew he'd hit a nerve by the silence that followed.

"You're unexpected, Tristan. By the way you so readily—and quickly, I might add—came to Samantha's rescue, I assumed you were falling for the mortal."

"It's the duty of the Dragon Kings to protect humans."

"Even when they start attacking you? Think hard about that one, lad, because you didna witness the war. You didna see the humans annihilate smaller dragons in one fell swoop. You didna hear the cries of the dragons as we raced to help them only to have Con hold us back because we might harm a human."

The hatred in his voice was so heavy and loud that

Tristan winced as it bounced around inside his head. *"Nay, I wasna there, but I'm a King now. I will do as we were meant to do. There are no more dragons for the humans to harm."*

"You're here."

"If you claim to no' be the one trying to expose us, what are you doing aligning with the Dark Fae and MI5?"

"Trying to stop Con. He is the one to blame for the way things are now. It was the Silvers who were going to take him and his Golds down before he convinced all the other Kings to send the dragons out of this realm."

"Con took away your magic so you would stop killing humans."

"I did kill humans. They were attacking dragons. We are dragons, first and foremost. What kind of creature are we to let our own kind be murdered as we protect the murderers?"

Tristan didn't have an answer. He hadn't been there, so he didn't know what he would do but he couldn't imagine sitting and watching his Ambers being killed and doing nothing about it.

"Con isna all he claims to be. He never has been. I learned that the hard way when I thought he was a friend. He betrayed me, he betrayed the Kings, but more than that, he betrayed all dragons."

The link was severed, leaving Tristan more unsure of things than ever before. Ulrik wanted him to join his cause, but what exactly was his cause?

The idea of Con being the one to expose the Kings was absurd. Con went out of his way to keep most mor-

tals as far from Dreagan as he could. He had even tried
to keep Kellan and Denae apart.

Tristan called out to Laith who opened his mind immediately. *"I suspect there's going to be an attack from
the Dark soon."*

"How do you know that?" Laith asked.

Tristan blew out a long breath. *"Ulrik told me."*

"What?" Laith shouted.

*"I'll tell you everything later. Right now we need to
keep Sammi away from them. I have a feeling if the
Dark get ahold of her she willna be as easy to find as
Kellan and Denae were."*

*"Nay, I doona suspect she will be. Surely the Dark
wouldna dare come on our land."*

"At this point I expect anything and everything."

*"The only place she'll truly be safe is in the moun-
tain."*

The mountain the manor was built into was a sacred
place for the Kings. It was also where they kept the
four sleeping Silvers that had been caught and trapped
before they could wipe out humanity. *"Doona give her
a choice. Just take her there."*

"Con will never allow it."

*"I'll deal with him. Just get Sammi, and I'll meet
you at the manor."*

Laith ended the conversation with a curt aye. Tristan
didn't waste any time flying toward the manor. Since
there were mortals about—working and visiting—he
made sure to shift back into his human form and run
the rest of the way.

He bypassed the house and entered the mountain

by a side entrance. As always, there were clothes stashed for just such emergencies.

Tristan found a pair of jeans and put them on before he made his way through tunnels to get to what could only be described as Kellan's office.

The cave was large and lit by dozens of torches on the walls. The entire back of the cave was lined with shelves where scrolls were shelved according to years. The scrolls eventually turned into books.

There were rugs placed all over the cave in a haphazard fashion. In the middle of the cave sat a large desk that looked as old as the Kings. An inkwell and a feather pen were situated on the left-hand corner. On the right was a wooden tankard filled with pens that had obviously been collected through the ages.

The most modern thing in the cave was the desk lamp that sat with its light shining on an open book, a book that Kellan had been writing of the history of the Kings.

A sigh passed Tristan's lips when he didn't find Kellan sitting behind his desk. He had hoped Kellan and Denae would have returned by now, but he had no such luck.

"Damn," he said and wiped a hand down his face.

Tristan looked at the scrolls and books and decided to find the facts for himself. He was standing before the shelves looking at dates when he heard a noise behind him. He turned and found Rhys leaning against the opening of the cave.

"What are you looking for? Maybe I can help," Rhys said.

Tristan glanced at the shelves again. "I want to know

what happened between Con and Ulrik, and I want to know about the war with the mortals."

Rhys straightened, his brows raised. "I thought we had already filled you in on all of that."

"You did. I want to read the account."

"You mean an impartial account."

Rhys might be a smartass and reckless, but he wasn't stupid. Tristan nodded. "I do."

"What's happened?"

Damn, but Rhys was perceptive. "Did you agree with Con in sending away the dragons?"

"Nay. None of us did, nor did we want to see them slaughtered. We did what we thought was best."

"And Ulrik? Did you agree with that?" Tristan pressed.

Rhys walked around to the other side of Kellan's desk and ran his fingers along the top. "It's no secret that I was against what Con wanted. Hell, Tristan, the Kings were completely divided."

"What united you?"

"Con. He's always had a way of uniting us. It's one reason he's King of Kings. Ulrik had that same ability."

"So Ulrik could have been where Con is?"

Rhys nodded slowly. "They were the best of friends, as tight as brothers. Ulrik was content to rule his Silvers. Con was the one who wanted to be King of Kings. Ulrik decided to step aside rather than have them fight each other for the position."

"Some considered Ulrik weak for that, did they no'?"

"Perhaps." Rhys smiled then. "But they soon learned their lesson. Ulrik was anything but weak. He was intelligent and had a sense of battle that I've never seen before. No one could ever win against him."

It all began to make sense to Tristan now.

"Why?" Rhys asked. "Why are you asking these specific questions?"

Tristan lifted his gaze to meet Rhys's. "Because Ulrik contacted me."

CHAPTER
EIGHTEEN

Very few times in Sammi's life had she been so completely blindsided. This latest one was a real kicker.

And she planned to throw a few punches of her own once her feet were planted on the ground again.

She looked up at Laith and glared at the black dragon. He paid her no heed as he flew them closer and closer to the manor house.

Flying didn't give her the same excitement as it had when Tristan had taken her. Then again, she hadn't been so angry she could chew nails.

She hadn't ever understood that statement until then. Now, she fully understood what her mother had meant. The closer she got to the manor, the more incensed she became.

More so because she had been gullible enough to believe Laith when he said Tristan had asked her to meet him at another cottage.

"Cottage my ass," she mumbled and propped her elbow on Laith's hand.

All too soon they arrived at the manor. At least

that's what she thought until Laith dipped behind a mountain to glide into the valley. She glanced at the mountain. On the other side of the manor was her sister and all the other Dragon Kings.

Sammi clutched Laith's black scales when he suddenly dove, his wings tucked against him so that they whipped through the sky like a missile.

She covered her eyes with her hands. Then she parted her fingers and peered through to see the wall of the mountain coming at her.

Before she could release a scream, Laith once more spread his wings and let his lower body drop. It halted them instantly.

She raked her hair out of her eyes as Laith landed, and still holding her in his hand, walked into the opening before them on three legs.

Sammi tried to take it all in. The opening might have been small enough that Laith had to duck his head, but once inside it was easily twice as tall as he was.

Tall enough for dragons to move about easily, she realized.

The light shining through the entrance quickly gave way to darkness, leaving her nothing to see. She blinked rapidly while hoping her eyes would adjust so she might glimpse something.

She swung her head from side to side, shifting in Laith's hand as she did. She was so busy trying to see something that she missed the flicker of light dancing on the stones until Laith stopped.

Sammi briefly saw the torches lining a corridor before Laith set her down. She turned to face him and glowered. "Some cottage. Why lie to me?"

"Because I told him to get you here however he needed to."

Her stomach quivered as it always did when she heard Tristan's voice. She slowly turned and found him standing in the shadows between two torches. Sammi hated that she couldn't see his face, not that he gave anything away through his expressions.

Tristan was a master at keeping everything carefully hidden. Much like everyone at Dreagan was. While the others had had countless centuries to do it, he'd had a few years.

"I told you I didn't want to come here," she told him to fill the silence since she refused to run and throw her arms around him.

"Things have changed. There is an imminent attack by the Dark against you. I had to get you to a place they wouldn't dare venture."

"In a mountain?"

He lowered his chin. "Aye. This isna a place we bring mortals."

"Not even Jane?"

"Jane is . . . one of us."

Sammi rolled her eyes. "Because she married into it?"

"Because she's Banan's mate."

There was something in Tristan's tone that made her shiver. "Laith explained what a Dragon King's mate was. If the Dark Fae are coming, you've now brought them to the manor where Jane is. Banan won't thank you for it."

"I'm doing what Banan asked—keeping you from the Dark."

"Why not just have Laith tell me the truth instead of deceiving me?"

"Because you wouldna have come," Tristan stated. "And doona tell me you would have, because we both know you wouldna."

She hated when she couldn't get the upper hand. She hated even more that she wanted to go to him and touch him to make sure the previous night had really happened and hadn't been a dream.

Why did he have to be so damned handsome?

"Am I to stay here?" she asked. When she glanced behind her Laith was gone. Whether he was in the shadows watching or gone she didn't know.

Tristan stepped to the side. "Nay. I have a more comfortable place for you. Follow me."

Sammi's legs felt as if they were weighted down, as if she were walking in waist-high water. She trailed after Tristan, but she didn't look around as before.

Everything she had told herself at the cottage about severing the link between her and Tristan had evaporated the moment she saw him.

Then he reminded her just how different their worlds were. He was immortal, powerful, and a shifter.

She was just Samantha Miller, a simple mortal who had lost everything.

It should have been like a douse of cold water. Instead, it made her want him all the more. If she reached out her hand, she could touch his back, feel his heat, remember the way his muscles stirred.

Tristan moved with the grace of a hunter. She watched him walk, wondering at the power within him. He had been tender, gentle with her at every turn.

But she knew there was a caged animal ready to pounce, a force that waited impatiently to be released.

She knew the size of him as a dragon, and she could only imagine the destruction he could cause if he so wished.

His head shifted slightly to put his face in profile. "You're unusually quiet."

"What's there to say?"

"You're angry we tricked you."

It wasn't a question, and she let him believe the lie. When in reality she was upset that he had left her. It was for the best. She knew that now because she was already becoming attached, but it didn't stop the hurt any.

Tristan halted and turned to face her. She pulled back so she wouldn't run into him. His dark gaze held hers and there was sorrow and a hefty dose of doubt reflected in his eyes.

"I'll do anything to keep you out of the hands of the Dark."

She swallowed, inwardly wincing at how loud it was. "You said Denae survived. Tell me what she did so if I do get taken I'll get out as well."

Tristan's gaze shifted to the side. "We doona know what she did."

"Oh." What else could she say? She had thought—expected—there to be a way to keep the Dark Fae away. "Everyone and everything has a weakness. Surely the Dark have one as well?"

"Nay," Tristan said. He reached out and touched her hair before he turned on his heel to continue walking.

First it was the Mob, next it was the Dark Fae, and then it was the two factions working together. Now was the realization that nothing could stop the Dark.

Tristan brought her to a small room with a chair and too many candles to count that lit up the space. Alongside the overstuffed chair was a table with an iPad.

"You'll be safe here. I'm sure Jane will be down soon to check on you. Until then, please remain in this room. I'd rather you no' encounter Con during all of this."

She touched the back of the chair as she walked around to stand at its front. "He won't approve of me being here?"

"Nay."

"What will he do to you?"

"You doona need to worry about that."

She met his gaze. "You put yourself in a difficult situation just for me?"

"I promised to keep you safe."

And with that, he was gone.

Sammi sat down with a sigh. After such a wonderful night in his arms, she hadn't even been able to touch him. She'd been too afraid of herself to wrap her arms around him and plant her lips on his.

To make matters worse, she was alone with her thoughts. That's the last thing she wanted. She needed her mind occupied or to do something with her hands, anything other than the nothingness that allowed her to think about Tristan and all that she wished for.

He rubbed his hands together. It hadn't been his intention to reach out to Tristan quite so soon. Still, it had gone exceptionally well.

Tristan had kept the conversation going, and no doubt there were questions he would demand Con answer. Con wouldn't, of course, and it would make Tristan all the more wary of the King of Kings.

From there it would take only a few more nudges to have Tristan on his side. After Tristan, he was sure others would gradually follow.

Fracturing the Kings from within. There wasn't a more fitting end to all that Con held dear.

As for Samantha, he wasn't sure yet how he would handle things. His alliance with the Dark Ones was precarious at best. He might have ventured into unknown territory that Con or the other Dragon Kings would never have done, but it had paid off.

To an extent at least. The Dark might agree to something, but they had their own agendas. Just as he did. They were too intent on their own pleasures, however, to realize it.

It wouldn't just be the mortals he got rid of, the Fae—all Fae—would go with them. The Kings would soon follow once they were divided and he started the war.

After they were gone, he would bring back the dragons. The realm would once more be as it should.

He smiled as he puffed on his cigar. His musings were interrupted by the ringing of his mobile phone. He rose from the sofa and picked up the phone to answer with a succinct, "Yes?"

"The Dark Fae came through, sir. They saw a King move Samantha Miller from the cottage just as you expected."

"They're so predictable. Where did they take Miss Miller?"

"To a mountain."

He squeezed his cigar until it broke in half. "Are you sure?"

"I'm relaying information given to us by the Dark, sir. We didn't see it ourselves."

"What else did our Dark friend say?"

There was a beat of hesitation. "He just smiled as if what happened was a challenge."

"To them it is, but they'll fail. No Dark would dare to venture onto Dreagan."

"Do we stand down then?"

"Aye," he barked. Then he cleared his throat and made sure his British accent was back in place. "Yes. As soon as you step on Dreagan land they'll kill you all."

"We could get more equipment from MI5 headquarters or hack into the satellite."

He leaned against his desk and reached for another cigar. He clipped off one end with the cutter. "A valid suggestion, but there is nothing at MI5 that can help us for the moment. We sit back and let the Dark do what they want."

"If they take Samantha, you'll never get to her."

"You're a fool if you think I wanted Miss Miller."

"But, sir . . . you blew up her pub."

He smiled remembering it. "That I did. She's done exactly what I wanted her to do, though it took her longer than I expected. She ran to Dreagan."

"If it isn't Samantha Miller, then who are you after?"

"Someone much more important." And who knew Tristan would find the need to protect the mortal? It was almost too perfect. "Any other news?"

"There are four new men I'll be interviewing tomorrow to fill in some of the spots we have open."

"Good, good."

"Will Mr. Calvin approve?"

"Yes."

He almost laughed. How silly these mortals were. They had no idea that all the names he used in his many resources and affiliations were all him.

It had taken him over five thousand years, but in that time he had gained access to the most influential and powerful humans. He ingrained himself into families so that he had to simply say the word and everyone in that family would willingly die for him.

He ran the Mob—all mobs on all continents. He was the one person who decided what drugs would go where and which of his lackeys he dubbed the current "drug lord."

He was the one who decided which king would rule and what country would win wars.

Everything he had done had been carefully planned out for one thing—the end of the Dragon Kings.

CHAPTER
NINETEEN

Tristan left Sammi and went to a cavern situated in the middle of everything. It wasn't the largest, and the torches were few. But inside was the greatest treasure the Kings had—the Silvers.

The sound of his boot heels was drowned out by the deep breathing of the four dragons in their cage. He stopped next to the enclosure and stared at the metallic shine of the silver scales.

The dragons were gorgeous. Ever since the others had brought him down here, Tristan made a point of stopping in at least once a day.

Sure he saw the other Kings in dragon form, but seeing these Silvers was different. They weren't able to become human. This was their one and only form. And they were spectacular.

He couldn't imagine not being able to look at them daily, which made him think of Ulrik. Ulrik was their King. He had essentially been kept prisoner on this realm with some of his dragons near, and he hadn't been able to see them.

It was beyond cruel. Combined with having his magic bound, not being able to shift into dragon form, or being with any of the other Kings, Tristan couldn't think of a more malicious, vindictive way to treat someone.

All because Ulrik had been protecting dragons.

Tristan squatted beside the bars and ran his hand over one of the dragons' wings. They slept, undisturbed by the vicious world around them. It was the magic of all the Dragon Kings and Dreagan that kept them asleep.

It was also the reason no King could stay away from Dreagan for long periods. Their combined magic was needed to hold the Silvers.

For hundreds of thousands of years the dragons hadn't moved. Then, two years ago, one did.

It was when he had become a Dragon King.

It was also when the spell Con had put over the Kings to prevent any of them from feeling deep emotions for humans somehow failed.

Hal fell in love with Cassie, a human. It was a few months later that Guy fell hard for Elena, which led Banan to Jane.

No matter how Con tried—and he had tried—he couldn't put the spell back in place. Once the Kings were in love, there was nothing he could do.

Then for almost two years life returned to what it had been. Until MI5 had sent Denae and her partner onto Dreagan to spy. They had woken Kellan, and to Con's horror, Denae became Kellan's mate.

Tristan wondered why Con went to such trouble to try and keep Kellan and Denae apart when he hadn't for Banan or Guy.

He continued to pet the Silver, his thoughts in a whirlwind about Con, Dreagan, and Ulrik as well as his role as a Dragon King. Or was he a Warrior?

Movement behind him had Tristan peering over his shoulder to find Rhys. It had been a mistake to tell Rhys about Ulrik, but the damage was done.

"I knew I'd find you here," Rhys said. "We all come here, some more often than others. I love looking at them, but there are a few who try to stay away."

"Why? Do the Silvers remind them of Ulrik?"

Rhys came to stand beside him and reached through the bars to caress the dragons. "I'm sure that's part of it. The main reason is that it's too painful to look at them and realize we'll probably never see our dragons again."

"But you know where they were sent," Tristan said as he stood.

"That was a verra, verra long time ago. We've no' had any contact with them to keep others like the Dark Fae from finding where they are."

"But others could have found them. They could be hurting."

Rhys's aqua eyes met his. "Aye, they could be. It's a chance we take to keep them free."

Tristan looked back at the sleeping dragons. The silver scales were shaded darker on the back of their necks. A row of tendrils ran from the base of the skull down to the tip of the tail the same darker silver as the shading.

He was told the Silvers had eyes the color of obsidian. Tristan wished he could see for himself.

"Will you tell me what Ulrik said to you?" Rhys asked.

Tristan shrugged and walked around the cage. "He said Con wasna the person we think he is. He said Con took away his magic because he was trying to stop the dragons from being sent away."

"That's a lie. I was there, Tristan. I know."

Tristan met Rhys's gaze from across the cage. "You were there through it all? You saw Con and Ulrik converse?"

"Well, nay," Rhys hedged. "Only Con and Ulrik were there."

"Then how does Kellan know what to write?"

Rhys's lips twisted in a rueful smile. "Ah, well, that's what happens when you agree to record the history of the dragons. Kellan sees what happens in his mind. He then records it."

"Did you read what he wrote?"

Rhys frowned. "Nay. I didna need to."

"Because you took Con's word?" Tristan guessed.

"Dammit." Rhys turned away from the cage and paced a short distance before whirling back around. "We killed Ulrik's woman because she betrayed him—and us. I saw him . . . ravaged at what we had done. And I saw Ulrik attacking the humans. Of course I believed Con."

Tristan began to wonder if he wouldn't have been just like Rhys and trusted Con after all that had been witnessed. "Do you wonder if you should ever read what happened between Ulrik and Con?"

"Sometimes."

Tristan was surprised at the response. "But you have no'?"

Rhys shook his head and casually strolled around

the cavern. "What's done is done. Do I wish I had stood beside Ulrik and fought the humans who killed our dragons? Aye. I do. There are nights that I lie awake and wonder if my Yellows would be here if I had stood with Ulrik. Or would I be banished like him, never to be in dragon form again and take to the sky. Aye, Tristan, I've thought about it a lot. I'm betting every King has."

"Why would Ulrik want me to join him?"

Rhys stopped cold, his eyes blazing with disbelief. "He actually asked that of you?"

"Aye."

"Banan went to see him to ask him to call off the Dark," Rhys said as he ran a hand through his long hair. "Ulrik refused."

Tristan leaned a shoulder against one of the thick bars of the cage. "Ulrik told me the Dark were coming for Sammi. On Dreagan land."

"What are we standing here for? We need to get to her," Rhys stated as he stalked to the entrance.

"I had Laith bring her here."

Once more Rhys halted. This time he slowly turned to Tristan. "Here? Where do you mean exactly?"

"She's down the corridor in an empty room."

"She's no' a mate. No one but Kings and their mates are allowed in the mountain, Tristan."

He walked around the cage to stand beside Rhys. "This was the only place I knew would guarantee Sammi was safe. Banan will agree with me, and if he doesna, then oh well. I doona fear Con or any of you. I had to make a decision."

"Do you care for her?"

Tristan was taken aback by the question. "What did Laith tell you?"

"Nothing. I've no' spoken with him. But you've no' answered my question."

How did he answer? If he admitted to feelings for Sammi, then Rhys might assume there was more to it than the lust that flared brightly whenever he thought of her. Then again, he couldn't deny there was something.

A man who felt nothing for someone wouldn't bring them to a private, secure location with the possibility of retribution.

"Aye," Tristan admitted. "I care for her."

"Obviously. How deeply?"

"I slept with her, if that's what you're asking."

Rhys waved away his words. "That was inevitable. We all knew it was coming by the way the two of you looked at each other."

"If you know all of this, why are you asking me questions to answers you already know?"

"To hear you say it," Rhys said.

Tristan clenched his jaw and looked away from Rhys. Was his uncertainty of who he was apparent to any who looked? He thought he had done a better job of concealing his indecision and doubt.

"There's no doubt you were born to be a Dragon King," Rhys continued. "You took to it as if you had always been a dragon. You think and fight like a dragon, but more importantly, you make decisions like a King. I know the matter with Ian and your past has rocked you."

"That's putting it mildly," he mumbled.

A ghost of a grin touched Rhys's lips. "Why worry

about it if you doona remember your other life with Ian and the Warriors?"

Tristan had always liked Rhys. He could be counted on with a wise-ass comment or sarcastic saying just to annoy. Rarely did the cocky smile leave his face.

He looked at Rhys and blew out a breath. "That's no' entirely true anymore."

"Interesting," Rhys said with raised eyebrows. "Do you remember Ian?"

"No' exactly. I get flashes of memories, seconds really."

"When did it start?"

Tristan rubbed the back of his neck and looked away. "After Sammi came and I tended her wound."

"I've no doubt Ulrik has people watching us. I'm sure he knows Ian is trying to contact you, and he knows you're the new Dragon King. You didna go through the wars with the humans or the Fae, so he figures your loyalty isna as complete as the rest of ours."

"So you're loyal to Con?"

Rhys smiled as he slapped him on the back. "I'm loyal to the Dragon Kings. Con makes mistakes just like anyone. He may like to think he's perfect, but he's far from it."

"Ulrik had compelling arguments," Tristan hedged. He hated to think that he might decide to leave Dreagan and join Ulrik, but the truth was, he didn't know who to believe or what to do since he knew only some of the information.

Rhys's smile died. "Ulrik was one of the best Kings. His Silvers would've done anything for him. Unlike some of us, Ulrik willingly took a human as his lover. He fell hard for her. There was no reason for him no' to trust her or any human. Hell, we all did. Ulrik had an amazing ability with words. He could talk anyone into anything."

"Isna that what Con did?"

"In a manner," Rhys admitted. "But Ulrik's was a true gift. Without even trying, he could change someone's opinion on a subject, any subject, no matter how inconsequential it might be."

Tristan glanced at the Silvers. "You think that's what he was doing to me?"

"Absolutely. It's enough that your twin from a past life is trying to get in touch with you, but I suspect there is more going on."

He wanted to confide all in Rhys, but would it only muddy the waters more? Rhys would try to convince him to remain at Dreagan.

"There is."

Rhys's smile was full of regret. "Perhaps you'll share what's going on with me or someone else. Ulrik is in your head now. You doona need to be pulled in different directions."

That's exactly what Tristan didn't want, and he already felt that way.

"I'm no' saying Con was right and Ulrik was wrong," Rhys continued. "But this isna about either of them. What we're fighting for now is to keep the Dragon Kings secret. We know our enemies now, and we know what they want. The only thing we need to focus on is staying united."

Rhys might have said Ulrik had a gift with words, but so did he. Tristan said, "Then let's unite and make sure when the Dark arrive that we're there to greet them."

Rhys busted out laughing as they walked from the cavern. "Now we're on the same page."

CHAPTER
TWENTY

Sammi opened the iPad and hit the music icon. Lana Del Rey's "Summertime Sadness" began a slow, sexy beat. Sammi began to sing along as she leaned back in the chair.

The song reminded her too much of her time with Tristan. The words got locked in her throat, clogging it until the emotion began to overwhelm her.

She quickly hit the forward button and Kings of Leon blared through the speakers. It helped to chase away the feelings she didn't want to face.

Sammi got to her feet and walked around the sparse room. She guessed it was a room. It looked more like a small cave, and since they were inside a mountain, she assumed that's exactly what it was.

"Sammi!"

She whirled around as Jane came running into the room, her arms wrapping around her tightly. Sammi closed her eyes and held onto her sister.

"Are you all right?" Jane asked.

Sammi nodded and tightened her grip. "I guess you know all of it?"

Jane laughed and pulled back. "We've known since before you left. You told Tristan and Banan everything."

"No, I didn't." She was sure she hadn't. She had gone out of her way to give them just enough to leave her alone.

It was the way Jane suddenly wouldn't meet her gaze that told Sammi something had happened, something she wasn't going to like.

"Jane, I didn't tell them."

Her sister dropped her arms and stepped back. "Laith told us that you know who Banan and Tristan are."

"Yes, but that's not the point."

"It is," Jane insisted. "If you know they're Dragon Kings, then you must also know that each has a certain . . . gift, you could say."

"Gift?" Sammi repeated, dread seeping into her pores. "What type of gift?"

Jane shrugged nonchalantly. "Each is different."

"What is Tristan's?"

Jane visibly cringed. "Don't be angry with him. He was doing exactly what Banan and I asked."

"Jane," Sammi urged.

"He can make you tell the things you wouldn't otherwise."

Sammi rubbed her forehead and desperately tried to contain the rage that bubbled within her. "So the night I felt calmer and more at ease . . ."

"Was the night you told them everything, yes," Jane said grudgingly. "He gave you some peace at least."

"And you all allowed me to sneak off?"

Jane bit her lip. "Sammi—"

"While they followed me?"

Of course. It all fit into place now. No wonder Tristan had found her so easily. She had believed she'd gotten away from the Mob, but in reality Tristan had been protecting her.

So much for her having the courage to face the time alone out in the wild. She hadn't been alone. She had never been in any danger.

That wasn't what riled her so. It was how easily Tristan had controlled her mind into spilling the secrets she had been protecting. If he did it once, he could do it again.

"Tristan tried to get me to come back here from the very beginning," she said as she glared at Jane.

Jane's smile was weak. "I begged him to return you any way he could."

Sammi began to laugh. What a fool she had been. While she had been trying to protect her heart from disaster, Tristan had been manipulating her into getting exactly what he wanted. And who knew if what she felt for him was real? After all, he could erase all her fears with a simple touch.

"There is no Dark attack coming, is there?"

Jane's forehead furrowed. "It's surprising all of us that the Dark would dare to come onto Dreagan, but it appears as if they are."

"Why? I'm no one. I wasn't involved with anyone at Dreagan except for you, and we might talk on the phone, but I had never been here before. Why would they use me? Why not someone else to get to the guys?"

"I don't know," Jane said in a low voice.

Sammi shut off the music. "The entire time I've

been here and around Tristan I've felt as if I'm given just enough of the truth to keep me quiet. I'm tired of it all. I'm tired of running for my life, I'm tired of my body hurting, and I'm tired of being used."

"Used? Sammi—"

"Used," she said over Jane. "I was used by Daniel to launder money in my pub. If all of you are right, then I've been used by the Mob—who are actually the Kings' enemy—to get to you, thereby to Banan. I was used by Banan to get information. I was used by all of you to flush out the people after me. And I was used by Tris . . ."

She couldn't even finish saying his name.

Her chest ached as she struggled to calm her breathing, but her chest was heaving and her heart pounded with dismay. She had given her body to Tristan, and she thought he'd felt something, anything for her by the way he touched her so passionately and loved her so thoroughly.

The truth was a cold bedfellow, and part of Sammi wished she was still trying to piece it all together.

"We did it to protect you."

Jane's heartfelt words did little to ease Sammi. Once more she had given a piece of her heart to someone— her sister. She hadn't wanted to, but Jane had been persistent, and Sammi had been so lonely.

All it proved was that Sammi really couldn't trust anyone. Not an ex-lover turned business partner, not her half-sister, and certainly not a mysterious, gorgeous man who could make her float with just a kiss.

"I'd like to be alone," she said and turned her back to Jane.

"Sammi, please," Jane begged.

But she refused to look at her sister.

She waited until Jane's footsteps faded to nothing before she peeked out of the doorway to see if anyone was keeping watch. Luckily, everyone thought she would stay put during the so-called threat.

How wrong they were. She hurried from the room, looking over her shoulder frequently.

Oh, she knew someone was after her, and she knew there was real danger out there in the form of Dark Fae. It wasn't that she had a death wish or wanted to push the limits, it was simply a matter of her taking control of her life.

Sammi got turned around so many times in the mountain that she lost count. Several times she had to hide behind boulders or duck into caves when she heard someone near.

It was only by sheer luck that as she was walking past an opening, she glanced inside to see the silver dragons. They were caged as they slept almost peacefully. She wanted to go to them, but there was a man with them. He had wavy blond hair, and was dressed in slacks and a shirt rolled up to his elbows.

She wisely skipped getting a closer look at the dragons and instead managed to find her way out of the mountain. Only to stop dead in her tracks as she saw how the manor was built into the mountain.

Sammi kept to the hedges and trees as she quickly made her way to the parking lot of the distillery. There had to be someone who would give her a ride out.

She rounded a corner and collided with someone. Sammi was knocked backward, but managed to fall into a hedge instead of onto the ground.

"Ow," came a muffled American accent.

Sammi looked over to find none other than Lily. She started laughing as she straightened and helped Lily to her feet. "Thank God it was you."

Lily dusted off her oversized shirt and skirt. "Sammi? Are you all right? You look better than when I saw you last week."

Had it really been that long? "Sorry I ran into you. You got the job, didn't you?"

"Yes." Lily beamed, her black eyes shining with excitement. "I'm really enjoying it too."

"That's lovely. Listen, Lily, can you give me a ride out of here?"

Lily nodded. "Of course. Is Jane busy?"

"Very much so. Do you mind if we leave now?" Sammi asked as she grabbed Lily's purse and ushered her toward the old BMW.

Lily's eyes grew troubled. "Where do you need to go? I need to be home at a certain time." She stopped and then gave a little shake of her head. "Sorry. I'm past that now."

Sammi was about to ask why a grown woman had a curfew, but she had more important matters at hand. "How far can you take me?"

"Wherever you need."

"Then take me as far as you can," Sammi said as she got into the passenger seat.

She listened to Lily talk of all the customers she had met while they drove from Dreagan. Still, Sammi didn't relax. She had thought she'd gotten away from Dreagan once before. For all she knew, she was being followed again.

Her hand tightened on the strap of the seat belt as she belatedly realized she had put Lily in danger. The Mob or the Dark Fae was probably watching her.

"Are there any cars behind you?" Sammi asked.

Lily chuckled. "No." Then she glanced at her and the smile vanished. "Are you in trouble?"

"More than you could possibly believe. I sorry, Lily. I shouldn't have involved you."

Lily just shrugged and looked in the rearview mirror again. "I gather since you're running from Dreagan that you'd prefer me not to tell Jane that I helped."

"I'd appreciate that."

"I thought I'd see you around the distillery these past days, but Cassie told me your wound needed tending and you were resting. The dark circles are no longer visible, by the way. I think the rest suited you."

Sammi looked out her window. It wasn't rest she had wanted. It was Tristan. How quickly time passed when she wanted to savor it. If only she hadn't fallen asleep she might have been awake when he left.

"Hindsight is twenty-twenty."

"What?" Lily asked.

"Something my mother used to say. Hindsight is twenty-twenty. I always found that saying so trite, but it's so damn true."

"Yes. It is."

Sammi jerked her gaze to Lily. Gone was the shy smile. The cautious, petite woman looked haggard, afraid, and disillusioned. An inner voice nudged Sammi to ask, "You have a curfew?"

"No," Lily said with a smile.

But that smile was forced. Sammi was conscious

that hers wasn't the only life that had gone to hell and back, but was Lily's one of them?

"Still no cars behind us."

Sammi nodded absently. "Cars. Right." She mentally shook herself. She wanted to help Lily, but first she had to help herself.

She leaned forward and looked up at the sky before gazing out of the side window.

"Are you looking for a plane now?" Lily asked.

Sammi shot her a smile. "Something like that. There are few clouds. A nice, clear day."

"That's good, I suppose."

"Very good," she said as she sat back.

The rest of the ride went by all too quickly. Sammi found she and Lily had a lot in common, and the only thing that made warning bells go off was how Lily easily diverted talk away from her past.

When Lily pulled the car over in a small village, Sammi spotted the bus stop just up the road. "Thank you. Get home safely."

"You stay safe as well," Lily called with a wave.

Sammi got out of the car and shut the door, waving as Lily did a U-turn and turned back the way they had come. She took a few moments to check her surroundings and look for anyone suspicious, letting out a sigh when the coast was clear.

Then she walked to the bus.

CHAPTER
TWENTY-ONE

Tristan finished filling his brethren in on what had transpired with Ulrik—at least most of it—and why he had brought Sammi to the mountain.

There had been mixed reactions, but Tristan had expected as much. He left Rhys and Banan to hash out details of how Sammi and the wives would be protected. Tristan had been itching to see Sammi again, to touch her and simply hold her in his arms.

Not that he knew what to say to her. She looked at him differently, as if she knew the turmoil within him. Laith had assured him that she hadn't been that upset at finding him gone, but a tiny voice inside Tristan told him that it had mattered a great deal to her.

He hadn't set out to hurt her. He'd needed answers, some sort of direction in the storm that had become his life. And she was part of it. It wasn't just the fierce, engulfing attraction—it was that somehow she released his memories.

Tristan wasn't sure if he was ready to face those memories or not. Then there was Sammi herself. She was . . . incredible. Her eyes were enchanting, her kisses intoxicating.

Her body enthralling.

With one inviting smile he had been ensnared, entrapped. Entangled. She made his palms sweat, his heart race, and his blood burn.

Tristan paused and scrubbed a hand down his face. His hands ached to touch her, but there were more pressing matters than slaking his lust, like keeping her out of the hands of the Dark.

The Dark. He hadn't fought them in the Fae Wars. In fact the only battles he had been in with the other Kings were with the Warriors and Druids. Yet he knew enough about the dragon he was and the others to know that they were powerful and effective.

The Dark—all of the Fae, really—had lost in the Fae Wars. The Kings hadn't been able to keep them out of the realm, but they were able to confine them. Even that was coming unraveled.

It's like there was some potent force whose single interest was blocking or collapsing all the Kings had done. It couldn't be Ulrik. His magic was taken from him. And this would have to be magic in order to fight against something as prevailing as dragon magic.

Ulrik had said he would stop the attack on Sammi if Tristan joined him. He wasn't afraid of the Dark. He was afraid of what they would do to Sammi.

Tristan leaned against the tunnel wall and hung his head. Ulrik offered an easy solution to the problem at hand. But if he left Dreagan to join Ulrik, Tristan knew he would be banished.

Con could try to take his magic and prevent him

from shifting into dragon form, just as he had done with Ulrik. Tristan didn't even contemplate spying on Ulrik. Ulrik would expect that and have countermeasures in place.

"Shite," Tristan growled.

He couldn't believe he was even contemplating such a drastic decision. If it had been any other mortal he wouldn't, but Sammi wasn't just anyone.

The idea of the Dark on Dreagan left a bad taste in his mouth. Dreagan was special, sacred. If the Dark wanted a war, then he would give it to them. If they wanted to take a King and any mortal connected to them, then he would take them in return.

He straightened and continued on to the chamber he had left Sammi in. He needed to see her, hold her, touch her—even if it meant more memories surfaced. Because right now, she was the center of the storm, the calm in all the chaos.

Tristan rounded the corner and stepped into the chamber as he called out, "Sammi."

There was no answer, and a quick look around the small chamber showed she was nowhere in sight. Tristan whirled around and ran back into the corridor as he looked one way and then the other.

He ran to his right, glancing into each entrance. When he didn't find her he circled back around, knocking into anyone who got in his way until he arrived back at the chamber.

Tristan was breathing hard, his mind refusing to believe what he knew had somehow occurred—Sammi was gone. She had left the mountain, Dreagan.

Him.

He let out a bellow and grabbed the chair as he threw it against the wall. It splintered into pieces, fabric hanging and crumpling as it crashed to the floor.

But that did nothing to ease his fury. Tristan backhanded the items atop the table before kicking the table itself and sending it to the same fate as the chair.

Before he could do more damage his arms were pulled behind him and held tightly.

"Easy," Laith said. "That was my iPad."

Tristan jerked against the grip. "Release me. Now."

"No' until you tell us what the hell is going on," Rhys said as he came around to stand in front of him.

"Look around. It's obvious."

Rhys's face twisted into a confused mask. "What's obvious is that you ruined my favorite chair."

Tristan gave another yank and pulled an arm free. He swung around, his fist aimed for Laith's face when he was once more stopped. He jerked his head around to find who had grabbed his arm and found himself staring into Banan's storm-gray eyes.

There was a soft gasp behind Banan as Jane stepped into the room. Her gaze shifted to Tristan. "Where is she?"

"Gone."

Banan released him. "Fuck!"

"I gather you mean Sammi?" Rhys asked.

Tristan nodded. "I've searched the entire mountain."

"It's my fault." Jane lifted eyes filled with tears. "I came to see her. She was upset, and I made the mistake of letting it slip about how we learned who was after her."

It felt as if a wrecking ball slammed into Tristan's gut. "You told her how I got the information."

Jane nodded and sidled closer to Banan. "She was furious."

"But why leave?" Laith said. "I told her the Dark was coming for her."

"I don't think she believed it," Jane said and wiped at her eyes before tucking her auburn hair behind her ears.

Banan gathered her in his arms. "We'll find Sammi, sweetheart."

"I hate to bring this up, but Con is going to lose his shit when he learns all of this," Rhys pointed out.

Tristan made a sound at the back of his throat. "Fuck Con."

"I'd rather you didna," Con said as he stepped into the chamber.

Tristan shoved past them all and ran to the back of the mountain. As soon as he reached the cavern, he shifted and flew out of the same opening that Laith had brought Sammi through just hours before.

He had to find her.

Because if he couldn't, he might very well be joining Ulrik.

Rhys sighed as he watched Tristan race out of the room. He knew exactly where Tristan was going, because he would do the same thing if he were in Tristan's place.

"What the hell is going on?" Con demanded.

Laith kicked at a piece of the broken table. "I brought Sammi here."

"What?" Con thundered, his black eyes narrowing in anger.

Rhys had expected just such an outburst. "It's no'

like Tristan had a choice, no' after Ulrik told him the Dark Ones were going to attack on Dreagan tonight in order to take Sammi."

Con's gaze swung to him, his nostrils flaring. "First Banan goes to Ulrik, and then Tristan does."

"You've got it backward," Banan said as he kissed Jane on the forehead and gave her a little shove out of the room. He waited until she had turned the corner before he faced Con. "I did go to Ulrik, but it was Ulrik who contacted Tristan."

All of Con's ire deflated as shock took him. "He . . . contacted Tristan?"

Rhys nodded. "That was pretty much our reactions as well. Turns out Ulrik wants Tristan to join his ranks. He offered to stop the attack if Tristan did just that."

"Is that where Tristan is going?"

Laith snorted. "Nay. He'll try and find Sammi first. But after that, I'm no' so sure. They have chemistry, those two."

A muscle ticked in Constantine's jaw. "Mates?"

"Maybe," Banan said.

Rhys crossed his arms over his chest. "Whatever is between Tristan and Sammi isna the point right now."

"You're right." Con looked at each of them. "The point is that Ulrik dared to contact one of us."

Laith's eyebrows shot up. "Dared? He's one of us, Con."

"He's banished. Doona forget that."

As if Con would let them. Rhys was as surprised as any of them that Ulrik had chosen now to contact them, and even more shocked that he had chosen Tristan. What were his motives?

Tristan was the newest King. He was strong, able, and powerful, but then so were all the Kings. The only advantage was that Tristan hadn't been involved in the past and all the horrible consequences. He was new to their world and their troubles, and he hadn't taken a side.

Not exactly. He had been delivered to Dreagan, and that's where he remained. But if he had to make a choice between Dreagan and Ulrik, Rhys wasn't sure which he would pick.

He hadn't lied to Tristan. Con had made mistakes. Hell, they all had, and they had to live with them. They shouldn't have killed Ulrik's woman, but Ulrik had given them no choice when he attacked the humans.

Ulrik had sworn vengeance on Con all those long years ago. Was the debt finally being called due?

"This is easily ended," Con said calmly from the doorway. "I kill Ulrik."

Rhys, Laith, and Banan exchanged a look.

"He's a King," Banan said. "Enough of us have died."

Con glanced around the room at the destruction. "Ulrik has caused enough trouble. I doona want to lose another King, but he's no' been one of us in a verra long time. He's out to reveal us to the world, all the while fracturing us from within."

"Aye," Laith said softly. "He's doing just that. But I willna be a part of his killing. We've taken enough away from him."

"Look what he's doing to us," Con said as he spread out his arms. "Our ordered lives are turned upside down. We're fighting mortals who are sneaking onto our land, and let's no' forget our favorite enemies, the

Dark. They're back. Do you remember the Fae Wars, Laith? Because I recall them all too vividly."

Banan picked up the shattered iPad. "There has to be another way to stop Ulrik than death."

"Like what?" Con asked. "You want to hold him prisoner with his Silvers?"

Rhys shrugged. "Maybe that's what we need to do. You knew letting him live back then would bring about this day. You knew he would scheme to kill you, to take away everything you hold dear."

"Which is Dreagan and the unity of the Kings," Laith said.

Con calmly slid his hands into the pockets of his dress slacks. "He was my best friend. I couldna kill him then."

"But you can now?" Banan asked.

Con nodded. "Aye. I'll kill him as I should've done to begin with, and then we go about unknotting his network. We'll return to the life we've had for centuries."

"That's no' possible no matter if we kill Ulrik or no'," Rhys said. "MI5 knows of us. No matter what precautions we take using Banan's friend Henry North or even Guy's ability to erase memories, we'll miss something."

Con lifted one shoulder, his face set. "It's better than what's coming if we do nothing. Doona kid yourself into thinking Ulrik will allow himself to be taken."

"There's one other option to keep Tristan with us. We need Broc," Laith said.

Rhys couldn't believe he'd forgotten about the Warrior. Broc could find anyone, anywhere. "What are we waiting for? Get him on the phone."

"Already on it," Banan said as he pulled out his mobile.

Rhys met Con's gaze. The battle everyone had dreaded between Ulrik and Con was coming. And this time Ulrik had no magic, no ability to shift into dragon form to fight his former friend.

This time Con would end Ulrik for good.

CHAPTER
TWENTY-TWO

Rhi fell in behind a heavyset woman as she exited the bus. She was still veiled, as she'd been since she happened to spot Sammi making a run for it.

She watched Sammi look around the small village trying to decide what to do. One day Rhi would have to admit to Sammi that'd she not so subtly pushed her to Ferness, but it didn't have to be anytime soon.

It was just a few small mental pushes, but it had worked to keep Sammi on the bus until Ferness. But getting her to Charon's village was just the first step. She then had to get one of the Warriors or Druids to somehow meet Sammi. All without Rhi playing a visible part in it.

"Why do I keep getting involved with the Dragon Kings and their business?"

She had asked herself that question for days now without any kind of answer. There was an answer. She just couldn't face the truth of it.

Not now.

Possibly not ever.

"I'm a sad, sad Fae," she mumbled to herself.

If only she could let go and move on, but that was impossible with her heart ripped out of her chest. She might not have gotten her happy ending, but if she could help the Kings while giving Con a kick in the balls, she would keep putting herself through the pain of being around the Kings.

She squared her shoulders, thankful she could keep the veil up as long as she could. It was a rarity in the Fae world. It was one of the few things she had gotten from her father.

Rhi followed Sammi across the street. She was about to nudge the mortal to visit Charon's pub when she spotted Dani entering a grocery store.

With a smile, Rhi focused on Sammi. "The store," she whispered, sending the thought to Sammi's mind. "Go into the store."

When Sammi didn't immediately comply, Rhi thought she might have to push her harder. It took a few minutes, but Sammi eventually turned and walked to the store.

Sammi had no idea why she went into the store. She didn't want to buy anything. In fact, she wasn't sure why she was in the village at all. She had wanted to keep going, but for some reason she couldn't explain, she had gotten off the bus.

She walked up and down the aisles wondering what to do since the idea of food made her nauseous. The clerk was eyeing her as if she was about to steal something, which only made Sammi uneasy.

After she turned down another aisle, Sammi glanced

out the window, looking for anything suspicious—and Tristan. She hated herself for wanting to see him again.

Despite learning everything she felt might have been done to her wasn't real, she still couldn't stop yearning for him, couldn't stop craving his kisses.

Couldn't stop longing to stare into his dark eyes.

She was pitiful. She had been used, and yet she wanted more if it. How pathetic that she didn't have the wherewithal to tell them all to go to hell.

Out of habit, she checked the window again and stumbled backward as she saw red eyes starting at her. Sammi tripped and slammed into a person. The basket went flying, cans of food clattered to the ground, and she became tangled with someone as they fell with a bone-jarring thud.

"Are you all right?"

Sammi winced as she rolled to her back and felt a can beneath her. She lifted her head to the window, but could no longer see the Dark Fae, if he had been there at all. She was seriously doubting her own mind now.

She looked at the woman she had crashed into. "I think so. I'm so sorry. That's the second time today I've run into someone."

The woman smiled widely as she laughed. "Perhaps you should wear pillows for safety."

"I think you're right," she said as they both laughed harder.

"I'm Danielle, but everyone calls me Dani."

"Sammi. It's really Samantha, but I prefer Sammi."

"Sammi and Dani," she said. "Women with male names. I think it was destiny that we meet."

Sammi liked her instantly. There was just something

about Dani that made you think everything was right in the world. It could be her unusual silvery blond hair or her emerald eyes, or that Dani had such a sweet personality.

Dani shoved cans aside as she got to her feet and held out her hand. "Come on. I think we could use a drink after this."

They gathered Dani's spilled items together, and Sammi found herself chatting as she waited for Dani to pay for them. The next thing she knew, Sammi was walking out of the store heading toward a pub with Dani.

"What brings you to Ferness?" Dani asked.

Sammi shrugged. "I just ended up here. It was the strangest thing."

"That happened to me the first time I came here. Odd how that happens, huh?"

"Very. Do you live here now?"

Dani's eyes crinkled in the corners as she smiled. "Aye, along with my husband, Ian. We've made Ferness our home for almost a year now. I've never been happier. I can't wait to introduce you to Laura. And then there's Aisley. She's not in Ferness as often."

Sammi merely smiled. She couldn't exactly tell Dani that she wouldn't be here come morning. It was nice thinking she had a friend. The last time had been . . . well, it had been a long time.

And there was a reason for that. Now more than ever she needed to be careful about who she trusted.

She stopped and put her hand on the door to the pub before Dani could open it. "Listen, you may think I've completely lost my mind, but . . ."

Sammi let the word trail off. How did she go about

asking if Dani was involved in the Mob or knew the Dark Fae? If she was, she'd lie about it, and if she wasn't, she'd have Sammi locked up.

Dani frowned as she reached out and touched Sammi's shoulder. "Are you in trouble?"

"You could say that. I'd like to have that drink with you, but I'm going to have to decline. I can't afford to trust anyone."

Dani didn't release her. "Wait. Please. I don't know what you're involved in, but there are people here who can help. Me for one. Tell me what's wrong."

"You wouldn't believe me if I told you." Sammi tried to walk away again, but Dani was stronger than she appeared.

"One drink. Talk to me if you want, or you can just listen to me blab on as I'm wont to do. Your choice," Dani said with a bright smile.

Sammi blew out a breath. She looked around for the Dark Fae or any sign of the Dragon Kings. She was so tired of being on her own, of wondering who to trust. Sammi didn't even remember what normal was. "One drink."

Dani opened the door and gave her a slight shove inside. The pub was like any other in Scotland. At least that was her initial take on it, but as soon as she sat down at one of the tables she had a sense that there was something more to this bar.

It wasn't a bad or scary feeling. If it had been, she'd have clawed her way out of the building. Instead, it was as if there was more to it, almost like it had seen things as amazing as she had over the last couple of days.

Sammi looked longingly at the bar. She missed her

pub, missed wiping down the bar and pouring drinks. She missed her rowdy customers and the smell of ale.

"I used to own a pub," she heard herself say when two pints had been set in front of them.

Dani sipped her ale. "You sound as if you miss it. Why did you leave?"

"I didn't have a choice."

"Ah," she said with a nod. "I had that happen to me once. It's not a pleasant feeling."

Sammi turned the glass around. She liked Dani, but that didn't mean she trusted her. Something could have been put in her drink.

"I got into a wreck in a snowstorm on a mountain," Dani said with a chuckle. "It was New Year's Eve and I was dressed for a party. I had to walk in the snow for hours. I was sure I was going to freeze to death."

"What happened?"

Dani's smile was slow and full of love. "I met my husband. He saved me from . . . well, he saved me. He was hiding in the mountains, and I had to talk him into bringing me. Ferness was the first village we came to. To be honest, I'd have been content to remain alone with him for months," she said with a laugh.

"What a story." Sammi was completely engrossed. "I gathered you stayed together after that?"

"There were a few bumps, but I knew from the first time I looked into his eyes that we were meant to be together."

Sammi leaned back. She was a complete romantic, even if she didn't want to get close to anyone. She still appreciated love and how it could change lives. "I'm glad for you."

Dani drank more of her ale and glanced at Sammi's untouched glass. "Do you have someone?"

"No. Maybe." What the hell was she saying? Tristan wasn't hers. He never had been. How could she say maybe? "No."

Dani's brows rose. "Ah. A complicated matter. Is that why you're here?"

"Something like that."

"Oh," Dani said, her face lighting up as she gave a wave to someone. "It's Ian. I can't wait for you to meet my husband."

Sammi turned to meet Ian and froze as she stared into dark eyes she knew all too well. It was Tristan. How had he gotten to Ferness so quickly? And why was Dani calling him Ian?

Thousands of questions darted through her mind at such a rapid pace that she grew dizzy. The room began to spin and she grabbed the table without ever taking her eyes off him.

"Tristan," she whispered.

His eyes narrowed for a moment before they filled with confusion and then understanding. "You know Tristan."

She blinked. "Know? It's you. Why are you doing this?" she asked as she got out of the chair and stepped backward, bumping into someone.

Sammi whirled around and found another man standing behind her with dark eyes and deep brown hair. Next to him was a woman who watched her carefully with moss green eyes, her wavy brunette hair pulled back in a ponytail.

"Sammi," Dani said slowly. "This is my husband, Ian. I told you about him."

She began to laugh. It was the only way to hold back the tears. "Ian? Wow. You move fast. I had no idea. So that's why you left me. You came to be with her."

Ian, or whatever his name was, held up his hands and softened his voice as if he were talking to a deranged person. "My name is Ian Kerr. I've never seen you before in my life. You must be talking about my twin, Tristan."

"Oh, please," she said with a roll of her eyes. "Do I look that naïve? You know what? Forget it. Forget all of it. It was all a game, wasn't it? The so-called Dark after me? The attraction between us?"

Why did her voice have to crack? Why couldn't she deliver a great speech and walk away with her head held high?

His lips, lips she had kissed, flattened. "I can prove I'm no' Tristan," he said and tore open his shirt.

Sammi glanced down, and it took a full two seconds for the lack of a tattoo to penetrate her mind. "Oh, God."

Her legs gave out, but the man beside her easily moved her to a chair. "Take deep breaths," he said. "I'm Charon and I own the pub. The beautiful woman with me is my wife, Laura. We're your friends, Sammi."

Sammi reached for her ale and began to drink, hoping the alcohol would dull the embarrassment. Twin. Tristan had a twin. She flinched when she realized all she had said.

Another ale was placed in front of her when she finished the first. She put her head in her hands and groaned. Would she ever stop making a fool of herself?

"I think we need to take this upstairs," Ian said.

Sammi didn't argue when Dani helped her to her

feet. Her mind was too shocked to do anything. She followed the two men flanked by Dani and Laura up the stairs and through a door. She was shocked to find herself in a lavish office.

"How do you know Tristan?" Ian asked before the door closed behind her.

Charon crossed his arms over his chest. "And what do you know of the Dark Fae?"

Sammi swallowed and looked helplessly around. She didn't know these people, but they obviously knew Tristan. And they knew of the Dark. Did that mean they knew what Tristan was? "Tristan and the others were helping me."

"What did you say your name was?" Laura asked, a frown marring her face.

"Sammi. Sammi Miller."

Laura suddenly smiled and looked at the others. "This is Jane's half-sister."

"You know Jane?" Would there ever come a time the surprises stopped? Because she was really getting tired of them.

Laura motioned to the couch as she sat. "I do. Very well, actually. We all know a lot about those at Dreagan."

Sammi looked from Laura to Ian, who was buttoning his shirt. He knew of the tattoo. Laura knew of Jane. Did that mean . . . ?

"They're dragons," Charon said.

CHAPTER
TWENTY-THREE

Sammi didn't know if she was happy that someone else knew who Tristan was or not. "What color is he?"

"Amber," Ian answered. "His dragon is amber."

"You really know about him?"

Dani chuckled as she glanced at Ian. "Oh, yes. We know of them. We've had many interactions with those at Dreagan."

Sammi swallowed and wished she had a drink. As if reading her mind, Charon walked to a sideboard and poured some whisky into a glass. He handed it to her with a nod.

She wasn't normally a whisky drinker, but the burn of it sliding down her throat helped her focus. As the whisky settled in her stomach, a warmth enveloped her but it didn't chase away the cold chill around her heart.

Despite taking a big gulp of the scotch, she knew it was possibly the best she had ever tasted. "It's Dreagan, isn't it?"

"Aye," Laura said.

Sammi laughed. "Even now I can't get away." She

squeezed her eyes closed. Would there ever come a time when she could look around and not think of Tristan, not long for his kisses—not wonder what a life with him could be like?

Ian sat on the coffee table in front of her. "How do you know Tristan?"

She opened her eyes and was struck again by how it appeared she was looking at Tristan. Sammi looked over Ian's face. At first glance, he was a dead ringer for Tristan, but now that she searched there were subtle differences.

Their smiles—Ian's was kind where Tristan's had a devilish, teasing air. Their eyes—Ian's held acceptance while Tristan's seemed to . . . search for something.

There was also the way Ian held his head to the right when asking a question. Tristan tended to lean his to the left. Their hair, while both long and the exact shade of light brown with gold threaded through it, Ian's was trimmed neatly while Tristan's had an untidiness about it that she found appealing. Then of course there was the dragon tat.

Sammi leaned back and cradled the glass in her hand as she looked down at the goldish liquid. "It's a rather long story. You see, I owned a pub myself. Unbeknownst to me, my business associate was laundering money for the Mob. He skimmed some for himself and they found out about it. They came calling one evening and killed him. I managed to escape out of my flat above the pub and into the water before they blew it up. I hid beneath the docks as they shot bullets into the water, and I got hit with one."

"Shite," Charon murmured.

Sammi licked her lips, the first vestiges of a grin pulling at her lips. With the four of them listening aptly, she imparted the rest of the story, although she omitted the night she and Tristan had spent together.

When she was finished, silence filled the room. She took a sip of whisky and looked between Charon and Ian, who wore matching expressions of apprehension.

"If this involves the Dark, we need Phelan," Ian said.

"Not until you tell me how you know of the Kings, the Dark, and everything that's going on," Sammi demanded.

Dani sighed and looked to Ian before she turned her emerald eyes to Sammi. "Laura and I are Druids."

Sammi started to laugh until she saw the seriousness of Dani's expression. If there were dragons and Fae, who was to say that there really weren't Druids?

"Druids?" she repeated.

Laura smiled and crossed her legs. "That's right. We're *mies*, which are Druids who use the magic they were born with. There are also *droughs*, who use black magic they get from giving their soul to the Devil."

"You can do magic?"

Dani nodded to the dark stain on her shoulder. Sammi looked to where her wound was. She had pulled the stitches again.

"Lift your sleeve," Dani urged.

Sammi dithered for just a second before she pulled up her sleeve. Laura winced as Dani's face scrunched. "I know it looks bad."

"It's been stitched tightly, or was until you pulled them," Charon said.

Sammi's thoughts once more turned to Tristan. He

had tended to her, his large hands on her skin. She pushed him out of her head and focused on Dani.

She motioned for Sammi to turn her arm more to her while Laura rose and moved to Sammi's other side. The Druids raised their hands over her wound, palms down.

Sammi wasn't sure if she was supposed to do anything. Her gaze lifted to Ian, who was watching her intently. She saw his eyes darken almost as soon as she felt something warm and bright move through her and settle in and around her wound.

Before her very eyes Sammi saw her flesh knit together, leaving the skin pink as if the wound had been stitched a month before instead of just days.

The threads of the stitches floated to the floor to land next to her feet. Sammi looked from them to her wound. "Your magic healed me?"

"Yes," Dani said, her eyes shining brightly. "We can do more as well."

Ian stalked to the sliding glass door and stared outside. "I want to know why they didna heal you at Dreagan."

"They did," Sammi said. "They got the bullet out and stitched me."

"Con could've healed you that night. You wouldna have had to walk around with such a wound," Charon said.

"Con." Sammi tested the name. "I think I heard mention of him, but I didn't meet him. There was Banan, Tristan, and Laith that I know of."

Laura's forehead furrowed. "Are they keeping her a secret from Con?"

Charon grunted. "That willna be for long."

"What's the problem?" Sammi was getting the distinct impression that she wasn't going to like Con.

Dani patted her leg. "Con is the King of Kings, the CEO of Dreagan."

"Their leader?" Sammi asked.

Ian kept his gaze focused outside. "In a manner. He keeps the Kings together, but he could no more tell them what to do than someone could tell me or Charon what to do."

"And why is that?"

Charon took her empty glass. "Well, lass, that's because we're Warriors. We've primeval gods inside us brought up by Druids when Rome attacked."

Holy shit balls. What else was walking around that she didn't know about?

Sammi wasn't shocked by his declaration. Anyone looking at Ian and Charon would know they weren't men to be messed with, but she hadn't expected this. "Are you immortal as well?"

"Aye. We've just no' been around nearly as long as the Kings," Ian said.

She frowned then as she stared at Ian. "If Tristan is your twin, how are you a Warrior and he a King?"

Ian turned to face her and she saw the haggard expression he had been hiding. "Because four hundred years ago while we were fighting a *drough,* Duncan was killed. That was his name. Duncan Kerr. We survived being imprisoned by the *drough* and tortured for decades. And in one instant he was killed."

Sammi could physically feel Ian's pain at losing his brother.

"At that exact moment, another *drough* in this century

pulled Deirdre to the present. Since she was next to
Duncan, I was yanked forward in time because of our
link as twins."

"He died?" she asked. "Are you sure?"

Ian's smile was sad. "Aye, lass. I was miles away, but
I felt it. We got confirmation from another Warrior who
was with Duncan who witnessed it all."

"I don't understand. How could Tris . . . Duncan
have been killed but be here now?"

Charon walked to the back of the couch and leaned
a hip against it next to Laura. "That's what we're all
trying to figure out. Duncan returned two years ago as
a Dragon King, literally dropping out of the sky, but he
returned with no memories of who he was."

Sammi couldn't sit any longer. She rose and began
to walk around the open space of the office. "He doesn't
remember you?"

"Nay." The grief, the desolation in Ian's voice was
difficult to listen to.

"Hasn't he seen you?"

Dani stood and went to Ian. She wrapped her arms
around him as she looked at Sammi. "Tristan refuses
to see him."

"This makes no sense. You all said you knew of the
Kings, that you had been there. How did you go to Dreagan and not see Tristan?"

"He was always in dragon form," Charon said.

"Oh."

Ian held Dani tightly. "Phelan has gone to Tristan on
my behalf. I get the feeling Tristan doesna want to know
of our life before."

"He's scared," Sammi said. "At least that's my guess.

I wanted no part of Jane when she came claiming we were half-sisters. She didn't give up on me though. And when I was in trouble, I knew the only person I could go to was her. Have any of you thought what he might be going through?"

Ian's face fell into lines of worry. "All he has to do is meet me."

"If he became a King two years ago with no idea of who he was before, he would do what anyone would, he would cling to those around him. He would embrace being a Dragon King and finding a place within their ranks."

Ian turned away from Dani and raked a hand through his hair. "The Kings kept Tristan away from me. They kept him in dragon form so I wouldna see him."

"I'm guessing to protect him," Sammi said.

"I want my brother back," Ian declared.

"You want Tristan to accept a past he can't remember. He's found a place with the Kings, but if he does accept you as his twin, where does he belong? Is he a King or is he a Warrior?"

Charon said, "He was a Warrior first."

"And now he's a Dragon King. I've only been around the Kings for a short time, but they are loyal to each other. They protect Dreagan and each other more fiercely than anything I've ever seen."

"Then why did you leave?" Dani asked.

Sammi should have seen that one coming. She wanted to wake up and discover this was all a dream. She wanted her pub back, to have her days be consistent and normal, like they used to be.

But if it was a dream, then that meant so was Tristan.

"The Kings have an enemy," Charon said. "He's set out to expose them, and it began several years ago. He's grown bolder by aligning with MI5 and the Dark Fae."

"So Tristan didn't make up the attack to get me back to Dreagan?"

Laura's mouth twisted in a grimace. "That we can't say for sure."

"The Dark Fae are dangerous," Dani said. "I've not encountered them, but Phelan has."

They had mentioned that name several times. Sammi was curious as to who this Phelan was. "What has he to do with the Dark?"

"He's part Fae," Ian explained. "Light Fae."

Charon pulled out his mobile and sent a text. "He was with Tristan recently in Ireland as they went in search of Kellan and Denae after the Dark took them."

"I've heard them mention Kellan and Denae," Sammi said as her mind whirled with the stories Tristan could probably tell. Had he been in danger with the Dark? Had they tried to capture him? At least she knew he had come out of it in one piece.

Laura briefly looked up at Charon. "The Dark want a Dragon King, and they managed to get their hands on Kellan. Denae was an MI5 agent who had been betrayed by her people. The Dark Ones, well, they wanted her."

That's all she had to say. Sammi knew exactly what Laura meant. "Why do they want a King?"

"That we doona know. But it can no' be for good," Ian said.

Sammi thought of Tristan, of running from Dreagan. He had said the mountain was the safest place for her. Would he come after her when he found she was gone?

Worse, had she just put him and every other King in danger by leaving?

CHAPTER
TWENTY-FOUR

Tristan had never felt so edgy or touchy. Nor had he ever felt so damned helpless. At least not that he could remember.

No matter how many times he flew over all sixty thousand acres of Dreagan, he couldn't find any sign of Sammi. Which left only one option—she had left Dreagan.

He couldn't understand why. Didn't she realize how perilous things were? Didn't she comprehend just how easily the Dark could get to her?

She didn't. He'd made sure of that by protecting her from all of it. He hadn't wanted to scare her, but that's exactly what he should have done.

It's exactly what he would do once he found her.

Tristan ignored the persistent calls of the other Kings to talk with him. He needed to be alone. All his hope had been in finding Sammi and doing everything he could to convince her to return.

The knowledge that he was the one that sent her running left him reeling. He had wanted to keep his distance from her, sure, but with her gone now, he was left with a cold, dark place inside him.

Tristan dipped a wing and circled back toward the manor. He'd wasted enough time searching Dreagan.

As he neared Dreagan, he saw a figure standing outside the back entrance to the mountain. Constantine. Tristan should have known the King of Kings would want more answers.

He thought back to what Ulrik had said about Con. The truth was, Tristan didn't know Con or Ulrik. He hadn't witnessed their dispute to take sides then or now. The one thing Tristan did know was that he would have to make a decision sooner or later.

The land rose up quickly as Tristan dove toward the ground. He waited until the last minute before he shifted into human form and tucked his head to roll. He stopped on his feet and slowly stood to face Con.

Without a word, Con threw him a pair of jeans. As usual, Con showed only the calm, collected man that he wanted everyone to think he was. He was a fool if he thought everyone believed that's what he was.

Tristan knew because that's what he'd been showing them since the moment he arrived on Dreagan, naked in the snow. But inside, he was a mass of anxiety, dread, uncertainty, and confusion.

Con's calm was as solid as ice. Inside must be something deep and dark.

"Banan put a call into Fallon."

Tristan frowned as he finished buttoning his jeans. "Fallon MacLeod? Why would we pull the Warriors in?"

"Because Fallon is the one who teleported Broc here."

Now the Warriors' involvement made sense. Broc

was going to use the power of the god inside him to find anyone, anywhere. At least they would locate Sammi quickly enough.

"Has he found her yet?"

Con turned and walked into the mountain. "He and Fallon just arrived. I'm sure by the time we reach them he will have."

Tristan lengthened his strides. Fallon and Broc were inside the manor in a front room along with Banan, Jane, Rhys, and Laith. Broc stood bent over, his hands on a table with his eyes closed as if he were in great concentration.

Jane sat looking ill while Banan hovered near her. Rhys stood with his arms crossed over his chest as he lazily looked around the room. Laith reclined on a sofa, his eyes glued to Broc.

Banan took notice of Tristan and immediately walked to him. "I tried to let you know," he whispered.

Tristan shrugged. All that mattered was finding Sammi. And praying she wasn't already in the clutches of the Dark Ones.

Rhys's mobile went off with Metallica's "Sandman" blaring, the sound a boom in the silence of the room. He answered it quickly with a soft, "Aye."

His gaze jerked to Broc's at the same time Broc's eyes opened. In unison they said, "Sammi is at Charon's."

Rhys disconnected the call and stuffed his mobile in his pocket. "That was Charon. Sammi is with them at the pub. Along with Ian and Dani."

Every eye in the room turned to Tristan.

"You doona have to go," Laith said as he fluidly jumped to his feet.

Fallon lifted a brow. "You came to the castle looking for Ian yesterday. Why would you no' see him now?"

"Well, well," Rhys said with a chuckle. "You're full of constant surprises, Tristan."

Jane got to her feet and asked Rhys, "Is there any sign of the Dark? What about mortals after her? Is she in danger?"

"She's fine or Charon wouldna have called," Banan told her. "Let us go get her and bring her here."

Con hadn't moved from the doorway. "If she's safe at Charon's, perhaps that's where she should remain."

"Because the thought that she could be my mate is too repulsive, aye?" Tristan asked him.

Black eyes as bottomless as the sea shifted to him. "If that was the case, Banan, Hal, Guy, and Kellan wouldna be mated."

"But it's true. You doona want us with humans."

"It's true. That's never been a secret. After what happened with Ulrik, I want to protect everyone from the mortals."

"And the Fae? What about Rhi?"

At the mention of the Light, anger shot through Con's gaze. "You know nothing of which you speak."

"Enough!" Banan shouted.

Rhys gave a snort and meandered his way to Tristan's side. "If Tristan is to be with us, he needs to know everything."

Tristan met Con's stare for several long, tense minutes. He couldn't sense what Con was after.

"Tell me," Con said. "How did Ulrik contact you?"

He frowned, taken aback by the question. "As any King would. Telepathically."

"Impossible," Con stated firmly. "His magic was taken from him, Tristan. He could no sooner speak to any King or dragon through our mind link than he could shift into dragon form."

"It was telepathically," Tristan insisted. "I was flying."

Laith scratched his chin, his gaze thoughtful. "Ulrik was always a crafty one when things called for it. He could've gotten some of his magic back."

"Then why has he no' spoken to his Silvers?" Con asked. "Communicating with our dragons is the first thing we would try."

Broc asked, "Who says he hasna?"

"Because the Silvers would wake," Rhys explained.

"You have dragons here?" Fallon asked, wide-eyed.

Con's nostrils flared as he huffed out a breath. "A precaution after our war with the humans. They were killing every human they could find."

"We stopped them and caged them," Banan said.

Laith nodded stiffly. "After we sent the other dragons away."

"Shit," Broc mumbled.

Rhys's smile was wide, but lacked any humor. "Exactly."

Tristan faced Con. If what Con said was true, then how had Ulrik made that mental link work? And what did that mean for the Dragon Kings? "Are you sure he couldna use the link?"

"Absolutely."

Trepidation rippled down his spine to settle coldly in his gut. Was it coincidence that Ulrik contacted him after he slept with Sammi? Was Ulrik spying on them just as the Kings spied on Ulrik?

The thought that his night with Sammi had been intruded upon by someone made him furious. That night was special in so many ways. It was meant to be private, shared only between him and Sammi.

"Are you sure it was Ulrik?" Laith asked.

It took Tristan a moment to realize Laith directed the question at him. "Aye." Then he paused as he thought back to their conversation. "He asked if I knew who it was. I said Ulrik."

"Did he acknowledge who he was?" Con asked.

Tristan slowly shook his head. "I can no' remember him conceding it, nay."

"Who else could it be but Ulrik?" Jane questioned.

Broc cleared his throat to get everyone's attention. "This does sound like a problem, but a more pressing one awaits."

Sammi. Tristan wanted to go to her and try to explain why he had used his power to pull the information from her. But he would have to face Ian. It was something he needed to do anyway.

Tristan bowed his head to Broc. "Aye. I'll fetch Sammi. If she'll even return."

"The Dark can't get her," Jane beseeched. "Sammi is defiant. They'll break her."

Not if Tristan had anything to say about it. "I'll bring her back, Jane," he vowed.

"Then let's get moving," Fallon said.

Tristan was turning to go back to the mountain when Fallon's words stopped him. "Excuse me?"

"You need to get there fast, aye?"

Tristan glanced at Rhys and nodded. "Aye."

"You can fly," Fallon said with a sly grin. "But I can jump you there quicker."

By jumping he meant teleporting. Tristan began to smile. "All right. Let's go."

Rhys moved to Fallon's other side. "I'm going as well."

Tristan raised a brow at Rhys, wondering what his friend was up to.

"Think of me as your wingman," Rhys said with a wink.

Con motioned to the others. "We'll be on alert and patrolling for the Dark. Get back here as quick as you can. I've no desire to have any more of us in Ireland."

"Jump us to a spot outside the pub," Tristan told Fallon. "I want to make sure there are no Dark around."

Fallon gave a nod and then placed his hands on Tristan and Rhys. In the space of a blink, the three of them stood in an alley across the street from a pub.

Tristan had never been to Ferness before, but he knew instantly the Knight's Bridge pub was Charon's. The building stood three stories tall with numerous windows to allow in light.

"They're on the second floor," Fallon said. "That's Charon's office."

Rhys rubbed his hands together. "Let's have a look around."

A Fae could remain veiled for a few seconds, and only a handful like Rhi could stay veiled for long periods of time. Tristan knew that if a Dark was about, it would be visible to everyone.

"The really powerful ones can mask their appearance," Rhys cautioned before he turned and went to the left.

It didn't take long for the three of them to make a

round of the small village. When they met back up at the alley, Phelan was there waiting for them. Somehow, Tristan wasn't surprised.

"I've been keeping watch. So far no Dark," he told them.

Tristan felt little relief. The Dark were a nuisance and trouble he didn't want, but the real issues were on the second floor of the building he stared at.

His lover and his twin.

They were both inside waiting for him.

What would he say to Ian? What could he say to a twin brother he didn't remember?

And Sammi? How did he even begin to explain what he had done? Would she even listen?

"Time's a wastin'," Rhys said.

Phelan grinned as he stepped in front of them. "As a precaution, I'll make sure we're no' seen."

"Too bad that little trick didna work in those tunnels in Ireland," Tristan said.

"Kiss my ass, Dragon," Phelan said, but there was a smile on his face.

The four hurried across the street and into the pub without worry of being seen thanks to Phelan's power to alter everyone's reality. Tristan didn't have time to think about what was coming as he followed Phelan up the stairs and through a door.

Before he knew it, he was standing in an office. Sammi sat next to Ian, laughing at something he'd said.

Rage, sinister and demanding, ripped through him like lightning. He took a step toward them as Rhys held him back. And then Sammi's glorious powder blue eyes met his.

CHAPTER
TWENTY-FIVE

Sammi's mouth went dry, her palms began to sweat, and her heart was pounding like a jackhammer in her chest. She stared at Tristan, her eyes soaking up every part of him.

Now, as he stood before her with his hair windblown and his chest bare, showing off the beautiful dragon tattoo while his dark eyes stared intently, heatedly at her, she wondered how she could have mistaken Ian for him.

He growled, a low, fierce rumble that was all dragon. Something inside her shivered and melted at the sound. She took a step toward him and wondered when she had stood.

Everything had come to a screeching halt when she noticed him. She forgot what Ian had said to make her laugh, forgot to worry about the Dark, forgot that she was angry at Tristan for tricking her—all because her body roiled with a dark, scorching passion she craved.

Her breasts swelled, her nipples tightened, and her sex clenched. No one else existed, no one else mattered. Sammi had to fist her hands not to touch him, to feel his warmth and his rigid muscles.

"You left."

Two simple words, but they were filled with anger and hurt. She swallowed to wet her mouth and recalled the stab of pain she had felt when she realized what he had done. "You tricked me."

He gave one shake of his head. "Never. You were in danger, and we were trying to help you without exposing you to our world and putting you in more peril."

Put that way she felt like a complete fool. Had she overreacted? He'd still used his power to make her reveal the very thing she had fought so hard to keep secret, and he had done it without her ever even knowing it. She would still be ignorant of it, if it hadn't been for Jane's slip of the tongue.

His eyes silently beseeched her to trust him, and damn her weak heart, but she was giving in. Tristan had a way of making everything seem trivial while sheltering her from the raging storm of life in the process.

The silence stretched on as she debated whether to go to him as she longed to do or keep her distance. The thought of never knowing the taste of his kiss again, of never feeling his body against hers made her ill.

"Will you return with me?" he asked.

Everything hinged on her answer. She could feel it in her bones, and yet she didn't have an immediate response. "Was the Dark attack real?"

"Verra."

Rhys cleared his throat and dropped his hand from holding Tristan back. Sammi jerked as she glanced around, remembering they were surrounded by people.

"He's no' lying," Rhys said. "The Dark could attack at any moment."

Sammi bit her lip. "I didn't know. I thought it was a ploy to get me to the manor as Jane wanted."

There was movement behind her as Ian stood. She watched Tristan's eyes shift over her shoulder. If she hadn't been studying him she would never have seen the slight stiffening of his body.

She crossed the distance separating them to lend whatever support he might need. Sammi couldn't imagine what Tristan was thinking, but the bland expression said what his lips would not.

"Dunc . . . Tristan," Ian said with a hopeful, joyous light in his eyes. "I never thought I'd see you again."

A man with long, almost black hair shouldered his way past Rhys and another man Sammi had just noticed to take the glass of whisky from Charon's hand. He drained the scotch in one swallow. "It's taken long enough to get the two of you together."

"Phelan," Charon said with a frown. Charon then looked at the two brothers. "The last time I saw the both of you together was in Cairn Toul. If it hadna been for Ian's hair being shorn, I wouldna have been able to tell you two apart."

Tristan had yet to utter a word. He was getting the look of a man who was trying to find his footing. Sammi slid her hand into his and interlocked their fingers.

When he squeezed her hand, she let out a relieved breath. She might not be happy with what he had done to her, but Tristan needed her right now.

She put her other hand on his arm. "I met Dani, Ian's wife, in the store and she brought me here. They told me what happened and why you don't remember him."

To her surprise, Tristan turned his head to her. "Are you ready to leave?"

Sammi blinked. Apparently Tristan had nothing to say to Ian, which in a lot of ways she could understand. Yet, Ian stood a few feet away from a twin he had been trying to see.

"Don't walk away," she whispered.

"The Dark could be closing in. We should get back."

He said it as if she hadn't just asked him to face his brother. Sammi glanced at Rhys, who wore a glower of disapproval. She was searching for a way to stop Tristan when he turned on his heel and dragged her to the door.

It was only because he wasn't expecting it that she was able to shove him around so that he hit a wall. She plastered her body to his and put her lips to his.

The kiss was meant to slow him, to stop him, but with one taste, the inferno inside her blazed. His arms wrapped around her, molding her to him as he ravaged her mouth like a starved man.

Sammi, for her part, was just as ravenous. She slid her hands into the silk of his hair and gripped the locks tightly. The passion, the soul-stirring need knocked her off her feet and kept her unbalanced, and yet she sought it out, yearning for more of it.

When he pulled back to end the kiss, she clung to him, not ready to stop the delicious desire coiling within.

"I can no'," he said in a voice so low she barely heard it.

She didn't need to ask to know he spoke of Ian. It

was too hard for him, just as it had been difficult for her with Jane. Sammi understood all too well.

Tristan knew he was holding her too tightly, but he couldn't seem to loosen his hold. Just having Sammi in his arms calmed the turbulence and turmoil of finding her gone.

"Then don't."

He'd expected her to argue the point in staying and talking to Ian, not to give him a pass. Tristan looked into her blue eyes and was drowning in the pale light.

Images filled his mind, memories pulled up from a deep crevice, of him and Ian. They stood side by side fighting, laughing, and living.

Tristan lowered his forehead to rest against Sammi's. The memories incessantly slammed into him on a playback so that he lived the same battle, the same fight in a mountain again and again.

Blood coated both him and Ian. He looked down to see his hands and the pale blue skin and claws he recognized. They slashed flesh and beheaded small yellow creatures that he knew were Deirdre's creation called wyrrn.

He saw Ian battling another Warrior as a second snuck up behind him. Tristan hadn't hesitated. He had let out a roar and attacked.

Sammi's hands caressed his face as she moved aside his hair. Her touch was cool against his heated flesh, and he dug his fingers into her back.

The sounds, smells, and sights of those memories were as clear as if he were in the middle of it. He lifted his head and met Ian's gaze.

The twin he wanted to deny stood watching him.

They were identical down to the small mole on the left side of their necks. Beside Ian stood a woman with silvery blond hair and bright green eyes.

That was Ian's wife, Dani. Was it coincidence that both he and Ian had women with male names? It had to be. Right?

Fallon gave a shake of his head. "I thought when you came to the castle that you were ready to see Ian."

Tristan thought he had been. Then he saw Ian and knew he wasn't remotely ready.

"It doesna matter," Ian said as he dropped his gaze. "We need to get Sammi back to Dreagan before the Dark show up."

Phelan elbowed Charon. "It's been awhile since we battled anything evil."

A brunette with moss green eyes shot Phelan a withering look. "After what you told me and Charon about fighting the Dark in Ireland?"

"Now, Laura," Charon said as he pulled her against him and nuzzled her neck. "You know we Warriors need battle to appease our gods. Besides, we'll just be helping the Kings if they need it."

Laura gave him a droll look before spearing Phelan with another hard look. "Have you told Aisley yet?"

"I'll handle my wife," Phelan murmured.

Rhys laughed, the sound loud and booming. "Oh, I'd like to see that. The Phoenix will have something to say, no doubt."

Phelan's forehead crinkled in a frown. "My wife understands my need to kill something evil."

Tristan noticed that Ian had yet to say anything. Dani was whispering something in his ear while he rubbed a hand up and down her back. Their love was strong, a bond unbreakable after all they had endured to give their hearts to each other.

He looked down at Sammi to find her eyes on him and full of worry. He understood her worry. "You doubt our night together was real."

"Yes."

"It was." He wound a lock of her wavy, sandy hair around his finger. "I think the kiss we just shared proved that when it comes to you, I have no control. I see you, I want you, and I have to have you."

"Lust. It's a powerful emotion."

"That it is." She seemed content to stay in his arms, and he was in no hurry to move.

Her tongue peeked out to lick her lips. "What are you going to do?"

"I'm going to take you back to Dreagan while we hunt the group of Dark who are trying to take you."

"That's not what I meant," she said with a lift of one brow.

He knew, but he wasn't ready to talk about Ian. That was a subject he needed more time to think on. Seeing Ian was a blow, but it was also like coming home.

"How do you know they're coming for me?"

Tristan ran his thumb over her lips. "Ulrik told me. He said he would call off the attack if I joined him."

"Ulrik? Is that who is behind all of this? Who is he?"

"He's a Dragon King who had his magic taken away by Con and can no longer shift. He wants revenge."

Her nails lightly scratched his scalp. "Apparently. This could be a trap for you or any of the Kings."

He had already considered as much, but he could

endure whatever the Dark had in store for him far more than Sammi could. "I'm sure it is."

"And you're still going to go?" she asked in surprise as she paused in her caress.

"I must."

"If you stop the Dark Ones this time, will it be over?"

Tristan had kept the truth from her, and it had made her run. It was time to stop lying to and evading her. "It's doubtful."

"I won't stay in that mountain the rest of my life."

"I willna let you."

Tristan had been thinking of how he was going to stop the Dark, and he knew there were only two ways. He could join Ulrik or he could let himself be taken by the Dark Ones.

Neither option was optimal, but neither was keeping someone as vibrant and beautiful as Sammi hidden away just to keep her safe.

"What are you planning?" Sammi asked suspiciously.

The entire room grew quiet as they waited for him to respond. He smoothed his hands down her hair and gently set her away from him. "Rhys, take Sammi to Jane and Banan."

"Tristan," Sammi said in a low voice.

He then looked to Phelan and Charon. "With the other Kings in the air scouting for the Dark, having someone on the ground with the woman at Dreagan will be helpful."

"Consider it done," Phelan agreed.

Tristan then turned to Fallon. "If you would be willing, I'd like for you to jump me to Perth."

Rhys let out a string of curses as he began to understand the plan.

Next, Tristan looked to Ian. "I've no right to ask . . ."

"Ask," Ian said with a firm nod.

Sammi forced him to look at her. "What are you
doing?"

"I'm ending this."

CHAPTER
TWENTY-SIX

Rhys prowled through the mountain in a fury. Tristan's plan had merit, but not when he was facing Ulrik alone. Especially after Ulrik had tried to recruit him.

Whether Tristan wanted to admit it or not, Sammi was important to him. It was just like Tristan to be honorable and sacrifice his freedom for Sammi.

Or worse—join Ulrik.

"Fuck!"

"I've never seen you at such a loss for words."

Rhys whirled around to find Phelan leaning against the entrance to the mountain. "Sod off, Warrior."

Phelan waited until Rhys walked past him before he fell into step. "You doona think Tristan's plan will work?"

"It might."

"Then what's got your knickers in a knot?"

Rhys stopped and glowered at the Warrior. "I counted on Con to put a stop to Tristan's plan."

"Ah," Phelan said, understanding dawning. "But Con isna."

"Nay. It defies reasoning. Con has never wanted any

of us to contact Ulrik. He about busted his scales when he learned Banan went to see him. Now he wants to do nothing when Tristan is doing the same?"

Phelan shrugged as they began to walk to the manor. "Who knows what's going on in that warped mind of Con's."

"If I have to, I'll go into the world of the Dark to find Tristan."

"And I'll go with you," Phelan said. "However, you're forgetting one important fact."

"What?"

"Tristan may join Ulrik."

After the way Tristan had spoken of Ulrik it was a distinct possibility, and that was why Rhys was so upset. He liked Tristan, not to mention he made one hell of a Dragon King.

If Ulrik managed to woo Tristan to his side, then Tristan would do in one fell swoop what Ulrik had been unable to do for thousands of millennia—undermine Con.

Was that why Con had let Tristan go?

"I see you've considered that," Phelan said.

"Aye."

Rhys stopped outside the manor and looked to the sky to see dragons circling. There were no visitors to Dreagan, and all mortal workers had been given the day off. But it wasn't a celebration they planned.

It was a battle that could be the beginning of the end of Dreagan.

"Deirdre, Declan, and Jason all tried to tear us apart from within," Phelan said. "We survived it all, and we were no' together nearly as long as you Kings."

Rhys looked into Phelan's blue-gray eyes. "Ulrik's banishment nearly tore us apart. I can no' see any meddling he does no' harming us in some way."

"Then let's no' let him meddle."

Rhys found a reason to smile as they entered the manor.

Tristan stood across the street from The Silver Dragon antiques shop and considered his plan. It was the only move he had, and yet he couldn't get the taste of Sammi's kiss out of his mind.

If only there had been time to strip off her clothes and make slow, sweet love to her. Her image was burned into his mind, as was the first time they had made love.

He couldn't keep his hands off her. It was a problem because Ulrik and the Dark would use her against him if his plan didn't work.

Kellan might have withstood the Dark as they threatened and harmed Denae, but Tristan wasn't so sure he could do the same. He had failed at being a Warrior, and somehow had been given a second chance as a Dragon King.

Was he going to screw that up as well?

Tristan pushed away from the building and ran across the street, dodging an oncoming car. Charon had loaned him a shirt and shoes, so it saved him from having to return to Dreagan.

He pushed open the door, and the tinkling of a bell sounded above him, announcing his arrival. He glanced around the shop for Ulrik.

It wasn't until his gaze lifted to the second floor that he spotted his target. Ulrik stood staring down at him with a bored expression. His long hair was loose, a contrast to the tailored suit he wore.

"Wipe your feet. I doona want my floors ruined."

As far as first words went, they couldn't have been further from what he expected. Tristan complied and wiped his feet on the rug while Ulrik closed the book in his hand and shelved it.

Tristan grew impatient as Ulrik continued to peruse the bookshelf that housed first editions and books dating back centuries.

"Are you going to just stand there, or are you going to tell me what you want?" Ulrik asked.

Tristan held back his retort and took a deep breath. "You're the one who contacted me, offering to stop the attack on Sammi if I joined you."

For several seconds Ulrik didn't move. Then he slowly turned to face him. "You want to take me up on that offer now, I suppose."

"And if I did? Does the offer still stand?"

Ulrik leaned on the railing and regarded him. "Sammi means that much to you that you would turn your back on Dreagan?"

"She does."

"A curious name for a female, do you no' think?"

"Samantha is her name. She goes by Sammi." Tristan cut his arm through the air. "What difference does her name make? Does the offer still stand?"

Ulrik bent farther and rested his forearms on the railing. "You didna answer my question, Dragon King."

"She's an innocent. You're using her to get to Banan."

"And yet you're the one standing before me."

Tristan clenched his jaw. "Because you offered me a deal."

"She's just a mortal. Why would you give up everything for her?"

"Does it matter?" he countered. Tristan wasn't sure why Ulrik was asking all these questions, but he was damned tired of it.

"A King turning his back on Dreagan for a mortal. Con must be seething. I'm surprised he didna try and lock you up. Or kill you." Ulrik straightened and started down the stairs. "He's watching you even now with one of his many spies."

Tristan wondered if Sammi was talking to Jane or thinking of him as he was her. "I know."

"You believe I'll honor my offer?" Ulrik asked as he reached the bottom step. He made his way to Tristan and stopped before him. "After what I know Con has told you about me, you trust me?"

"I'm here, am I no'?"

Ulrik's gold eyes narrowed for a moment. "That you are. Did Constantine actually let you read the accounting of what happened? Or did he prefer to tell you what occurred himself?"

"He told me."

"As I figured." He put one hand in the pockets of his slacks and turned to walk behind the Louis XIV desk he used as his own.

Tristan reined in his temper when Ulrik picked up some papers and began to read through them. On his desk were several mobile phones stacked neatly beside each other. "Are you going to honor your offer?"

Without looking up, Ulrik said, "If you think I can save Sammi from the Dark, you're mistaken."

For a moment Tristan seriously considered reaching across the desk and wrapping his hands around Ulrik's throat. Instead, he threw open the door and stalked out. He had hoped Ulrik would keep his word, but Tristan hadn't expected it. It would have been easier, but there was a contingency plan in place.

He walked down the street and cut through an alley to get to the next street. Tristan continued to zigzag through the streets until he found Fallon.

"It didna work," he stated as he walked up.

Fallon straightened from lounging against the building. "You knew it might no'. Back to Dreagan then?"

"Back to Dreagan."

Ulrik straightened from his crouching position atop the building where Tristan had met up with none other than a Warrior, Fallon MacLeod. Interesting.

He didn't notice the rain as it began to drizzle, soaking his clothes. It appeared Tristan was set to go to any extremes to save Sammi.

"A mortal," he said aloud.

That must be a thorn in Con's side. Four of his Kings already mated to humans.

Ulrik's smile was cold and calculating. Everything Con had built would be destroyed. Ulrik would see to it himself. After all, he owed Constantine.

He turned and jumped from building to building, making his way back to The Silver Dragon. There was much Con didn't know about, no matter how many spies he put on Ulrik.

"Soon, old friend. Soon, you will feel my wrath. I've thousands of years of revenge to pay you back for."

Sammi tried to sit, but every time she did, she would jump back up.

"You're making me dizzy with your pacing," Ian said from the window with his back to her.

She threw her hands up. "I can't help it. Why did you agree to this? Why is Dani all right with you putting your life on the line?"

"Because it's for Dunc . . . Tristan. He asked it of me."

Sammi shook her head and wished for a very tall glass of wine, whisky, or anything to calm her nerves. Ever since Tristan had laid out his plan, she had been a mess, a complete bundle of nerves that got worse as the hours ticked by.

It didn't help that they were once more back at the cottage. The same cottage where she had spent a glorious night in his arms and woke to find him gone the next morning.

She couldn't even go into the bedroom. It was too painful to see the bed with sheets still rumpled from their passion-filled night.

Ian turned his head to her. "It's a good plan."

"A plan that uses you for bait."

"Only if Ulrik doesna accept him."

Rhys had related the entire story of how Ulrik's lover, a human, had betrayed him and led her people to kill dragons. The Kings had responded quickly and killed her, but without telling Ulrik what they were doing.

According to Rhys, Ulrik had gone a little insane.

No one was sure if it was because his lover had been murdered or that she'd betrayed him.

Either way, Ulrik began to send his Silvers to kill humans, and not just the ones hunting dragons. The Silvers killed all humans.

That's when Con and the rest of the Dragon Kings had united their magic and taken away Ulrik's. He was doomed to walk the earth as an immortal, but without any of the benefits of being a Dragon King.

It was a sad story really. In some ways she could completely understand why Ulrik wanted retribution against the humans as well as Con.

Then she remembered he was the one who'd sent someone to murder Daniel, destroy her pub, and kill her. The idea that he was also in league with the Dark was mind-numbing.

Now she knew why the Dark wanted a Dragon King. It was for Ulrik.

And Tristan had just served himself—and Ian—up on a platter.

CHAPTER
TWENTY-SEVEN

Tristan found himself at the cottage in less time than it took him to think of it. He looked at the stone structure and the double doors he had followed Sammi through as his desire had flared.

Remembering that night, the passion, the sighs, the pleasure, sent his blood heating. How in the world could he be here with her and not give in to his need?

"Are you sure you know what you're doing?" Fallon asked.

Tristan shifted his gaze to him. "You mean, can I put Ian in danger?"

"Aye. He has a wife, a home. A life."

"You doona think I realize that?"

"Nay, I doona. I think you're so wrapped up in the workings of the Kings that you'll sacrifice anything and anyone to get to the endgame."

Tristan raised a brow at the unspoken leader of the Warriors. "Tell me, Fallon, when I was supposedly this Duncan, did we get along?"

"We did. Why?"

"Because I'm finding it hard not to put my fist into your jaw."

"Enough," Ian said as he walked out of the cottage.

Tristan barely spared him a glance as his gaze landed on Sammi. Worry lines bracketed her mouth, and her powder blue eyes were filled with doubt and indecision.

He understood exactly how she felt. His plan would work, but that didn't mean he liked any of it. There was a large chunk of it that he hadn't shared with any of them, because if they knew, none would have agreed to the plan.

Ian stopped several feet from Tristan. "How did it go with Ulrik?"

"No' as I'd hoped."

Sammi let out a relieved sigh. "He didn't want you. Thank God."

"He didna have much to say, actually," Tristan said as he walked to her. He couldn't keep any kind of distance from her. She drew him much like the sun drew flowers.

She looked up at him, her hand on his chest. "Now comes the waiting, right?"

"I doona think we'll have to wait long," Ian said as he moved around them to enter the cottage.

Tristan looked at Fallon to see him staring angrily. Fallon was furious that he was willing to put Ian's life on the line. Odd that he wasn't irate with Ian for being prepared to do it.

"If you have something to say, say it," Tristan demanded of Fallon.

Fallon's dark green eyes narrowed dangerously. "Ian is one of ours. You Kings may be cavalier with your own lives, but we can no' be. You may no' remember who you once were, but the rest of us do, especially the man you're so casually using as bait."

As soon as the last syllable left Fallon's mouth, he jumped away. Tristan drew in a long breath and returned his gaze to Sammi.

"Why didn't you tell me about Ian?" she asked softly.

He shrugged. "Probably for the same reason that I wouldna see him."

"No one can know what you're going through, so don't let anyone try to tell you that it's wrong. You have to decide what's best for you. You're a Dragon King, Tristan. I'm not saying the Warriors aren't important. They are."

"I know," he said and slid his fingers into the cool locks of her hair. "And thank you."

"I didn't think you were coming back."

"I shouldna have, but I had to see you."

She pulled away and out of his arms. "There's no need to say such things. I know you need me to help set the trap."

"You think I'm lying?" He was so taken aback that he could only gawk at her.

"This isn't the time. Good luck," she said and walked back into the cottage, closing the door quietly behind her.

It would've hurt less had she slammed the door, but her calm acceptance of what she thought he had done was enough to snap his control.

"Let her go," Ian said from behind him.

Tristan whirled around to find Ian on the porch that came off the master bedroom. He glanced at the door, but knew going after Sammi now would only cause more damage. Ian let his gaze look around him. "Spectacular view. Now I know why the Kings chose this place. But there is something about this cottage that has Sammi tied in knots. Her frequent looks into this bedroom," he said and pointed with his thumb over his shoulder, "tells me everything. No' half as much as your reaction when you found her with me, however."

Tristan swallowed. What did he say to the man who was his twin? A man he saw bits and pieces of through memories as fleeting as sand through his fingers.

"You should've seen her reaction when she first saw me. Sammi thought I was you. Whatever you did to send her running must have been bad."

"I did it to save her life."

Ian nodded absently. "And possibly crushed whatever was blooming between the two of you in the process."

"How can I have her in my life when I doona even know who I am? Am I Tristan, the Dragon King? Or am I Duncan, the Warrior?"

"Why can you no' be both?"

Tristan opened his mouth to answer, but he quickly closed it. Could he be both Dragon King and Warrior? Could he accept his past as twin to Ian and still give himself to the Kings?

Ian rubbed his hand on the back of his neck. "I doona expect anything from you. I just wanted to see you. I wasna there when Deirdre had you killed. I've regretted every day since that I remained behind at the castle."

"I doona know how I died, and I'm no' sure I want to know."

"It doesna matter. None of it does anymore. It's enough that you're here. Whether you ever regain your memories or no', I'm once more complete knowing you're alive."

Tristan looked into eyes the same deep brown as his own. Ian was giving him a way out so he wouldn't have to have any more contact once this was over. Is that what he wanted? He wasn't so sure now. "This plan could go all pear-shaped."

"That could be said for any plan. Just remember Dani will have your arse if anything happens to me," he said with a smile.

But Tristan couldn't smile. He knew the possibility that the very worst could happen was high. "Go home to your wife."

Ian's smile was replaced with incredulity. "Pardon me?"

"Fallon was right. You have a wife. Go home to Danielle."

"And what will you do?"

"Whatever has to be done."

Ian grunted, affronted by his answer. "Even if that means letting the Dark take you?"

"Even then."

"Nay," Ian said with icy fury. "I wasna by your side the last time. I'll no' leave it now."

Tristan looked to the sky. The Kings were keeping their distance from the cottage so the Dark Ones would think they were safe to attack. "We willna be together now. The Dark can no' see two of us."

"Exactly. Get your ass moving."

"Standing in for me willna change the past."

Ian crossed his arms over his chest, his expression flat. "I'm immortal, you ass."

"But you've no' see what the Dark Ones can do. Immortality will only make their torture last longer. Now that Ulrik has refused me, my place is here. I'll be the one to confront the Dark and keep them away from Sammi."

"I'm no' leaving. I agreed to your plan. Let us carry it out so Sammi can be safe and you can prepare to do some serious begging for her forgiveness."

Tristan had no other argument to sway Ian away. He hated that he liked the guy. Whatever reason he had, Ian readily countered it. There was nothing for him to do but accept that Ian wasn't going to leave, and make damn sure that he was ready when the Dark came.

Because they would come.

"Stay vigilant. The Dark are no' like any of the Druids you've fought. They're much more devious, and will appear in the room before you've even realized they're there."

Ian dropped his arms and nodded. "Anything else?"

"They like to show off. They want a Dragon King, so they'll make a big show of attempting to take Sammi. I'll be near to step in before they can take either of you."

"You hope."

Tristan looked away. He did hope. He couldn't stay too close to the cottage for fear the Dark would see him and Ian, but he couldn't be too far away and not get to them in time. It was a huge chance he was taking, but he was also prepared to follow them back to Ireland and comb those tunnels to find them.

"Good luck," Tristan said. He started to walk off when Ian held out his hand. Tristan looked from his outstretched hand to his face before he clasped Ian's forearm.

Ian's hand tightened on his forearm as a smile appeared. "It's good to have you back, whether you're Duncan or Tristan."

With that, Ian turned on his heel and walked into the cottage.

Tristan turned to the mountains and the growing darkness. The Dark Ones could come at any time, but they preferred the night. It was no wonder so many people were afraid of the dark. They knew what was inside it—the Dark Fae.

Rhi whistled a made-up tune as she walked the halls of Usaeil's home, a grand thirty-two-room castle built out of granite on the coast of Donegal Bay and surrounded by gardens that reached as far as the wooded hillside beyond. It wasn't the colossal, vast palace in the Fae world, but it suited her queen perfectly.

Her rubber-soled biker boots made nary a sound as she walked the black and white checkerboard floors. Usaeil had been calling her for some time now. As one of the Queen's Guard, Rhi had to have a good excuse for ignoring her queen.

Explaining that she was helping the Dragon Kings wouldn't win her any favors. Then again, with the Dark rising, the Light needed friends.

Not that Rhi wanted any of the Dragon Kings as friends. The history between Rhi and the Kings went back a long way, and the hurt ran deep—on both sides.

They blamed her, and she blamed them, well, one in particular—Con.

She didn't notice the murals of the Fae world painted along every corridor. She had been down this hallway too many times to pay them any heed now. Though she could remember the first time she had seen them. They had been painted to remind the Fae of their glory years, a time when they dominated any and all realms they chose to visit.

A time before the Dark attacked the Light.

Everything the Fae had gained fell apart like a kid knocking over blocks. It crumbled into dust, their power fading as quickly as Rome's did on Earth.

She returned to the Fae realm, but not nearly as often as she once had. When her family had died there had been nothing to pull her home.

The closest thing she had to a home was her cottage, her secret place warded against other Fae, Dragon Kings, Druids, mortals, and any other supernatural being that might try and find her.

It was her refuge, her sanctuary. Her asylum.

Rhi came to the doors that separated her from her queen. As she reached them, they swung open of their own accord. It was one of Usaeil's tricks in her unlimited bag of magic.

As soon as she saw Usaeil on the small leather bench with a fan blowing her hair and lights staged around her, Rhi rolled her eyes and took a seat to await her turn after the photo session was over.

Few knew that Usaeil moonlighted as a famous movie star. This current photo shoot was for some US magazine Usaeil had wanted the cover for. And as with anything her queen wanted, her queen got.

As soon as Usaeil saw her, she waved away the photographer, who just happened to be another Fae. Oh, how the Kings would be furious if they knew just how deep the Light had embedded themselves into the lives of mortals.

"Where have you been?" Usaeil demanded as she rose and stalked toward her.

Rhi looked over the black leather pants and white silk shirt that was open and see-through to reveal a sexy black bra. "I like the outfit."

"Thanks, but don't change the subject." Her queen sighed. "Rhi, times are changing for all of us, even the mortals, though they don't know it yet."

Rhi looked down at her freshly polished nails, painted a toasty warm brown color called I Knead Sour-Dough and a design of swirls in gold and black. "I was lending a hand to the Kings."

"Good. And you need to get back there ASAP."

Rhi frowned as she looked at her queen to see if she had sprouted two heads. Not once had Usaeil ever told her to help the Kings. "What?"

"The Dark are planning to attack, and the Kings think they can handle things themselves. You and I both know that isn't the case. Now get moving, and be sure to report back to me as soon as it's over," she ordered and walked away, calling to the photographer as she did.

Summarily dismissed, Rhi hesitated only a moment before she teleported to Dreagan.

CHAPTER
TWENTY-EIGHT

Taraeth looked his men over as he walked up and down the line they had formed in the great hall of the castle he had taken over centuries ago. "There is a Dragon King who thinks he can make deals, a Dragon King who believes he can control his own destiny. Tonight we will take him from the sanctuary he imagines is safe from us on Dreagan. Tonight, we will have a Dragon King!"

The hall erupted with shouts from his men. Not all would be going on this important mission, because there were other assignments, but Taraeth had picked his best men to go to Dreagan.

"What fools the Kings are to think we would keep off their precious Dreagan," Taraeth continued when his men had quieted down. "We had one Dragon King in our grasp, and we will have another. This time, there will be no escape for the King called Tristan."

Taraeth rocked back on his heels and smiled. The Kings were fools if they didn't consider the Dark a worthy opponent, but Taraeth would show them how wrong they were.

He had waited a long time to retaliate against the Dragon Kings after they defeated the Dark during the Fae Wars. The Kings thought themselves above every other creature throughout all the realms.

Not anymore.

They had weaknesses, most especially their human mates.

He hadn't wanted to believe his new ally could force the Kings to do his will, but that's exactly what the Dragon Kings had been doing for two years.

The only thing no one had expected was a new Dragon King. It didn't concern him, but his ally had been stunned.

To Taraeth it was just another King to bring down. Any enemy could be brought low once he found a weakness. The Kings had been strong, impenetrable.

Until Con's magic preventing the Kings from having feelings for humans was shattered and they began to fall in love.

"The Kings are not as strong as they once were. They still believe themselves the fiercest beings of this realm. Let's show them who is going to rule now!"

The cheers were deafening as the Dark shouted their excitement.

Out of the corner of his eye, Taraeth saw Balladyn standing near the wall, silent and still. It hadn't taken much of a nudge to have the former Light turned to Dark. It was the idea that none of his comrades came looking for him that sent Balladyn over the edge.

One more ace up Taraeth's sleeve. Balladyn wasn't a

Dark anyone wanted to tangle with. Tristan would learn that soon enough.

Taraeth gave Balladyn a nod. The Dark merely looked at his men, and as one they filed out of the great hall. Taraeth's other lieutenants stepped forward and handed out assignments to some while others got the night off to enjoy whatever human they had brought in.

Still others would guard the castle. There was no chance of a human falling into their home, and anyone else would have to find the doorway that was carefully hidden, which wasn't impossible—and why they had guards.

Taraeth rubbed his hands together. He was counting down the minutes until Balladyn returned with Tristan.

Sammi tried to read, but her mind was too caught up in everything to pay attention to the words. It wasn't until she read the same page five times that she gave up.

But she couldn't just sit and do nothing. She reached for the iPad on the table and found Angry Birds Space. It felt good to knock those piggies over and blow them up. For a few minutes it gave her the feeling that she was in control.

All too soon that wore off as well. She set aside the tablet and sighed. Ian glanced at her, a small grin turning up his lips.

"Waiting is the hardest," he said.

She dropped her head back onto the sofa. "I think I have to agree. We should have the bad guys text us a time we should expect them."

Ian chuckled and moved from the window to the chair opposite her. "What will you do after all this is over?"

"How can you ask that? I'm in knots wondering if I'll live or not."

"You'll live. Never doubt that. Tristan willna allow anything to happen to you."

She licked her lips and raised her head. "You make it sound as if we will get out of this."

"I could be here for days telling you stories of how each Warrior was able to get out of a scrape with the *droughs* we fought. We had each other, and we were fighting for the love of our women. There were times it was dire and things could have gone differently, and yet here we all are with our wives. Everyone except Duncan."

The sadness Ian was always careful to keep hidden around Tristan was blinding. "He spoke with you. He'll come around. It's not like time is a problem for either of you."

"True," Ian said with a laugh, leaning forward to rest his forearms on his knees. He clasped his hands together and looked at them. "What I'm trying to say is no' to give up hope. No matter how bad things look, you have to believe in something."

"Like my sister?"

Ian's dark eyes met hers. "Or Tristan."

That Sammi didn't know if she could do. "That's asking a lot."

"Why? Because he used his power to learn what you were keeping hidden in an effort to save you?"

She shrugged, shifting uncomfortably under his direct gaze. "I admit, I was angry about that at first, but it's hard to stay that way when I know why he did it."

"Then why are you pushing him away?"

"Because I don't want to get close to anyone." Sammi couldn't believe she told him that so easily. She hadn't ever told anyone that, but there was something about Ian that made her feel . . . secure, like he was a big brother she could lean on.

"What happened?"

"My mother died. We had each other, and it was always just the two of us. Then she was just gone. I still feel that pain."

"Just as I feel the pain of losing Duncan. That kind of closeness isn't shared by many, but as a twin, I know exactly what you mean. It's hard for most to comprehend the depth of our despair."

"You moved past it."

Ian gave her a ghost of a smile. "Dani helped me. I'd still be in that cave if she hadna appeared. She gave me something to focus on, but I willna sit here and tell you it wasna frightening to love someone again. I might have wanted to push her away, but I loved her too deeply to ever try it."

Love. Why had the topic turned to that emotion? Sammi had never said anything about being in love. She didn't even know what being in love meant since she had never let anyone get that close.

"Why no' give Tristan a chance?" Ian asked.

"I'm not that strong." She laughed at her own words. "I'm really not. The only reason I survived my mum's death was because of the pub. We bought it together, so I did everything to make it the best it could be."

"And now it's gone," Ian said softly. "You could be letting something magnificent pass you by. Have you thought of that?"

Every damn second of every day, but she wasn't going to tell him that. There were only so many secrets he would pull out of her. "There isn't just one person for each of us out there."

"Whoever told you that is full of shite," Ian said angrily. "The people who say that have never loved deeply, they've never found the other half of themselves."

"Some are destined to be alone."

He gave a shake of his head. "Nay, lass. Those are the people who doona see love when it's standing right before them, they are the ones who turn their backs on happiness, the ones too afraid to get hurt. How can you know what love is if you doona get hurt?"

"I've hurt enough for ten lifetimes," she said defensively.

His face crumpled into a frown. "Everyone feels the pain of loss, Sammi. That's part of life. You're no' doing yourself any favors by shutting yourself away."

"I know. I can't stop it though."

"Do you want to?"

That was the million-dollar question, wasn't it? Did she want to allow herself to feel deeply for—and possibly fall in love with—Tristan?

She thought of the way she found it easy to go to him, to let his arms wrap around her and hold her. How she needed his kisses as much as she needed food to sustain her. How she craved his body to a degree that it frightened her.

"I don't know."

There was a brush of air and Sammi felt a hand over her mouth as a scream welled within her. Ian jumped to his feet, his face a mask of fury.

"No need to bother," said a man with a heavy Irish accent behind her. "We've come for you, but I'll be taking this pretty thing as my reward."

Ian laughed. Sammi's eyes grew large the longer he laughed. She began to wonder if he'd lost his mind, but when she noticed the Dark eyeing each other with wariness she realized what Ian was doing.

"Nice try," Ian said. "You willna be going anywhere with her, and I'm certain I willna be going with you."

Sammi jerked, startled when Rhi appeared in the chair next to Ian's. She sat nonchalantly with her legs crossed and one high-heeled foot swinging. Rhi had on slim white cargo pants and a gold-and-white top with a harlequin pattern. She looked ready for a night out on the town, not a battle.

"We meet again, Balladyn," she said, her gaze never leaving the Dark behind Sammi.

Sammi chanced a look up. Her heart hammered as she recognized him as the man she had run into in the store and the face she'd seen in the stream. This was the Dark after her?

He had long black hair that hung midway down his back with thick strips of silver running through the obsidian locks. His eyes glowed red as he focused on Rhi.

"I warned you I'd have to kill you if I saw you again," he said.

Rhi sighed dramatically. "That you did, big guy. Since this is the second time we've . . . met . . . since then, you'll see how I don't believe you."

There was a second of silence, a beat of stillness, like a moment before a hurricane hits or a bomb detonates.

And then all hell broke loose.

CHAPTER
TWENTY-NINE

It took every ounce of Tristan's considerable control not to shift into dragon form and ram the cottage. For one, he could injure Sammi, but there was also the fact he needed to confuse the Dark Ones.

He kicked open the back door and stormed into the house to see Rhi and a Dark One in hand-to-hand battle. Every time he tried to use magic, she knocked it aside. Every time she reached for her sword, he kicked it out of reach.

Tristan's gaze swung to Ian, who had Sammi behind him while he faced five Dark who were inching toward him, lobbing magic.

With Ian's ability to sense magic as a Warrior, he was able to warn Sammi in time to keep them both from getting hit.

No one had noticed Tristan yet, and he had a difficult time deciding whether to announce his presence as he had planned or rush to Sammi's side. He hated that she was surrounded by the Dark, but if everything worked out, that wouldn't be for long.

"Someone looking for me?" he bellowed.

The five Dark surrounding Ian and Sammi turned their heads to him before looking confused. His gut wrenched when Sammi's gaze shifted to him and he saw the stark fear reflected in her depths.

He wanted to take her into his arms and fly her far from the danger within. How foolish for him to believe he could handle seeing her in such a predicament in order to save her. How utterly wrong he had been to think he would be calm in such a situation.

It had been a rash, reckless idea. He was wound as tightly as a drum, every fiber of his being sizzling with the need to shift into dragon form and defend Sammi as only he could.

The five Dark continued to look from him to Ian and back. At least they were no longer attacking. Rhi and her assailant had yet to pause, though she did glance at him and begin to laugh.

It was the laugh that caused her foe to grab her by the neck and slam her against a wall, but Tristan knew Rhi was anything but subdued or helpless.

The Dark Fae's red eyes turned from Rhi to him before sliding over to Ian. "What is this?" he demanded.

"I'm Tristan," Ian said. "How dare you come onto Dreagan."

Tristan stepped forward. "Nay. I'm Tristan. You'll answer to me for trespassing on Dreagan and breaking the treaty."

Rhi kept laughing, though there was anything but mirth shining in her silver eyes. "I think you've got yourself into a quandary, Balladyn."

"I've been in many, pet. I'll get out of this one too."

"Not going to happen." All the laughter was gone. Rhi's voice was hard and cold, determined.

Tristan shared a look with Ian. Rhys, Banan, Laith, Con, Phelan, and Charon were waiting for his signal to storm the cottage. There was no way the Dark were leaving with anyone.

Balladyn roughly squeezed Rhi's neck, but she never stopped glowering at him. Rhi knew this Dark Fae, and knew him well. There seemed to be endless secrets to Rhi.

"Who'll be the first to answer to me?" Tristan demanded.

Balladyn let out a low, gravelly growl that stopped a Dark in his tracks. He set his red gaze on Tristan. "How are there two of you? What kind of magic is this?"

"No magic," Ian said. He pointed to Tristan. "I doona know who that is. I'll be the one to take your life though."

Tristan gave a derisive snort. "I'll be the one killing him. I am a Dragon King after all."

Balladyn's gaze then focused on Sammi. "We take them all and sort it out later."

"No need," one of the other Dark said. "The Kings always have a tattoo of a dragon."

Balladyn's smile was cold and ruthless. "Take your shirts off."

Tristan was the first to tear off his tee. Ian was a second behind him. The magic Con had used to fake the tat on Ian's chest was so good that for a moment Tristan began to wonder who was the real King.

"I'm tired of talking. It's time to fight," Tristan said. "Death comes to any Dark who dares to venture onto

Dreagan. The treaty has been broken. If it's war you want, then it's war you'll get."

Balladyn's smile was as frigid as the arctic. "Oh, it's definitely war we want, Dragon King, but this time, you'll be the ones to leave this realm."

Tristan had heard enough. Rhi gave him a wink to let him know she was ready. Tristan let out a roar as he dove for the Dark nearest him.

Sammi was aghast at the melee before her. No sooner had Tristan attacked than Ian punched a Dark and dove to the floor. When he got to his feet he had Rhi's sword in hand.

As for Rhi, she and Balladyn were once more rolling around on the floor, colliding into furniture and walls alike as they beat each other.

A moment later, the front door flew open as Dragon Kings and Warriors came pouring in. Sammi smiled, because she knew they would be victorious.

She quickly went to stand between Laith and Phelan while the others attacked the Dark Fae. Sammi couldn't see the magic being thrown around by the Dark and Kings, but the air was electric with some unknown charge that could only be magic.

Three Dark lay dead, their lives taken by Ian, who swung Rhi's sword as if it was a part of him. He wasn't the only one with a sword, however.

Tristan also held one. She had no idea when he had gotten it or how, but it was beautiful in its simplicity. The blade was straight and the pommel leather wrapped with enough room for a hand and a half as he swung it.

The tide was quickly turning in their favor. Sammi

looked at Laith to see the Dragon King's face was grim. "What is it?"

"Two more Dark are here."

"What?" she asked in confusion.

Then she saw them. The two Dark that quickly turned into six and then ten. It had been a trap, but not set by the Kings. This one had been set by the Dark.

Sammi lost count of the new Dark Ones appearing. Laith left her next to Phelan as he joined the others in the battle. Beside her, Phelan was fisting his hands and growling as he yearned to get into the thick of things.

"Go," she urged.

He shook his head. "I can no' leave you alone."

No sooner were the words out of his mouth than his skin shifted into gold and gold claws shot from his fingers. He let loose a long, vicious growl and ducked a blast of magic before he speared the attacking Dark in the throat.

Blood sprayed Phelan as well as Sammi, but she didn't bother to move. She had worked herself into a corner with Phelan now standing in front of her ready to defend her against a steady stream of Dark.

It wasn't long before Charon returned and the two of them kept the Dark at bay. But for every Dark they killed, three more replaced them.

"Duck!" Charon yelled at her.

Sammi's mind was still processing his request, but her body went into action. Her legs folded and she ended up on all fours on the floor with a smoldering hole in the wall where her head had been.

"Bloody hell," she murmured and decided to stay

lower to the ground. She put her back into the corner again and pulled her legs against her.

Her palms were sweaty and her mouth dry with fear. She searched the area for Tristan and found him fighting three Dark Ones with an ease that should have relieved her mind.

Instead, it made her all the more nervous, because Tristan was like a madman as he fought. He would fight until there was nothing left. He would put himself in peril, put Dreagan in peril.

There was a crack as if a strain on the wooden beams of the ceiling. Sammi easily found the source. It was Laith. He had shifted into dragon form. He stood, a wall of black scales against the Dark.

With a roar he busted his head through the roof. His tail took out two Dark Ones as well as the left half of the cottage. Sammi covered her head with her hands as debris began to rain down.

No sooner had Laith shifted than Banan joined him. Black stood next to Blue, and between the both of them the roof was completely demolished.

Boards bounced next to Sammi, one hitting her shoulder. It wasn't until she looked up and found Phelan and Charon standing over her like shields that she realized why she was all but unfazed.

Charon let out a furious growl when his right leg crumpled and he went down on one knee. The air around him was charged higher, letting Sammi know magic had been used.

The Dark responsible was soon fighting Phelan. Sammi looked at Charon's leg to see a ragged hole the size of a football burned into the lower back half of his jeans. The skin bled amid the burns. To her shock, his wound began to heal right before her eyes.

"If only we healed as quickly as the Kings," Charon said with a wink.

He was up and fighting alongside Phelan again a moment later. Her mortality hit home like a sledgehammer. Every being, excluding herself, was immortal to some degree.

Her life could be snuffed out in an instant. A blast of magic from a Dark hitting her would most likely end her life. There would be nothing inside her to heal such a wound.

She stood in a room full of supernatural beings, immortal and powerful. They were fighting a war she had no part in, a war that she had been pulled into against her will.

But now that she was in it, Sammi didn't think she could leave. How could she return to Oban and her pub knowing what existed on Dreagan?

There was no way any man would ever compare to Tristan. He was wild and fierce, untamed and ferocious—and she couldn't take her eyes off him.

The raw, visceral power left her astounded and dazed.

The brutal, primal strength was startling and remarkable.

The fierce, potent energy of him made her heart pound and her soul come alive.

Tristan was the epitome of a Highland warrior. He was ruthless, merciless as he fought.

She was so in tune with him that she slowly stood to go to him. One step away from the corner and everything changed.

Perhaps Sammi should have paid more attention to the room at large rather than seeing Tristan with new eyes. Maybe then she would have realized there was a new Dark One in the room.

An arm wrapped around her from behind and grabbed her neck. Some unknown, unseen force was preventing her from speaking to warn Tristan or even Phelan and Charon that a Dark had her.

"Well, well, well," said a deep, husky Irish voice in her ear. The male laughed softly. "Ah, but this was too easy. Tell me, dear, do you know which one is the real Tristan?"

Sammi shook her head. It didn't matter what they did to her. She wasn't going to tell them anything.

"No matter," he whispered, his voice lowering even more. "Soon, Tristan will be coming to me. You see, I have what he wants. You."

Terror, unyielding and inexorable, engulfed her. She had made a critical mistake, one that could be the end of her. Her gaze looked past the groups fighting to what was left of the bedroom.

The white linens were barely visible from the collapse of the roof. In her mind, however, the bed was clean and on it were her and Tristan locked in a kiss with their limbs tangled as they learned each other's body.

It was the last thing she saw before the chilling, horrifying darkness.

CHAPTER
THIRTY

The Dark Tristan was fighting disappeared before he could land the killing blow. It was just like the cowardly fuckers to pull that kind of stunt.

He whirled around, ready to take on the next Dark One, but there was no one other than the Warriors and Kings. Until his gaze landed on Balladyn and Rhi still locked in battle.

This time Rhi had the upper hand. She stood with one gold heel of her shoe on his throat and her sword at his groin. "It's over, Balladyn. Call off your dogs."

His slow, evil smile sent a chill of foreboding down Tristan's spine.

"Look around, pet," Balladyn prodded her.

Rhi paused before she looked up, her gaze clashing with Tristan's before she slowly surveyed the room. "Where did you send them?"

"Where else? We got what we came for."

Tristan's heart squeezed as if a fist had plunged into his chest and wrapped around it. He couldn't catch his breath. He turned his head to the corner he had spotted Sammi in to find it empty.

Phelan and Charon turned as well, their puzzled expressions saying what words could not.

"That's right," Balladyn said.

Tristan jerked his head to the Dark to find his red eyes staring at him.

Balladyn's smile grew. "We have her, Dragon King. If you want her back, you know where to find us."

He teleported out just as Rhi was bringing down her sword. The blade cut through the rug into the wood floor while she cursed.

Tristan knew what they would do to Sammi. He knew all too well what awaited her in the depths of the Dark Ones' home. His plan had been to protect her.

Instead, she was now in the hands of his enemy.

Tristan threw back his head and roared all his fury, his ineffectiveness. His vehemence.

Hopelessness slid into his gut like a snake, coiling its cold skin around him until he was drowning in it.

It had been pure luck, Rhi, and Kellan's quick thinking that had gotten Kellan and Denae out of the Dark Fae's prison last time. At least Tristan had Rhi. He hated to ask her to go back to such a place, but he had no choice. He had to get Sammi back.

Even if it meant he changed places with her.

"It was all a damned trap," Ian growled.

Rhys said, "We were too damn confident in our success."

"How did they know our plan?" Phelan asked.

Banan and Laith shifted back into human form, but

Tristan couldn't take his eyes off the last place he had seen Sammi.

"Do they have someone who can stay veiled as long as Rhi who might have spied on us?" Banan asked.

Laith made a sound at the back of his throat. "Why would they risk so much by coming onto Dreagan?"

Tristan had no answers for them. His mind was in a whirl of rage and ire over how he could have messed up so badly that Sammi was taken.

Somehow he had to pull himself together, to become a cold, calculating machine so he could go into the depths of the netherworld to find her.

Just how the hell he was going to do that was something he hadn't figured out.

Rhi didn't think she had ever seen someone as desolate as Tristan. The shock and surprise at finding Sammi gone showed plainly on his face.

"Tristan," Ian said as he walked to his brother's side. "We'll find Sammi."

Rhi felt eyes on her and turned her head to Phelan. She, Phelan, and Tristan had been in the tunnels outside of Taraeth's fortress recently, and Rhi would be content to spend eternity without seeing them again.

That wasn't going to happen though. She would be going back into the awful place because she knew Tristan would ask it of her. As much as she wanted to refuse, she couldn't. She was a romantic, a sucker for love.

Sammi and Tristan might not have realized it yet, but they were made for each other. Just as she and her dragon lover had been.

They hadn't survived, but Rhi would do all she could to help Tristan and Sammi.

The war had begun, and there would be casualties—there always were. Rhi was afraid that this time, the humans were going to be dragged into it.

And that would be the downfall of the Kings.

That didn't mean the Light Fae would get to share in the spoils of the realm with the Dark. There would be another civil war. She was so tired of fighting, so tired of being the one to put what she wanted on hold.

It was in the Light's interest to join the Kings. Rhi knew she could talk her queen into it. Constantine was another matter, but then she knew how to go around that.

She would speak to the other Dragon Kings and let them convince Con. If she asked, he would say no just to irritate her, and there wasn't time for that. He was a first-rate ass, but this war went beyond her hatred of him.

Right now she was more focused on Balladyn. Rhi had thought fighting him would be difficult with their history. It should be hard to battle someone she had considered a brother and mentor.

Balladyn, however, had made it easy for her. His jabs about losing her lover hadn't made her lose her cool as he had hoped—as it would have done before. This time, it made her more focused.

She ran her fingers through her hair to smooth it out of her face and got a strand caught in her nail. "Damn," she mumbled when she saw her nail was split, her new polish chipped in multiple places.

A nice long visit to her favorite salon was in order once Sammi was back in the safe confines of Dreagan Manor with Tristan by her side.

That was going to be the problematic part. The Dark would offer to trade Sammi for Tristan. And Tristan, the noble fool, would do it.

Rhi began to formulate several plans that might keep both Sammi and Tristan out of the Dark's clutches, but every one was chancy and required fate to be kind.

When fate was anything but.

The air moved behind her, and before Rhi could turn, a blade was pressed beneath her chin. She stilled instantly.

"You should've remained on guard. Did nothing I taught you stick in that bullheaded mind of yours, pet?" Balladyn asked in her ear.

To Rhi's surprise, the only one looking at her was Con. His black gaze was blank, uncaring that a Dark had her in his grip. Rhi knew then that this was the end for her.

Even if she called out, even if she tried to get away, Balladyn would kill her. There was nothing anyone could do to help. She was well and truly doomed.

What irked the most was that this wasn't how she was supposed to go out. In the midst of battle for sure, not being taken by surprise because she'd let her guard down like some stupid youngster.

"I've been waiting for this for a long time," Balladyn whispered.

Fear was too strong. She wanted to live! Rhi sucked in a breath to call out for help when Balladyn teleported her away.

She found herself in the dark in the next second. Before she could ask what he was doing, Balladyn hit her on the back of the neck, sending her to her knees.

Rhi fell into a puddle of water that made her gag— the stench was so terrible. She was then roughly yanked around and shackles put on her wrists and feet.

"These are the Chains of Mordare. I know you've heard of them, of just what they can do to a Fae. No Light magic can free you."

Her head was spinning, her eyes unable to focus. She wanted to demand that Balladyn tell her what his plans for her were, but she couldn't get the words past her lips.

"It's your time to suffer. Pet," he said contemptuously.

Then there was only silence. And the dark.

It was the worst kind of hell for a Light Fae.

"Shit!"

Tristan jerked at Con's explosion. He forced himself to look at Constantine to find the King of Kings pacing in an agitated state.

"Where the hell is Rhi?" Phelan demanded angrily. "Did you send her away, Con?"

Con stopped pacing and spun to face Phelan. "Nay. She was taken. By Balladyn. Who is that son of a bitch anyway? He calls her pet as if they know each other."

"I think they do," Phelan said, his face lined with worry as he bent to collect Rhi's blade that she must have dropped.

Tristan drew in a deep breath. "There's no doubt they know each other. Those two were fighting as if they had a long-coming grudge to settle."

"Our way into the Dark's holding is gone," Charon said.

Rhys righted a chair and kicked at a dead Dark. "No' exactly. Phelan can find a way."

"And I'll be beside him," Tristan stated.

Ian rubbed his chest as the dragon tattoo vanished. "I'll be with you. If nothing else, we can try to fool them again."

Tristan was shaking his head before Ian finished. "Nay. Balladyn knew who I was. He looked right at me. That ruse willna work again."

"What did you say to Ulrik?" Banan asked. "Did you accidentally say something that would tip him off to your plan?"

"Never. I went out of my way to keep the conversation on me."

Laith gave the broken sofa a kick away from a small closet and took out two pairs of jeans. He threw one at Banan and kept the other. After shoving one leg in the pants, he said, "Tristan's plan was sound. The only way they could've known what was going down was to be privy to it."

"No' necessarily," Ian said. "They were thoroughly confused when they saw both me and Tristan. They didna know of that."

Con sighed loudly. "Which means they guessed and had the extra Dark on standby much as we were. Fuck me!"

"You all can debate that for as long as you want, but I'm going after Sammi. I can no' leave her there any longer than necessary," Tristan said.

Con's eyes, black as coal and cool as a yawning abyss, caught his. "You know they willna exchange her for you, no matter what they've said."

"I know. Just as I know that I'm no' coming out of there." It was a fate he resigned himself to.

He had mucked up being a Warrior, and when some-one had counted on him, he had royally screwed up being a King. As second chances went, he had fucked up beyond measure. This was his penance.

Phelan stepped forward. "It's no' just Sammi we need to look for. There is Rhi as well. Balladyn took her for a reason."

"And no' a good one," Con said angrily. "I know what they do to the Light. You might as well forget Rhi. If she survives, she'll become Dark."

"If?" Ian bellowed. "You're no' giving her enough credit."

Banan walked to the doorway and glanced at the broken front door. "And you Warriors have no' seen how they break a Light Fae. You know what the Dark do to mortals. It's ten times worse for a Light."

"I'm no' going to give up on her so easily," Rhys said. "She's helped us when there was no reason for her to. The least I can do is search for her."

Charon gave a brisk nod. "I'm in agreement."

"Time is of the essence, gentlemen," Con said. "You'll be lucky to find one of them, if either. I'm coming with you."

Tristan couldn't have been more surprised than if Con had beheaded Phelan.

The last time he had snuck into Ireland it had just been him and Phelan. This time, the Dark were going to feel the fury of the Kings and Warriors.

CHAPTER
THIRTY-ONE

Sammi shuddered and wrapped her arms around herself, her eyes tightly shut. She was freezing. And wet. Where was she? More importantly, why was she squeezing her eyes shut?

Then it all came back in blazing Technicolor. Her heart missed a beat and her stomach dropped like a stone to her feet. She shivered, this time in panic and dread.

The Dark had her.

Insidious, menacing. Devious.

They were the boogeymen, the things mortals instinctively knew resided in the shadows waiting to strike. They were monsters, demons of the dark with enough magic and power to wipe out every last human.

Tristan had told her what they did to mortals, and her vivid imagination released dozens of scenarios she wished she could wipe from her mind.

Sammi couldn't stop shaking. The terror had such a grip on her that even her teeth were chattering. The mind-boggling, unimaginable despair and trepidation sapped every smidgen of warmth from her body.

No amount of hoping the situation would all be a dream was going to help her. If she wanted a chance, she was going to have to face what was around her—no matter how petrified she was.

She opened her eyes expecting to find herself in some dark prison. Instead, lights blazed around her, blinding her so that she had to blink several times to adjust. Sammi drew in a shaky breath wishing her heart would stop beating against her rib cage.

A quick look around showed her several things. The room was narrow but long, the shape of a rectangle. There were no windows, just dozens of lights that seemed to hang in midair since she couldn't see the ceiling.

And she was alone.

For the time being.

Sammi took that small measure of good news and held on tightly. She wasn't a fool. They had taken her to get Tristan. In his duty as a Dragon King, he would come for her. Until then, the Dark would take their entertainment—on her.

How she wished Tristan wouldn't come. It wasn't that she wanted to stay with the Dark, but once they took her soul, she wouldn't know the difference. At least they wouldn't have a King.

But Tristan was too devoted to the Kings to do anything other than his loyal obligation.

"I see you're awake."

Sammi jumped when Balladyn suddenly appeared in front of her. She hated that they could do that. It would mean she had to constantly stay on guard. She let the hate fill her. It warmed her, chasing away the fear enough so she could think straight again.

"Bastards," she mumbled.

One black brow lifted, his gorgeous face hard as granite. "Excuse me?"

She just stared at him, trying not to let his red eyes freak her out any more than she already was. If a woman could get past the red eyes, he would be considered a prime catch. Not only was Balladyn's body tall and sculpted and almost as fine as Tristan's, but he had the face of a movie star, a Daniel Craig type that left women panting.

"Don't test me," he said in his thick Irish accent. "Your room is lighted, but I can change that."

Sammi thought it wise to keep her sarcastic remark to herself. She wasn't brave enough to provoke a Dark Fae. A pity really, because she had some awesome comebacks she really wanted to toss his way.

No one had frightened her as he had, and she loathed him for it. The hate and fear mixed inside her until it was a ball of writhing, twisting angst.

"Defiant." There was a small, sardonic smile on his face. "Odd since most mortals fall over themselves to be with us. What makes you different?"

"I know what you are."

"So do they," he retorted. "Taraeth will be in to see you soon. I'd suggest if you don't want to be stripped and have every Dark have his way with you that you continue to hold that sharp tongue of yours."

Sammi swallowed, hating that it was loud even to her ears. She despised bullies, and that's exactly what Balladyn and the Dark were. Tyrants, tormentors. Intimidators.

He smiled knowingly. "You humans are so pathetic,

letting every emotion you feel be shown to the world. Why do you think we chose you to take as ours?"

"We have a choice too. We can say no."

"You can try. It's not very successful."

"Denae did it." Sammi bit the inside of her mouth to keep from smiling when she saw her words had hit a sore spot.

He took a step closer, leaning over her so that she had to tilt her head up to look at him with his red eyes narrowed dangerously. "If you want to live, don't mention that name to Taraeth."

The warning came in a low, dangerous voice that sent coils of fear, numbing her body once again.

She waited until he straightened and turned away before she said, "You've made a mistake in riling the Kings."

"It's time they had their scales ruffled. They've ruled this realm for far too long."

And then he was gone, leaving Sammi in the room with nothing but her thoughts. She looked around feeling like a lab rat on display.

All four walls were stone, but she had the distinct impression that she was being watched, as if one wall was nothing more than a mirror that she couldn't detect.

"Bastards," she whispered.

Tristan clenched his teeth as Con shouted for him to wait. He glared, feeling every second that went by and he wasn't on his way to get Sammi was a second they could be touching her, marking her as one of the Dark's.

Con's gaze was on the group of Warriors. "You've painted a big target on yourselves by helping us tonight."

"So?" Phelan said with a shrug. "I'm no' going to let them keep Rhi. She helped me. I'll be there for her."

Con let out a long breath. "Phelan, you're part Fae. The Dark willna think much about you interfering, but the same can no' be said for other Warriors."

"I welcome the target if it means helping Tristan," Ian said.

Tristan, however, knew what Con was getting at. "Con's right. Perhaps you all should return to your women. There is no telling what the Dark will do."

Charon barked with laughter. "Then they doona know our Druids."

"The Druids and Fae never battled," Rhys said thoughtfully. "Who knows what could happen? The Druids are strong."

"No' as strong as the Dark," Banan said.

Laith shrugged. "They'll hold their own is my guess."

"We should warn everyone," Phelan said as he looked from Charon to Ian.

Tristan could barely stand still as the three took the time to place calls to their wives. He was wound tight, and he would need to calm down or risk Sammi's life.

"Banan, return to the manor," Con said. "You'll want to be with Jane, and the more Kings that remain on Dreagan the better."

Banan's lips compressed tightly. "I'd rather be going to Ireland, but the thought of Jane in the Dark's hands is enough to keep me here."

Tristan shared a look with Banan as an unspoken

promise passed between them. When the Warriors had finished their calls, Tristan walked out into the open so he wouldn't hit anyone when he shifted.

He gave no one time to say anything as he transformed and then lowered his head for Ian to climb on the back of his neck. As soon as Ian was situated, Tristan took to the sky.

One by one, Rhys, Con, and Laith shifted. Rhys carried Phelan while Laith carried Charon. Con took the lead, sending a message through their link that they were headed to Ireland and to be on the lookout for more Dark.

Tristan didn't have to tell Con to hurry. They all flew as if the edge of the cosmos was nipping at their tails. All Tristan could think of was Sammi and what a fool he'd been to walk away after their night of passion.

She stirred a riot of feelings—not to mention memories. As turbulent and alarming as that was, he hungered for her in a way he knew—deep down in his very soul—that he had never felt for a woman before.

He didn't know why he had become a Dragon King, and it no longer mattered. He was a King.

Yet he had also been a Warrior. No longer could he try and deny that. Fighting alongside Ian had proven that when he knew, instinctively, what Ian would do before he did it. They had fought the Dark as if they did it every day.

That kind of familiarity and awareness didn't just happen. That came from a lifetime of knowing someone.

Tristan didn't know how a relationship with Ian would

work, or if it even could. But he owed it to the both of them to try. Just as he would try everything in his considerable power to free Sammi.

He thought of her smile and her sharp wit. She had stood on her own for years. It made her tough, tough enough to survive weeks on the run from the Mob.

Or really Ulrik.

That was a hard pill to swallow. Ulrik had been playing him from the very beginning. The fact Tristan had gone to him was like acid burning his stomach.

It no longer mattered about Ulrik's past and what had been done. It was the present and his actions. Ulrik had to be stopped. Maybe Con was right in wanting to kill him.

Tristan could see the edge of Ireland with his dragon vision. They were close. He hoped Sammi knew he would come for her, that he wouldn't leave her with the Dark.

He flew faster, Ireland coming closer and closer. Tristan could almost feel Sammi.

Suddenly there was a loud buzzing in his head like white noise. Tristan roared as pain exploded in his head. He tried to remain in flight, but he could feel himself tilting. And then Ian slipped off.

Tristan attempted to find his brother, but he kept reaching for thin air. The static grew louder, the pain unbearable. Any moment he expected his brain to explode.

And through it all he heard laughter. Ulrik's laughter.

It was only belatedly that Tristan realized he was no longer flying—but falling.

* * *

Con dove down for Ian the moment Rhys bellowed through their link. With Ian in hand, Con could only watch as Tristan plummeted to the water.

"What the hell!" Phelan shouted from Rhys's back.

Con looked down to find Ian searching the water for his brother. The fact Tristan had sunk quickly was worrisome. Dragons were some of the best swimmers. Many dragons had lived in the water.

"*Stay steady,*" he told Rhys and Laith.

Ian looked up at him. "Where is Tristan? Why are you no' going to get him?"

In order to respond Con would have to return to his human form. Instead, he set Ian atop Laith's back and tucked his wings as he dove for the water.

He hit the water as fast as a torpedo, slicing through it like a hot knife through butter. Con spotted Tristan's amber scales. He was floating downward, unconscious.

It took little effort to reach Tristan, but pulling him out was another matter. Something had ahold of him, something magical.

Con used his tail as well as all four limbs, and it took all of his considerable strength to yank Tristan from whatever had taken him. As soon as Tristan was free, Con swam them to the surface. The moment they broke the surface he took flight, not wanting to wait around to see what else might try and take Tristan.

Rhys and Laith moved to either side of Con. Anger simmered and seethed. How dare Ulrik attack one of the Kings? It was him that Ulrik was after. His old friend was about to get his wish too.

As soon as this latest issue with the Dark was resolved

and Sammi recovered, Con would do what he should have done all those millennia ago.

He was going to kill Ulrik.

Con made sure to hide his rage as they reached the shores of Ireland. He set Tristan down upon the sand and landed beside him. Rhys and Laith were quick to do the same.

Ian had jumped off Laith and was running to Tristan before Con could shift into human form. The only King who remained a dragon was Tristan, and the fact he hadn't stirred caused worry to swirl in Con's gut.

"What happened?" Rhys demanded.

Con looked over Tristan. "It's no coincidence that magic was used just as we were reaching Ireland."

"Had Tristan been alone . . ." Ian couldn't finish, and he didn't need to. Everyone knew exactly what he left unspoken.

Phelan growled low in his throat. "This is shite."

"At least we know who to blame. Ulrik," Rhys stated.

Con rubbed his jaw as he considered their options. "The longer Tristan remains unconscious, the longer the Dark have Sammi."

"He'll never forgive himself," Charon said.

That's exactly what Ulrik wanted. Con didn't bother to tell the others that. Ulrik was his problem to correct. It had been their friendship that stayed his hand the last time.

For so many centuries he'd lived with the regret that Ulrik was not a Dragon King in the truest sense of the word.

Now Con lived with the regret that he hadn't killed him and saved everyone this trouble.

Con moved to stand at Tristan's head and put his hands atop the huge dragon head. His magic had always been strong, and it had only gotten stronger when he became King of Kings.

It was going to take that magic to wake Tristan.

CHAPTER
THIRTY-TWO

Kiril was on his second glass of passable Irish whisky. But he longed for a bottle of Dreagan.

Just as he longed to return to the land.

He had no idea how long he would be in Ireland spying on the Dark Ones. He was in the *an Doras* pub. It would make things easier if he came every night, but it would also make them suspicious.

So Kiril made sure to visit two other pubs as well. Just to keep the arses on their toes.

He swirled the liquid in his glass as he reclined in the booth. The pub was busy, busier than usual actually. There was an undercurrent of excitement through the building. What it was he hadn't discovered yet.

Kiril picked up a conversation behind him. He kept his gaze on his glass, but all his attention was on the two Dark males talking.

"Did you hear?"

There was a grunt and then the thud as a glass was

set down heavily on the table. "They had a Dragon King once before."

The first laughed, the sound grating on Kiril's nerves. His voice was higher pitched and annoying. "Taraeth is stronger than you think."

"He had his arm cut off by a human," the second man said gruffly.

"Ah, but this time he'll keep the King."

Gruff grunted again. "I'll believe it when he has him."

"Taraeth has set a trap for him." The laughter became higher pitched. "The war has begun. We'll have this realm to ourselves in no time."

"You look like you could use a refill," came a voice next to Kiril.

He jerked his gaze up and into the red eyes of a Dark Fae. Some tried to conceal their eyes while others didn't bother. He gave a nod to the Dark who set down the glass of whisky and slid into the bench opposite him. "Appreciate it."

The Dark smiled. "I've seen you in here a few times. The name is Farrell."

"Kiril," he answered. So they had noticed him. Would they know he was a Dragon King, however?

"What do you think of our pub?" Farrell asked.

Kiril brought his drink to his lips and drank. He returned the glass to the table before he said, "I find it interesting."

"That's not an Irish accent I hear. Tell me you aren't a Scot."

He smiled though it was tight. "Hate to disappoint."

Farrell laughed and leaned back as he got comfortable. "We have a few Scots come in now and again.

You, we can handle. It's the damn Brits that get under our Irish skin."

Kiril joined in the laughter, but he was on full alert. If they expected to nab a King, could they be referring to him? He was going to have to be extra vigilant if he expected to leave the pub that night.

Farrell continued to talk, taking control of the conversation as he spoke of Ireland, Cork, and the benefits of being Irish.

Kiril was nodding at something Farrell said when he felt Con push against his mind. He opened the link between them while keeping eye contact with Farrell as he spoke of their famous crystal.

"The Dark have taken Sammi. We were on our way to Cork when magic was used to bring Tristan down."

"I've bought several pieces of Waterford crystal," Kiril said to Farrell. *"Where are you now?"*

"In Ireland. Rhys and Laith are with us. Phelan, Charon, and Ian also tagged along."

Warriors and Kings. There really was a shit storm coming. *"Is it true? Has the war begun?"*

"Aye. Watch yourself, Kiril. They'll target anyone they think is a King."

The link severed, Kiril drained the rest of his whisky and reached for the glass Farrell had brought. "Tell me, Farrell, what's with the red eyes?"

"They're special contacts. The women go crazy for them," the Dark answered as he leaned on the table.

Kiril might look like he was listening raptly, but in fact he was surveying the pub looking for any threats coming his way. The Kings might need him, so he wanted to get back to his house soon.

But not yet.

"I'll be in Cork for a while on an extended holiday," Kiril said.

Farrell smiled widely. "We'll have to be sure to meet up again."

Just what Kiril wanted. He might finally have an in with the Dark.

Tristan came awake as if he'd been slapped. When he opened his eyes and found Con standing over him, he knew that's exactly what had happened.

"About damn time," Rhys said brusquely.

Tristan sat up and found himself nude on a beach. He looked up and met Ian's worried gaze. "What happened?"

"You doona remember?" Phelan asked.

He shook his head and rubbed the back of his neck, which was sore. "I remember a strange sound in my head that was excruciating."

"You fell," Laith said. "Into the water. Con had to pull you out."

Tristan didn't know why everyone was upset. So he had fallen. It wasn't the best thing that could happen, but it wasn't as if he could've died.

"Something had you," Con said.

That was enough to cause him to frown. "Had me?"

Con nodded solemnly. "It was magic."

"How long have I been out?" Tristan asked as he gained his feet.

Charon kicked at the sand. "A few minutes."

Everyone attempted to act normal, but Tristan got the distinct impression that there had been something major going on with him. He turned to Ian, who he knew would tell him the truth. "What really happened?"

"You fell," Ian said and glanced at the water. "Con had to go in and get you, and just like he said, there was magic used. It was anchoring you to the bottom of the sea. Con got you out and on the beach, but you wouldna wake."

Tristan rubbed his neck again. It was a dull ache, one that made him feel as if he'd been clubbed in the back of the head. "And?" he urged.

"It took Con's magic to break the hold over you so you could wake."

Con's magic. That meant that whatever magic was used on him had been particularly strong. His gaze swung to Con. "Thank you."

"They intend to have you one way or another," Con said. "Let's no' give them what they want."

Laith slapped Tristan on the back. "Agreed. Now, can we get our naked asses back into dragon form and find these sons of bitches?"

"I'm all for kicking some Dark Fae ass," Rhys said. "The sooner, the better."

Phelan smiled and nodded. "Oh, aye. Let's get moving."

Tristan looked out at the water. The mental link was used only by dragons, but even then, he could decide whether to listen to whoever was trying to talk to him.

Whoever had gotten into his head had done it without his authority. He didn't like the vulnerability . . . or the weakness. He could be a detriment to the others.

"Nay," Ian said as he came to stand beside him.

Tristan glanced at his twin. "What?"

"You willna be a disadvantage in battle. You know what was done to you, and you willna let it happen again."

"You sound awfully sure of me."

Ian smiled. "I am. I know you as no one else does. You will triumph just as you always have."

"Then let's go."

With a mere thought, Tristan was once again in dragon form, his mind completely closed off. After the Warriors were settled on the backs of the Dragon Kings, the company took to the skies, toward Cork.

Toward the Dark.

Sammi should've known she wouldn't be left alone. Just as Balladyn had said, Taraeth, the king of the Dark, stood before her.

He thought by towering over her he could show her how weak she was. Sammi chose to remain seated on the ground. The Dark fed off of her strength.

Besides, they wouldn't suspect her of anything if she appeared weak and helpless.

She watched Taraeth rub his shoulder where his arm had been cut off. Sammi sent up a silent shout of joy to Denae for managing to pull that off.

Taraeth wore black leather pants and a red and black Affliction tee that had a skull on the front. By all accounts, he was just an average guy who kept his hair long and had red contacts.

Only, she knew the truth of how deep the evil resided inside him.

"I like your fear," Taraeth said as his red gaze raked over her. "That means you know of us."

Sammi gave a slow nod and looked at the ground.

Out of the corner of her eye she saw Balladyn on her left and some other Fae to her right.

It was just the three of them. Sammi had taken on bigger men in her pub, but they had been drunk. And they hadn't had magic. She couldn't attack them head-on. She was going to have to come up with some other way to beat them.

If you can.

She told her subconscious to shut up and concentrated on what Taraeth was saying.

"I'll give it to the Kings. They have a knack for picking pretty women. A pity that the women always end up with me. You do realize that you're mine now?"

Sammi winced when his finger lifted her chin. When had he squatted before her? He must move as quickly as the wind. She was at a disadvantage if she couldn't even see them.

"Tristan will come for you, but it'll be too late. I'll have marked you."

She turned her head away from his touch only to have him roughly grab her chin and force her head back to him.

"What do the Kings do to make you turn away from us?"

Sammi frowned. "I don't know what you mean."

"First Denae, and now you. No other human has ever turned away from me. It has to be something the Kings are doing, some kind of magic being used."

Sammi tried to stop it, she really did, but the laughter just burst from her like a balloon popping. And once started, she couldn't stop.

"We'll see who's laughing when I take you with

Tristan watching. You'll scream in pleasure. You'll scream for me." He leaned close and whispered, "You'll beg."

The laughter was gone. Sammi didn't question that Taraeth could do just as he said. They were gorgeous specimen. Every last one of them.

It was no wonder human women fell to their knees and begged the Dark. Sammi might have done the same thing years ago, but she was different now.

Tristan.

She was different because of her time with Tristan. He'd walked her through a world of dragons and Fae and magic. He'd stood beside her, holding her, sheltering her.

And she had wanted him.

The need had been great, the hunger overwhelming. Only Tristan had been able to relieve the ache within her, to ease her body with a night of languid loving.

"If he comes," she said.

Taraeth's smile was cold. "He'll come. The Dragon Kings are meant to protect the humans. How could he ignore the need to save you, the sister of his friend's mate? If he doesn't come, Banan will. It doesn't matter which King I get in the end."

He stood and adjusted his shirt with an eager smile. "Get ready. It's the beginning of the end for the Dragon Kings."

CHAPTER
THIRTY-THREE

The darkness didn't scare her.

It was a lie Rhi repeated silently over and over in her mind. In fact, she was more terrified than she had ever been in her life.

No Light Fae had ever come back from torture with the Dark, so no one knew exactly what was done. The fact none had returned said it all though.

Rhi thought back to the dozen new nail polishes she'd recently bought. There was the bright green called Gargantuan Green that she couldn't wait to wear. Hearts & Tarts, a soft pink that called to her Fae side. Cha-Ching Cherry that would go amazingly with her new shirt. Then there was a stunning deep blue called Keeping Suzi at Bay that begged to be worn. But her favorite was a Chianti red called I'm Not Really a Waitress.

She had to get out so she could try each and every one of her new collection. Panic infused her, distress pouring off her in waves.

Fear she had known before, but this went deeper than fear. This was pure terror. The kind that had her heart knocking against her ribs and her blood turning to ice.

"How do you like your new accommodations, pet?"

She tried to hide her alarm at Balladyn's close voice. He had snuck up on her without her even knowing. This didn't bode well.

At all.

"If you want to torture me, then what are you waiting for?" she taunted in what she hoped was a stronger voice than she felt.

His laugh sent a sinister chill down her spine. "That will come. I owe you, after all."

"Owe me?" She couldn't believe he blamed her for his becoming a Dark. She wasn't the one who had pushed him to the edge.

"Oh, yes," he said, not bothering to hide his delight. "I've waited years for this. Years of thinking what I would do to you if I ever had you in my grasp. I didn't think I'd get the chance, not once I heard you made the Queen's Guard. I should've known. You've never done what was expected of you."

"What did you expect from me?" She hated that the question was past her lips before she realized it.

"You left me!"

The walls vibrated with his fury. She shrank away, despising herself all the more because of it.

She could hear his harsh breathing all around her, making it impossible for her to pinpoint where he was. He was Dark. The darkness was part of him, allowing him to use it to his advantage as well as see in it.

"I saw you fall." Her voice shook, and she cleared her throat, hoping it would tamp down her fear. "I tried to get to you, but I was stopped. That's when they told me you were dead."

"And you didn't check yourself?"

His rage had vanished. It was replaced with cool indifference.

Rhi didn't know which bothered her more. Gone was the Fae who had held her, comforted her after her brother's death.

Gone was the kindness and laughter that had always been Balladyn's traits.

Gone was the Fae who had stood guard outside her room when she lost her Dragon King lover.

She shifted, the sounds of her chains loud in the silence. "We were in the middle of war. When the battle was done I went back for you, but your body was gone. For a while I thought you might be alive and wounded. I searched everywhere."

"Not everywhere."

Rhi closed her eyes. "It never entered my mind that the Dark had you."

"Even if they did, no one ever comes to rescue a Light."

His words were twice the blow, because he reminded her that she was well and truly alone. No Light Fae would dare to venture into the Dark's territory.

"So as revenge you'll turn me Dark?" she asked.

His answering chuckle was as icy as the temperature. "Oh, I have something else in mind. Perhaps centuries from now you'll become Dark. Until then, I plan to have my fun."

"And how will you do that?"

The eerie silence that followed only heightened her already frayed nerves.

"Balladyn?"

Again there was no answer. He had left her to her own thoughts, allowing her imagination to think of ways that he could hurt her. There were many.

That in itself made her want to scream.

By leaving her alone—in the dark—he was making her endure the cruelest torture of all.

Tristan and the others landed in the field that had seen their first battle with the Dark in seven thousand years. He didn't relish being back in Ireland. It might be a beautiful country, but it didn't hold the wild ruggedness of Scotland.

He returned to human form and slowly examined the area. He couldn't see any doorways created by the Fae, nor did he see any Dark.

"They're here," Phelan whispered.

Con stood tall, his nakedness not bothering him. "Where?"

"Hard to place them exactly."

Urgency rode Tristan hard. "Do you see a doorway?"

"I see six." Phelan turned his gaze to Tristan. "Each of them could lead to the tunnels we were in last time."

"Or somewhere else," Tristan finished.

Rhys narrowed his eyes. "They were expecting us."

Tristan looked from Con to Rhys to Laith. The Dark wanted him. If the others remained there was a chance the Dark could get lucky and nab a second King.

"Take to the skies," Tristan told them. "The farther you are from here, the less likely one of you will be captured."

Laith snorted loudly. "I'd like to see them try to take one of us."

Tristan didn't bother to tell them he planned to give himself to the Dark Ones. He could survive with them. Sammi couldn't. And Jane would never forgive him if Sammi wasn't returned.

Rhys gave a vicious shake of his head. "You can no' be serious!"

Tristan didn't pretend not to know what he meant. "There isna another way to find Sammi. We had Rhi last time. It was only because of Rhi that we found Kellan and Denae. Look around," he said and spread his arms. "There's no Rhi. We'll be guessing with whatever doorway we take. It could lead us anywhere. We could be stuck for weeks, months. Do you know what will happen to Sammi in that time?"

Rhys turned away and glared off into the distance. Laith kept shaking his head. The only King who would meet his gaze was Con.

"She means that much?" Con asked.

Did she ever. Tristan wished he had known just how far Sammi had wormed her way into his psyche and his soul. He'd had an inkling of it when he saw her with Ian. His reaction should have been a sign, but even then he was trying to ignore it.

If only he had realized how much he did care for her, then he would have protected her more. The only way he could make up for what he'd done was by rescuing her from the Dark.

"She does," he answered.

Con's nostrils flared as he took in a deep breath and slowly released it. "I'll come with you. They'll most likely come after me and give you time to find Sammi."

"Are you insane?" Laith asked angrily.

One side of Con's lips twisted in a smile. "Quite possibly."

"Nay. The Kings need you. Dreagan needs you," Tristan said.

Con gave him a droll look. "Each King makes their own decisions. I've made mine."

"I'm going in with Tristan as well," Ian said. "I didna come all this way to sit on the sidelines."

Tristan nodded. "I was hoping you'd say that."

"Count us in," Charon said of him and Phelan.

Phelan chuckled and stared at something to his left. "At least we know what's in those damn tunnels this time."

"Would Taraeth no' have moved?" Tristan asked.

Con's smile grew cold and calculating. "Taraeth would only move his palace if it was completely destroyed. The battle was here last time."

"Wait," Charon said, his brow puckered in a frown. "I thought Taraeth's compound was on this realm."

"It is," Con said. "Just hidden. Earth provides humans for the Dark to enjoy, but the realm doesn't give them everything they need." He motioned around him with a sweep of his arm. "So Taraeth finds a place he likes, cloaks it in magic so no one sees it, and then peels back the layers between realms until part of the Fae world is visible beneath his great house. It gives him a seat of power, or so he thinks."

Ian rubbed his forehead thoughtfully. "When we go through one of those doorways we could be in the Fae realm?"

"Potentially," Rhys said.

Laith turned his back to them. "I think each King should take a doorway until we find the one we want."

"Too risky," Tristan said. He quickly looked at Phelan. "Do you remember the doorway Rhi made?"

Phelan squinted. "I might be able to pick it out."

"Good. Search for it." Tristan then looked to Laith and Rhys. "We'll have to work hard to get out of the tunnels this time. The Dark Ones will have things in place to prevent it. You two will be our cover once we do come out."

Rhys punched him hard in the shoulder. "And you better come out along with Sammi. Doona make us come back in there for you."

He smiled and let them think he agreed. Tristan knew how hard they had worked, and the luck that had been on their side when they'd freed Kellan and Denae from the Dark.

The Dark had followed them out of the doorway, and it was only with the help of the Kings that they won that skirmish.

This time the Dark were prepared. This time they expected him. And this time there wouldn't be a way out. Tristan had accepted that. He just hoped the others did as well.

"I doona think I can leave you in there," Ian whispered as they watched Rhys and Laith shift into dragon form and take to the skies.

Tristan lowered his gaze. "You're going to have to. Just as you'll have to convince the others no' to come back in for me."

"I lost you once before. Now you're asking me to let you go after I've just found you again? You're my brother whether you're a Warrior or a Dragon King."

He faced Ian and smiled grimly. "I doona have a choice this time. Sammi needs me."

"Is it love?"

"I doona know. Maybe. I think about her constantly, and I can no' stand to be away from her. I crave her touch and her kisses as if there were no tomorrow."

Ian smiled ruefully. "I do believe you've fallen for the lovely Samantha. You never looked at a woman as you do her."

"I never . . . had someone?" He had been afraid to ask, afraid that he had left behind someone important.

"Never. There were women, but none that ever held your attention or your affections. The same can no' be said for Sammi."

"How did you know you loved Dani?"

Ian smiled at the mention of his wife. "When the idea of living life without her by my side seemed pointless. Doona do as I did and fight what's between you and Sammi. Take hold of her and love her, brother."

"Even when I doona know why I was made into a King?"

"Even then. Love can no' be understood. You've been given a second chance all around. Will you really throw your chance with Sammi away to let the Dark have you?"

Tristan didn't want to. He wanted to go on enjoying life—and Sammi.

"Understand," Con said quietly as he stood beside Phelan and Charon. "The Dark are waiting. They doona plan to do any kind of trade." He turned his head and looked at Tristan. "If we're going to win this day, we need a plan they'll never see coming."

CHAPTER
THIRTY-FOUR

Sammi hated the feel of wearing wet jeans. It was about as disgusting as mud slipping through her toes. She shivered just thinking about it.

It was hard not to think of miserable things when she felt so dismal. Wet jeans, damp shirt and hair, along with the icy temperatures were enough to put a saint in a foul mood.

And she was far from a saint.

At least her thoughts had taken her from the Dark Fae. They were a terrorizing lot to be sure. She leaned her head back against the stone wall, hating that she was so helpless. But what could a mortal do against the magic of the Fae?

Sammi climbed to her feet and stretched. She groaned when her jeans stuck to her leg. "Ick," she murmured and made herself walk around the rectangular room.

If only she had magic to toss at the Dark Fae she wouldn't feel so powerless. As it was, she felt like an inmate on death row waiting to be executed.

She prayed Tristan came for her, but she also hoped

he didn't. There could be nothing good of the Dark having a Dragon King. Nor could she imagine Tristan locked away as she was.

He would long to see the sky and ache to take flight. He was a glorious specimen in human form with his chiseled features, hard muscles, and the tat on his chest.

But as a dragon, his amber scales gleaming in the sunlight, he was magnificent. He glided effortlessly upon the wind, his massive wings spread wide while he moved between mountains.

How could someone like that be kept in the dark? How could someone like that survive with the Dark Ones?

Tristan was immortal, but that didn't mean he wouldn't be affected somehow, someway. That thought chilled her. His obligation would send him, and he would be stuck in this evil place.

"Do you love him?"

Sammi shrieked as she whirled around to find Balladyn leaning a shoulder casually against the wall as he watched her. Once more he had come upon her without her knowing. How she despised that. "What?"

"Tristan? Do you love him?"

"You want me to say yes so you can use him against me?" She rolled her eyes. "Please. I'm not that guileless."

His smile didn't reach his red eyes. He had changed into all black—black jeans, black boots, and a black BKE long-sleeved tee. His hair was pulled away from his face and secured at the back of his head, hanging down his back in a black and silver cascade.

"For someone who wants to destroy my world, you

sure like the fashions," she pointed out. "Are those Bed Stu boots?"

"Answer me, mortal."

His voice was as hard as granite, as unforgiving as the arctic. Sammi was petrified of him. Her first instinct was to cower and tell him anything he wanted. It was also her plan to make them think she was scared.

Easy since both went hand in hand.

"His power lured me," she said, hoping Balladyn bought the lie. Though it wasn't a complete lie. There was something mesmerizing about the Kings, but Tristan more than any other.

Balladyn narrowed his eyes on her. "It's not wise to lie to me."

"I don't love," she blurted out. Tears stung her eyes as the truth of her life came back and slapped her in the face.

She didn't love. Anyone. She hadn't even let Jane as close as Jane thought she was. Sammi had taken her calls and texts and exchanged e-mails, but every time Jane wanted her to visit, Sammi had an excuse. Same for when Jane tried to see her.

Sammi could keep her at a distance with electronics. It was more difficult when someone stood before you. Tristan had shown her that. She'd tried her damnedest to keep him at arm's length.

And failed.

If the Fae realized she had fallen for the Dragon King, they would use it against both her and Tristan. She was weak as a mortal against the Dark, but she could do her part to make them think it was nothing more than a King protecting a human.

"You spent the night in his bed," Balladyn said, breaking into her thoughts.

Sammi wrapped her arms around her middle to help keep her warm. "It was one night. That doesn't mean anything."

"It does. It can."

"Not with me. Besides, if he cared for me, would he have put me in danger back at the cottage? Would a Dragon King who loved a mortal have had her anywhere near where a potential attack would come?"

She inwardly smiled when she saw Balladyn frown and hesitate before speaking. She had hit the nail on the head.

What was worse, she was thinking how true her words really were. She might have fallen in love with Tristan, but he didn't return her feelings.

The emptiness inside her yawned like a gaping black hole threatening to swallow her. That same hole had nearly taken her when her mother died.

This time she wouldn't be able to outrun it.

This desolation, hollowness . . . this sadness was why she had made sure never to get close to anyone. The pain was too intense to bear.

"You see I'm right," she said as her heart crumbled into a thousand pieces.

"Yet you expect him to come."

It wasn't a question. Sammi tilted her head to the side. "The main purpose of the Dragon Kings is to protect humans. Isn't that why there were the Fae Wars? He will be doing his duty as a King. Nothing more."

"You're lying."

"You know I'm not."

Balladyn pushed away from the wall and gradually walked to her, eyeing her the entire time. "Your words make sense, but I saw the way he looked at you when Taraeth took you."

"I'm Jane's sister. Banan had Tristan watch over me. I'm nothing more than an obligation, a duty."

"So you say," he said.

He kept walking around her, making Sammi turn to keep him in her sights. "Why would I have need to lie?"

"Because you love him?"

She forced a laugh she didn't feel. "Oh, how wrong you are. Tristan is nothing to me. He was someone to fill my bed because I enjoyed what he looked like."

"You could be lying."

"I could be, but I want to go home. You scare me. This place scares me. My connection to Jane and Dreagan is what landed me here. What loyalty to the Kings do I have? None."

Balladyn took a step toward her, bringing his body close enough that she could feel the heat of him. "Kellan was quick to deny his feelings for Denae, and yet they were mates."

"I'm not Denae, and Tristan isn't Kellan." She was running out of things to say. If only he would believe her and step away. She needed to be alone in her misery.

"Maybe."

Sammi looked to the ceiling before she met his red gaze. "Look. I don't know how to make this any plainer. What do you want from me?"

Before she could guess his intentions, his hand snaked out and grasped the back of her head while his lips descended upon hers.

The kiss wasn't horrible, but it didn't make her blood burn or her skin tingle or make her long to strip off his clothes and wrap her legs around him as it did when Tristan kissed her.

Balladyn ended the kiss quickly and looked down at her. "You are a cold one. If Taraeth doesn't thaw your body, I'll get my chance."

Sammi was so shocked she could only stare at him. "I'll never see my home again, will I?"

"Never. It's not so bad down here. You'll get used to it soon enough. All the others do."

She turned her back to the wall and tried to control her breathing so she didn't hyperventilate. This couldn't be happening. She didn't want them touching her or kissing her, but Balladyn made it sound as if she wouldn't have a choice.

"All this because I knew the Kings?" she asked in one last desperate attempt in hopes they let her go.

He tugged at her hair. "That's part of it. Then there's the fact you walked away from me when we bumped into each other."

She was aghast. "Of all the conceited things. Do you really expect women to fall at your feet?"

"They always have. I'm Fae. It's what we do."

"I don't care about anyone, and I don't love. I'm a cold one, as you put it. There's your answer. Some humans are meant to go through life alone. I'm one of those."

He ran a finger tenderly along her jaw. "We'll see. Taraeth will keep you awhile until he tires of you. If you want to survive him, I suggest you not make him angry."

Her lips parted to respond, but he disappeared. She

fisted her hands and ran across the space to the opposite wall and slammed her hands against the stones again and again.

"I'm not part of the Kings! I don't care about any of them!"

Tristan was right behind Phelan as they stepped through the doorway and found themselves back in the tunnels. Ian, Charon, and Con followed.

They had taken just a few steps when Sammi's voice, yelling that she wasn't part of the Kings bounced along the walls of the tunnels.

The Dark knew they were there, and they wanted him to hear her. Her words stung, but at this point, Tristan wouldn't hold anything against her.

Fear most likely ruled her, and anyone would say whatever was needed to try and get freed. Sammi had yet to realize that the Dark never willingly let anyone go.

"She sounds tired," Ian whispered.

Tristan squatted next to the wall. It was once more pitch black, but neither the Warriors nor Kings had trouble seeing in the dark. "She's terrified."

"Do you think Rhi is being held here as well?" Phelan asked.

Tristan had no answer. It was Rhi who had found Phelan before he knew he was part Fae. A strong friendship had developed, and Tristan was glad to see someone was worried about her.

He would be as well if it wasn't for Sammi. As much as he wanted to find Rhi, he had to get to Sammi first.

"There's no way to know," Con answered.

Charon looked down the tunnel where it split into three. "We'll cover more ground split up."

"Agreed," Phelan hurried to say.

Ian nudged Tristan. "We'll take the left side."

Phelan and Charon exchanged smiles. It was Charon who said, "We'll take the middle."

"I'll take the right," Con said with a nod. "I can communicate with Tristan, and he with me, but there's no way we can let Phelan and Charon know it's time to get out."

Tristan looked at Phelan. "Con's right. We have to have some way to communicate."

"Use magic," Phelan said.

Charon nodded in agreement. "Aye. Down here in this muck, it'll feel different enough to know it's one of you."

With a nod, Con stood and hurried down the tunnel to disappear in the fork that branched to the right.

Together, the four of them approached the other two entrances. There was a silent look exchanged between them before Charon held out his arm. "Whether you go by Duncan or Tristan, and regardless of whether you're a Warrior or a Dragon King, it's a pleasure to be fighting next to you again."

Tristan clasped first Charon's, and then Phelan's forearm before they split into twos and went their separate ways.

Sammi—and the Dark Ones—waited.

CHAPTER
THIRTY-FIVE

Tristan and Ian walked silently through the tunnel. Instead of being infested with the grotesque animals he and Phelan had battled the first time, there was nothing.

The Dark had set the stage to be sure. A warning voice in his mind caused him to stop and listen. Silence. Absolute, sheer silence.

Last time the tunnels hadn't been filled with noise, but they hadn't been as unearthly still and soundless as they were now. It set him on edge, and he wasn't the only one. A glance at Ian showed he was just as unnerved.

"Something isna right," Ian said in a hushed tone.

Tristan looked around and nodded. "They know you are no' a King, but I doona think they realize you're a Warrior and can sense their magic."

"What are you thinking?" Ian asked with a sly grin.

It seemed as if he and Ian had always been together. It wasn't just that Ian looked exactly like him. It went deeper than that to a feeling as if he was a part of Ian, and Ian was a part of him.

There had been no more memories, and maybe that

was a good thing. They tended to make him try and piece together what happened before or after the memory.

Tristan pointed down the tunnel. "I'm going to go ahead. Stay behind me a ways. Let them think I'm alone."

"I can stay out of sight for sure, but I'm no' liking the part of you going to them alone."

"There's no other option." Tristan sighed and looked down at his hands, hands that had once sprouted claws with skin that had turned a pale blue. "Use your power as a Warrior when it comes time."

"And that time will be?"

"When they refuse to release Sammi."

Ian's lips flattened. "I can no' talk you out of letting them have you?"

"There's no other way. I'm no' going to willingly give myself to them. I'll fight, but in the end, it's about Sammi. Promise me that you'll get her out."

There was a pause before Ian nodded. "Doona make me come back for you, brother."

Brother. Tristan felt something deep inside him warm and expand as if just coming alive. He was no longer just human. He was a dragon first and foremost. He was part of something huge and powerful, something important.

Yet a part of him would always be a Warrior, a man who had a twin that could read his thoughts and know his every action.

It was exhilarating to know he would always have Ian. He wasn't just part of Dreagan, he had roots at Mac-Leod Castle as well.

The Dragon Kings and Warriors had become strong

allies. His connection just strengthened what was already there. He didn't want to give all that up to be bound in a prison by the Dark, but he didn't see a way out.

Not only were the Dark expecting him, but they were in their territory. They outnumbered the Kings fifty to one. It was bad enough Tristan was going to give himself to the bastards. No other Kings needed to be caught as well.

He started to walk away when Ian dragged him back and enveloped him in a tight hug. For a second Tristan couldn't move. Then he returned the embrace.

"Give them hell," Ian said as he released him.

Tristan's throat was tight from the depth of his emotion. He couldn't get any words past, so he tried to smile and hurried away.

Every little sound made Sammi jump. She couldn't rest, couldn't stop her heart from plummeting to her feet again and again.

It was like being in one of those Halloween haunted houses, but she couldn't find the exit. Her mind was already going. She would find herself thinking about Jane and reliving their conversations.

Then there was Tristan. She could have sworn he was behind her as she sat on the ground, one shoulder leaning against the wall.

She felt his heat, smelled the wind and power that was distinctly his. He had even touched her, pulling her against his chest and holding her close.

But when she turned her head to look at him, she was utterly alone.

Hours later—or what felt like hours, it could have been minutes—she closed her eyes and rested. All her mind could conjure was Tristan and their steamy, passion-filled night of love.

His kisses had sent her reeling.

His body had been a work of art.

His hands had caressed her, teased her until she writhed with need.

Then he had joined their bodies. It was one of those perfect moments, as if everything in the world had come together just for them.

It had been special, exceptional.

Extraordinary.

And, like a fool, she had run from it. If only she had run to him, to what the safety of his arms provided.

If only . . .

Those were the words that would be etched on her tombstone. She had been aloof and cold to anyone who could have meant something to her just because she couldn't handle the pain when that person left.

How many relationships had she let slip away that could have sweetened her life? Even if just for a few weeks? How many friendships had she let fade to nothing that could have been there for her?

Jane would never know how much Sammi needed her as a sister and a friend. Sammi had been selfish and unkind during their last conversation.

Now Jane would think that Sammi didn't love her. Her own sister? How could Sammi have put Jane through that all those months? Jane, her sweet soul, had never given up on them.

Sammi rewarded her by saying some nasty things

and running away from the only people who could have kept her safe. If only she had remained in the mountain she might not be held by the Dark wondering if it was the place she would die.

It was a sobering thought, especially when she wanted to tell Jane she was sorry and that she was the worst sister ever. There would never come a time she could make it up to Jane.

Worse, Sammi would never be able to hold Tristan again, to kiss his lips and fall under his spell. She wouldn't get to tell him that somehow he had broken through her walls and made her feel again.

He had made her love again.

Love. That word was frightening and . . . exhilarating. It was freeing and liberating.

It gave her strength and hope.

It was a love she would never get to experience, a love she would never know.

Sammi opened her eyes. No longer was she in the brightly lit room. She was on the mountainside in the middle of a patch of heather. Above her she heard a whoosh. She looked up and saw Tristan flying, his large dragon form blocking out the sun as he circled above her.

She laughed and jumped to her feet. His apple green dragon eyes watched her expressively. There was love shining there, as well as happiness.

He landed, shifting into human form as he did. Sammi drank in the sight of his glorious body, tight muscles, and the black and red dragon tattoo covering his chest.

She ran to him, no longer able to be apart from him.

He laughed as he easily caught her against him and kissed her roughly, urgently.

With his arms locked tightly around her, he laid her down on the grass and ripped her dress off.

"Mine," he whispered while lovingly gazing down at her.

"Yours. Always."

Sammi pulled him down for another kiss, and just as their lips met, he faded to nothing. The sunshine, heather, and mountains disappeared into the damp room.

It was too much for her. She screamed, jumping up to slam her hands against the walls, not noticing when her bones broke or when blood coated her.

Kiril finished off his fifth glass of whisky and pushed it away. He hadn't had an update from any of the Kings since they landed in Ireland, and he was getting antsy.

"Another?" Farrell asked.

Kiril held up a hand, palm out and glanced at the bar to the pretty brunette he had spoken with outside the pub hours earlier. "I'm going to have to pass tonight."

"You don't plan on leaving?" the Dark asked with a grin. "There's going to be a big party here in a few hours."

Kiril knew then that Farrell realized he was a Dragon King. What Kiril didn't know was if Farrell knew that he knew. Either way, Kiril was going to have to be extremely careful in whatever he said and did.

He slid from the booth and stood. "As much as I hate to miss it, I'll be otherwise engaged."

Farrell stood as well. "Trust me, this party will be better than anything you might be doing."

Just as they'd planned earlier, the brunette sauntered

up and wrapped her arms around him. "I was getting lonely," she said, looking up at him.

Kiril placed a hot, lingering kiss on her lips. "I told you I wouldna leave without you, lass."

"You mean you've been sitting with me while this lovely thing has been waiting?" the Dark asked with a wink to the brunette.

Kiril held the woman tighter when he felt her began to sway to Farrell. "I was waiting on her to meet me here. When she saw us talking, she opted to wait for me."

Farrell whistled. "Amazing. I willna keep you from your night then."

Kiril leisurely walked out of the pub and put the brunette in his car. He would have to take her back to his house since the Dark were watching it.

As calloused as it was, Kiril didn't want to know the female's name. He would make sure he always had a different woman on his arm so the Dark didn't try to target any one woman he was with.

It was the only way to keep the females safe and continue with his cover.

"I wouldna advise ever going to that pub again," he told the brunette as he drove away.

Kiril looked in his rearview mirror and saw Farrell standing in the doorway of the pub watching. His next step would be to invite his new friend over.

He hated dealing with the Dark Ones, but it was worth it if he could help end whatever uprising the Dark were trying to pull.

"I like that pub," the woman said sullenly. "The men never let me sit for long without a drink."

Kiril sped the Mercedes SLS AMG faster down the

narrow road. "Do you want to have a long life with the possibility of a husband and children down the road?"

"Aye. Someday."

He had a hard time believing the residents of Cork were really that unaware of the Dark. Or was it that the people liked the Dark Fae and their appeal?

"You'll no' have any of it if you return to *an Doras*."

He pulled into his driveway and slowly drove down the gravel-lined drive until he stopped at the front. Kiril shut off the engine and looked at the pretty female.

There would be no going to help his brethren, not this time. His work was here—and just as dangerous. All Kiril could do was hope they checked in with him while he continued his spying.

If he didn't find some way to take his mind off what was going on, he might do something to tip the Dark off. Too much was at stake for something that thoughtless.

"I'm famished," he told the woman.

Her frown disappeared, replaced by a smile. "I'm pretty hungry as well. Do you have any cheese?"

"I wasna talking about that kind of hunger."

Her smile widened. "What are we still doing in your car then?"

CHAPTER
THIRTY-SIX

Rhi could feel her essence fading away. Light Fae were creatures of happiness and pleasure. Just as the Dark could survive in the light, the Light could survive in the dark.

Except this wasn't just any dark. The place was weighted with evil, subjected to pain and grief until the walls fairly bled with it.

In any other event, she could withstand the way the fortress affected her. This time was different. This time Balladyn had put the Chains of Mordare on her.

They were supposed to have been lost during the Fae Wars.

Just as Balladyn was supposed to have died.

How many other things was she told that were untrue? Not that she would get the chance to speak her mind about being lied to. She was going to suffer right where she was until she died, turned Dark, or until the end of time.

Rhi thought over what Balladyn had told her. He blamed her for his being Dark. Maybe she should have gone into Taraeth's stronghold and searched for him, but it never entered her mind that Taraeth would actively seek out Balladyn.

The former mentor and friend was no longer the same. Balladyn's mind had been twisted into something she no longer recognized. His face might look the same, but inside, he was a different Fae.

He was Dark, which meant he was lost to her.

He wasn't the first to be taken. There was her father, her brother, her mother . . . and the most painful of them all . . . her lover.

Maybe Balladyn was right and she was to blame. She was the common denominator to all of them. She was the one to be left standing, so to speak.

The thought of turning Dark scared her. She would rather die, to cease to exist than have her world ripped apart and become something evil, something monstrous.

A loud squeak shouted into the silence, announcing Balladyn's approach. Rhi kept her head turned away from the door. She couldn't stand to look at him anymore.

"You look diminished," he said coolly. "And filthy. You were always so put together, pet, so perfectly made up. How pitiful you look now."

The weight of the Chains of Mordare held her arms down, making it difficult to move. The ones shackling her ankles were even worse.

"Get on with whatever you want to do to me, and just shut up," she told him.

Instead of angering him and forcing him to begin the torture as she expected, Balladyn squatted in front of her. "You forget how well I know you, Rhi. Have you ever seen what happens to a Light when we torture them?"

She hadn't, and he knew it.

His cocky smile grew larger. "I can smell your fear. The great Rhi, captured by me. I'll become a legend when I turn you to the Dark."

"I thought you wanted to punish me for leaving you. Making me a Dark Fae won't accomplish that."

"I didn't say I was going to turn you Dark now. In time, remember. There's no need to rush. There is plenty of . . . time."

She looked at the ground and the puddle of water he stood in. For centuries she had mourned him and the Fae he had been, the friend.

"You were a hero to the Light. Once." She smiled when she saw him stiffen. "I told Usaeil you were a Dark One the last time I saw her. Your name was stricken from the Hall of Heroes."

There was a beat of silence. "As if I care."

"I think you still do." She lifted her gaze to his. "I remember how revered you were, how the females begged for your attention in the hopes of catching your eye and being your mate. I recall how you were chosen to lead the squadron. The queen shouted your accolades to all the Light."

"Nice try, pet. You should've remained at your family estate and married a handsome Fae and had many children."

"I wasn't going to be left alone anymore. I refused to be the Fae who waited for news of loved ones and friends from the war. I would be the one to decide my life."

He tapped the chains with one finger. "And look where that got you. First you do the unthinkable and mix with the Dragon Kings. Did you really think taking him as your lover would work? Did you really think he would stay? With you?"

His words were like weapons, slicing open her wounded heart. He of all people knew how she had mourned for her lover, how she had tried in vain to get him back.

"You see?" Balladyn asked. "All these centuries later you still mourn him. Does he even know? Have you told him yet that you still love him? Perhaps I should be the one to tell him, and then bring him here so he can watch you turn Dark. I bet he wouldn't even help you."

"You need someone to blame for what you've become. I'm an easy scapegoat. If I hadn't been there, you would've found someone else to blame."

Balladyn leaned close until they were nose to nose. "No one else exchanged a promise with me never to leave each other behind."

"Look at that," she said as she lifted her hand up with great effort, her arm shaking from the weight of the chains. "My polish is chipped. What a bummer. I'll have to get that fixed."

With a growl, Balladyn rose and spun away. He stalked away before he walked back to her, once more in control of his emotions.

"You want torture, pet? I've got it for you."

Rhi watched as he spread his arms wide and a black cloud, yawning and dense, which sucked up the meager light in the darkness billowed from his hands and barreled right at her. She bit the inside of her mouth, tasting blood, in her effort to hold back her screams.

The cloud was suffocating, stifling. It beat against her in a disgusting, gloomy mass. Again and again it hit her without hands, slapping against her body until she was thrown against one wall and then another.

Every time she tried to call to her magic, the Chains of Mordare would send an electrical current straight into her brain.

Phelan, along with Charon, crept slowly through the tunnels. Part of the tunnel was so low they had to crawl on all fours to get through it, while other parts were tall enough Phelan was certain any of the Kings could stand upright in dragon form.

Charon thumped him on the arm to get his attention. Phelan looked to the narrow opening in the wall. That's when he spotted Constantine walking through the tunnels confidently, casually, as if he had been there many times before.

"Was it coincidence he took the tunnel on the right?" Charon asked.

Phelan watched until Con was out of sight. "He might be looking for Rhi."

"You told me yourself they hate each other."

It was true. Was Con really there to rescue Rhi? Or make sure she was never found?

Phelan clenched his jaw tightly. "Damn."

"As soon as we locate Sammi, we'll start the search for Rhi."

"We should've brought Broc," he mumbled as he continued onward.

It didn't matter if Con hated Rhi or not, she wouldn't get left behind if Phelan had anything to say about it. No matter how much Con might hate her, Rhi would get saved.

Tristan wasn't surprised when he turned the corner and found Balladyn leaning against the wall, twirling a long blade of grass between his teeth.

As soon as Balladyn saw him, he smiled. "I knew you'd come. Of course, you took your time finding us once you entered the tunnels."

"I'm here now."

"So you are."

"Show me Sammi."

Balladyn chuckled and straightened. "In time. I have to admit, I'm surprised that you're willing to give yourself to us in exchange for a human."

"That is if Sammi is really here."

He held his hand over his heart mockingly. "You wound me, Dragon King."

"And you're trying my patience, Dark One."

"I think you and I both know it will be pointless to release the pretty Samantha back into your world. She's tasted us. She'll never be the same."

Tristan knew it was going to be hard to keep his feelings for Sammi locked away, but he didn't expect to be tested so soon. The raging frenzy to attack Balladyn was heavy in his chest, and it took every ounce of control to remain calm. "You couldna keep your hands off her, could you?"

"She does have the most tasty lips," Balladyn said

with a knowing smile. "Tell me, Dragon, why are you really here?"

"She's my responsibility. I failed to keep her out of your grasp."

Balladyn tsked. "She's just a mortal. You're willing to be locked away with us because of one human? Did Kellan not adequately explain what we're after?"

Tristan knew, all right. Kellan had information that the Dark wanted. Only the Dark thought all Kings knew whatever secret it was that Kellan held. They would soon learn the truth.

"I see he did," Balladyn said and tossed aside the grass. "Are you prepared to give up that information?"

"Are you prepared to die?"

"Such confidence. Bandying words with you will be better than with Sammi."

"And Rhi."

Balladyn's smile was sly and secretive. He turned away without answering. "Come, Dragon. It's time for you to see Sammi."

Tristan didn't have to look behind him to know that Ian was there. In fact, he could pinpoint Ian's exact location—hanging by his hands and feet flat against the ceiling of the tunnel.

No one ever looked up.

Tristan sent a quick message to Con letting him know he was with Balladyn and being led to Sammi. There was no reply back from Con, but he didn't take that to mean anything. There was no telling what Con was involved with at that moment.

He followed Balladyn through a door and then a

maze of corridors and a dozen more doors. Finally Balladyn stopped in front of what looked like a wall, but
as Tristan drew closer he could see it was actually a
mirror.

"She doesn't know it's a mirror," the Dark Fae explained. "To her, it's simply a wall."

Tristan knew he was about to be put to the ultimate
test. The Dark wanted to know if he truly cared for
Sammi, and if he let one shred of reaction show, one
slip of indignation, he and Sammi were both doomed.

He kept his gaze on Balladyn as the Fae watched
him with a shrewd grin. "Have a look," he bade.

With a tight control on his emotions, Tristan slowly
turned to the mirror. At first he saw nothing but a handful of Dark Fae standing around.

Then he saw a bare foot. That's when he realized
there was a woman lying on the floor with the Dark
Ones around her. Two of the Fae shifted, giving Tristan
a glimpse of a Fae atop her, pleasuring her.

Sammi.

It was Sammi. He'd know those sandy waves of her
hair anywhere. Tristan couldn't see her face, but then
he didn't need to. Balladyn wouldn't bring him to anyone but Sammi.

She moaned, her legs lifting to wrap around the
Dark Fae as he filled her. The others began to quickly
undress as they waited their turn.

"Unlike Denae, Sammi wanted us. She begged. Repeatedly. We hunger for the pleasures of the flesh as
well as the hope within mortals. Odd. Sammi had very
little hope, which Taraeth fed off of, but her body was
willing."

Tristan couldn't stand to watch another minute, but he couldn't pull his eyes away either. The anguish and desolation ran deep within him.

He had been too late. He had taken too much time. He had failed her as he had promised not to do.

Sammi had held out for as long as she could. Tristan didn't blame her. He blamed himself.

"Does it pain you to see her this way after you've had her in your bed?"

Tristan inhaled deeply. The icy calm that took him centered all his hatred and despondency on one person— Balladyn. Tristan began to plan how he was going to kill the Dark One.

"It pains me to see any human in your clutches. You bleed their souls dry so they can never return to their families."

Balladyn shrugged. "None of them complain."

Tristan was about to turn away when he spotted a small heart tattoo on the outer ankle of the woman. He had seen every inch of Sammi's body. She didn't have any such markings.

He swiveled his head to Balladyn. "That isna Sammi. Where is she?"

CHAPTER
THIRTY-SEVEN

Balladyn's answering grin made Tristan want to smash his fist into the Dark Fae's face. It had all been a trick. But why?

"Are you sure that isn't your Sammi?"

"She isna mine," Tristan said in an even tone. He couldn't show his anger, no matter how much he wanted to. "Sammi doesna have any tattoos. Take me to her. Now."

"As you wish," Balladyn said and turned on his heel.

Tristan stayed just one step behind him. No other Dark followed, which put him more on edge than ever. The Dark obviously had a plan. They didn't try to force him into a room or shackle him. Yet.

It would come. He wasn't about to lower his guard just because he was being treated as a guest. The Dark wanted something from him. They wouldn't get it, but they could certainly try.

As they walked down the corridor, Tristan let his gaze wander around. The lighting was dimmed, the furnishings opulent to the point of gaudy.

The place was immaculately clean, but nothing could dispel the cloud of evil the Dark brought. They lived off humans, draining them of love, hope, and happiness—and leaving behind a shell of nothing but an insatiable hunger for sex with the Dark.

"You don't approve," Balladyn said, his Irish accent thickening, a small tell that he was annoyed.

Tristan shrugged when Balladyn glanced at him over his shoulder as they turned a corner. "It's no' exactly my decorating taste."

"I'm not referring to the furnishings, Dragon."

"And I'm no' talking about this place, Dark."

Balladyn stopped walking and shifted to the side to look at Tristan. "How does it feel to be the newest King? Have your brethren told you all of their conquests? How about their failures?"

"I know enough. I've got a lot of years to catch up on."

"Thousands upon thousands. You're a fool if you think they've done nothing but good."

Tristan kept his voice mild as he said, "The humans are still here, are they no'? The same willna be said if your kind take over as you want."

"The humans are nothing more than cattle. They destroy this realm with the carelessness of a child. And yet you defend them. They ran your dragons out, hunted them one by one."

"That they did. And what will you do the mortals?"

Balladyn's smile was pure evil. "We'll hunt them down one by one."

"You just want the Kings to step aside?"

"You should be thanking us for doing what none of you could. What kind of race of beings would send their own kind away to save ungrateful, ungracious, vain, self-absorbed, vicious, destructive creatures? Only the Dragon Kings. You've alienated yourselves."

"You went to all that trouble to capture Kellan and now me just to ask us to step aside? I think no'."

Balladyn began walking again, this time more slowly. He waited until Tristan was even with him before he said, "Of course not. There is something we're looking for."

"With all your magic, you can no' find it?"

"No," he said flatly. He motioned for Tristan to turn right. "It was hidden by the Kings."

Tristan stared blankly as Balladyn searched his face. He had no idea what the Dark was going on about, but he would play along for the time being. "There's a reason for that."

"It was hidden before Constantine became the King of Kings. It was hidden by the first King of Kings and protected by his successors."

Tristan wracked his brain for what it could possibly be, but he came up empty. "Why do you want it?"

"Do you ever wonder how Con became the King of Kings?"

"He was the strongest of the dragons."

Balladyn shook his head. "Ulrik was stronger, but Ulrik didn't want to rule everyone else. He wanted the Kings to rule themselves, but I'm getting ahead of myself. I'm talking about Con. Do you know how a King of Kings is chosen?"

"Of course."

"Do you?" he asked thoughtfully. "There were four before Con, and each of them had very short reigns."

"They were challenged by another Dragon King."

Balladyn halted before a door. "Precisely. Ask Con what he did to be the next in line."

Tristan hated that another person was putting doubt in his mind about Con. As far as he knew, Con was doing good in leading the Dragon Kings and running Dreagan.

But how much of the past didn't he know? The others took it for granted or didn't care. While Tristan was naïve because he was so new.

Ulrik had put the first seeds of doubt into his mind, and Balladyn was spreading them.

Damn but he hated the suspicion that now rose like a giant within him. Con and the others had welcomed him at Dreagan, they had shown him what it was to be a Dragon King.

But no one was perfect. Everyone made mistakes.

That included Con.

"Show me Sammi," Tristan demanded again.

Balladyn gave a bow of his head and opened the door. It swung open and Tristan expected Sammi to come running up or hear her voice.

Instead, he saw her floating in midair on her back, her glorious mane of hair softly drifting as if the wind were stirring it.

Rage exploded inside him at the same time a healthy dose of trepidation churned in his gut.

"What did you do to her?" How he kept the fury from leaching into his voice he'd never know.

Balladyn stepped into the room and went to her, leisurely walking around her until she was between them. "We had no choice."

"Explain that." Tristan followed him in, but stopped

when he reached Sammi. She looked peaceful, as if she were simply asleep.

But he knew better.

"Her mind snapped. She was hurting herself. She broke every bone in both hands. When we went in to calm her, she grew more uncontrollable. It was either this, or . . ."

Tristan met his red eyes over her body. The Dark didn't need to finish. Tristan knew exactly the other option they could've used. He wasn't sure why they hadn't.

"It was a gesture of goodwill," Balladyn said.

He had known it was coming, just not so soon. "What do you want? I'm already turning myself over to your custody in exchange for you releasing the mortal."

"I want the location of what we seek."

"And if I doona have it?"

"Then I'll wake Sammi and allow the Dark to have her. You saw what they did to the other mortal. Can you imagine what they'll do to her? A woman who has been with a Dragon King?"

Tristan reassessed his thoughts on Balladyn. The Dark One was clever, and he was banking on Tristan's feelings for Sammi to get him what he wanted.

All Tristan wanted to do was gather Sammi in his arms and run like the wind. With her in her current state, she couldn't hear or see him. Which could be to his benefit.

He could test his theory and turn and walk away, but he wasn't likely to get very far. Besides, he had come in exchange for her. He couldn't change his mind now.

"What will it be, Dragon King? Will you give me the location?" Balladyn pressed.

"You ask too much."

"Is it so difficult to agree to wipe out the humans?"

Tristan sent a shout to Con through their link as he said to Balladyn, "It is. We were charged with protecting them."

"Have you found Sammi?" Con asked.

"Aye. They have her deep within the palace. Lock onto my location and you'll find us."

"How is she?"

"They've used their magic to make her sleep. Balladyn said she lost her mind and they had no choice. He's threatening to wake her and give her to the Dark if I don't give him something in return."

There was a loud snort from Con. *"What does he want now?"*

"The location to something he seeks, something he says was hidden by the King of Kings long before you."

There was silence after his statement. That worried Tristan even as he pretended to listen to Balladyn lament about the humans.

"You know what he seeks." Tristan stated the obvious, hating that Con didn't trust him enough to tell him what it was.

"Aye."

"But you willna tell me."

"Tristan, you must understand that few of the Kings know of it. Kellan does because he records our history. I do because I'm the King of Kings."

It made sense, and it also made Tristan feel better that he hadn't been intentionally left out. *"What is it?"*

"Something you better hope never falls into their hands. It was hidden for a reason, Tristan."

"I need to give him something so that he might let Sammi go."

There was a long pause before Con said, *"I'll take care of that."*

"Well?" Balladyn urged. "Are you going to give me what I want, or shall I call in my fellow Dark?"

Tristan started to make up a lie about a location the object could be when shouting rang out through the palace. Balladyn's eyes narrowed as he ran around Sammi's body to the door.

"It's Constantine!" a Dark shouted as he ran by.

Balladyn whirled around to glare at him. "Is this some trick?"

"Do you want me or do you want Con?"

"I'll have both," Balladyn snarled before he stalked out of the room, the lock clicking loudly into place.

Tristan spun about and reached out to touch Sammi. He hesitated, unsure of what kind of Dark Fae magic had been used to put her in such a state.

With a growl of frustration, Tristan tucked his arms beneath her and pulled her against him. Instantly, the magic holding her evaporated and her body slumped.

His anger grew when he felt the dampness of her clothes. She had been wet and cold, and the Dark had done nothing. He glanced at her hands to find them covered in dried blood. Had the Dark healed her broken bones? He doubted it. More worrying was Balladyn's insistence that Sammi had lost her mind.

There was no telling what the Dark had shown her or done to her. A mortal, even one as strong as Sammi, could only take so much before they snapped.

Tristan turned to walk to the door when it crashed

open and Ian filled the doorway, the pale blue skin of his god giving off an eerie light.

"You found her," his brother said with a relieved smile. "Con let himself be known. The Dark are after him."

Tristan hurried to Ian. "Only for so long. Balladyn wants both of us. He'll be back soon."

"He willna expect you to have gotten out of the room," Ian said with a sly grin.

"What did you do?"

Ian held up his pale blue-skinned hand and the long light blue claws as they raced down the hallway. His smile showed the fangs protruding, and his eyes were the same pale blue from corner to corner as his skin. "I may no' be able to do magic, but I can sense it. The Dark, or more precisely, Balladyn's is interesting. Getting through his magic was like picking a lock."

"That's fascinating since the Dark can prevent us from shifting into dragon form. How are you no' affected by it?"

"I didna say that," Ian said while wrinkling his nose. "The Dark are worse than the *droughs* we battled."

There were no more words as Ian moved ahead of him and scouted out approaching Dark. They found the hallways clear of everyone. Tristan just hoped Con would be able to get out. He didn't want to return to Dreagan and tell everyone the King of Kings was being held by the Dark.

"Wait," Tristan said to stop Ian. When Ian faced him, Tristan carefully placed Sammi in his arms. "Find the others and get out of here. If I know Sammi is with you, then I can fight the Dark as I want."

"You're going after Con."

"I am."

Ian nodded gravely. "Be careful."

"Take care of her, brother," Tristan said before he turned away.

CHAPTER
THIRTY-EIGHT

Ian used the speed of his god to get him out of the palace and back into the tunnels in record time. It helped that the Dark were more concerned with catching Con than patrolling the corridors.

As soon as Ian entered the tunnel he started backtracking the way they had come. He had gone twenty steps before he encountered a huge beast that resembled a worm. It inched its way through the tunnel, lifting its head as if sniffing the air.

Ian slid his back against an outcropping of stone and watched the worm-creature slowly move past. As soon as it did, he moved around the outcropping, but he moved more cautiously. Who knew what he might encounter next.

He held Sammi tightly, all the while wishing he was with Tristan, fighting beside him. But Tristan has given him something to guard, something that was precious to him—Sammi.

Ian had to get Sammi out to the other Dragon Kings. Once they had her, then Ian could return to Tristan's side. He had lost his brother once, and by some miracle had him back again. He wasn't going to lose him a second time, not if he could help it.

He reached the main tunnel where they had branched off into three groups without incident. Ian had taken one step before he was grabbed roughly by both arms and shoved to the right.

Ian's gaze clashed with Phelan's before he looked over and found Charon. Charon put a hand to his lips and then pointed over his shoulder.

There Ian saw an animal he couldn't make out, on its back with all twelve of its legs bent in death. But if it was dead, why were they being quiet?

"We killed the baby," Phelan whispered.

The scream of outrage from the mother as it nudged its baby was earsplitting.

"We need to get out now," Ian told them in a hushed tone.

Charon jerked his chin to Sammi. "Where is Tristan?"

"With Con."

Phelan tamped down his god, his gold skin, claws, and eyes changing back to normal. "What happened to her?"

"They used magic," Ian explained.

Phelan let one claw lengthen as he sliced open his wrist and let a few drops of his blood fall into Sammi's mouth. Ian waited impatiently. With Phelan being half-Fae, his blood could heal anything, except death.

Ian just hoped it worked against the magic of a Dark Fae.

"Damn," Charon muttered when there was no change in Sammi. "Why is there blood on her hands?"

Phelan shrugged. "We get her back to the Dragon Kings now."

Charon smiled as he looked at Phelan. "Looks like we've got to kill us the mother."

"Let's get to it," Phelan said as he walked to the beast while he released the primeval god within him.

Ian could do nothing but watch Phelan with his gold skin and Charon with his copper skin battle the creature. Even with both of them, it took longer than Ian expected, which proved how formidable the animals from the Fae world were.

Ian was standing beside his friends when the mother fell beside her baby. The three immediately started for the doorway. There was no time to think about what they might encounter next or to wonder where Tristan and Con were.

"There," Phelan said and pointed ahead of them. "That's the doorway."

Ian couldn't wait to get through it and out of the world of the Dark Fae. Before they reached the doorway, a dozen Dark surrounded them.

All Tristan had to do to find Con was follow the mass of Dark Ones running through the palace to the great hall. Tristan sidled up against a wall and peered over the side down to the middle of the hall where Con lounged in a chair as if he were a regular guest.

"Constantine," Taraeth said as the crowd parted for him to walk to Con.

Con looked like a king, even as he sat with nothing on but a pair of ripped, faded jeans. "Taraeth. I wondered how long it would take you to come to me. The last time I saw you I put the scar on your face. Then I saw nothing but your ugly arse as you ran away while the rest of the Dark were slaughtered by my Dragon Kings."

Tristan saw Balladyn on the opposite side of the hall, leaning over the railing on the same floor as Tristan. Balladyn looked amused more than angry, like the rest of the Dark.

"Aye, but who's ruling the Dark now?" Taraeth taunted.

Con glanced down to Taraeth's missing limb. "A Dark who had his arm cut off by a mortal wielding the blade of a Light."

"She will pay for it."

"No' likely. She's the mate to Kellan. They've been bound, Taraeth. You know what that means."

The Dark hissed, his red eyes flashing dangerously. "I already have Tristan. Now I have you."

Con's laugh made the Dark shift uneasily, their worried glances telling Tristan just how much they feared Con.

"You doona have me," Con said.

Taraeth spread his arms wide. "You're in my palace, Dragon King, surrounded by my men. I have you, all right."

"Is that right?"

"You know it is. You can no' escape us."

Con slowly stood. As one, the Dark took a step back. Tristan grinned. The Dark Ones talked big, but they feared the Dragon Kings, most especially Con.

"Are you out?" Con's voice filled his head.

"I'm watching you. It's quite a show you're putting on."

"Where is Sammi?"

"With Ian. I alerted Rhys and the others to expect them soon."

"But we doona know if they've gotten out."

"Is that what you're waiting on? Trust me. Ian will get Sammi out."

"You trust the Warrior that much?"

"He's my brother," Tristan answered.

"Let's get out of this place then."

Charon let out a bellow and attacked the Fae. Phelan was right behind him. Ian ducked a blast of magic as he realized he couldn't fight with Sammi in his arms, but neither could he put her down.

There was a loud crash and the unmistakable sound of a dragon's roar. Ian looked up to find Rhys in the tunnel, his yellow scales bright in the darkness as he reared up on his hind legs and swiped at the Dark with his front.

In a flurry, the Dark began to attack Rhys, their intent to make him shift back into human form. But Ian could help with that.

He handed Sammi to Phelan. "Get her out now. Rhys and I will follow shortly."

Phelan didn't argue as he made his way to the doorway thanks to Rhys's dragon body blocking it from the Dark. Ian stepped in front of Rhys and used the power of his god to block the magic pelting Rhys. Then he deflected it back at the Dark.

Together, he and Rhys turned the tide. Charon beheaded two Dark before he followed Phelan out of the doorway.

"Go!" Ian bellowed to Rhys.

Rhys receded out of the doorway with Ian walking backward while continuing to block the magic. As soon as they were through, Charon tackled him to the ground while Laith dove from the sky to attack any Dark Ones that tried to follow.

Ian scrambled up and ran to Sammi where Phelan had laid her on the grass. The sun was coming up, its golden rays hitting the grass.

Phelan tamped down his god and was talking as Ian approached, and that's when he saw Sammi's eyes open. Ian quickly let his claws and fangs retract while his skin and eyes returned to normal.

"It's all right," Phelan said soothingly. "You're all right, Sammi."

She looked from Phelan to Ian. "This isn't real."

"It is, lass." Ian smiled as he helped her sit up. "Look. You're out in the fresh air."

"I was before too," she said as her voice rose and she tried to scoot away.

Phelan easily held her as he glanced at Ian. Ian took a deep breath and grabbed Sammi's shoulders. "You're really free, Sammi. Tristan went in and found you. He's the one who asked me to bring you out."

"Where is Tristan?" she asked as she looked around.

There was a wildness still visible in her gaze, but she had calmed down. "He went to help Con."

Her forehead furrowed deeply. "Con?"

"He came to help rescue you," Phelan said. "We all did. Look around, lass."

As if just noticing the battle, Sammi's eyes widened and her mouth slackened. "Bloody hell."

"Come on," Ian said as he got her to her feet. "We need to get you out of here."

She yanked her arm out of his hold. "Not without Tristan."

Ian considered her for a moment. Tristan loved this woman, but did she love him? "Why?"

"Because . . . because I need to see him."

It wasn't a confession of love, but there was something there. Ian suspected that Sammi wasn't used to voicing her feelings, and if anyone was going to hear those words, it was going to be Tristan.

The Dark drew closer to them, and this time it was Sammi that grabbed his arm. Phelan flanked her other side to protect her when a Dark got through the Kings.

"You honestly think you could hold me?" Con asked Taraeth.

The king of the Dark sneered. "I've been preparing for this day for a long time. You have many enemies, King of Kings, some even within your ranks."

Tristan saw Con's confident smile right before he grabbed the Dark One near him and broke his neck. He then threw the Dark over the side and watched the others scatter as their comrade landed with a thump on the tile.

Across the way, Balladyn's red gaze landed on him. Tristan smiled as realization flashed across the Dark's face. Below, Con and Taraeth were facing off.

The entire castle of Dark was trying to decide whether to attack Con or let Taraeth battle it out. Tristan's attention was diverted from below when Balladyn jumped on the stone railing and then leapt across the entire width of the great hall to land in front of Tristan.

"You killed one of my men," Balladyn said.

Tristan shrugged. "You took Sammi."

There were no more words as Balladyn attacked by ramming his shoulder into Tristan and then hitting him with magic repeatedly in the stomach.

Tristan kneed Balladyn twice in the face and flipped him over. Instead of landing on his back, the Dark One easily shifted his body and alighted on his feet.

Balladyn snarled and attacked again. This time Tristan dodged a blast of magic only to feel the Dark's fist against the side of his head.

Tristan turned to the side and then reared back with his elbow, smashing it into Balladyn's face before extending his arm and swinging it backward to slam his fist into the Dark's nose.

Out of the corner of his eye, Tristan saw golden scales as Con shifted into dragon form.

"You're not leaving!" Balladyn bellowed as he wiped away the blood and focused on Tristan once more.

"You'll never find that which you seek," Tristan promised.

Balladyn smiled coldly. "There will be one of you that breaks. There always is."

"You thought it would be me?"

Two balls of magic appeared in Balladyn's hands. "I still do. You're the newest, Tristan, the one who doesn't have the ties that the others do."

"Then you'd be wrong."

Tristan kicked out with his foot, connecting with Balladyn's chest just as the Dark released the magic.

He dodged one, but the other hit him in the side as pain sizzled along his skin.

Chaos and shouts from below drew everyone's attention as Con lashed out with his tail and with fire. Smoke quickly filled the great hall, blinding everyone.

Tristan held his side and searched for Balladyn. He saw the Dark come at him. He felt the dragon within yearn to break free. Just before he shifted, someone grabbed his arm and yanked him away.

"Time to go," Con said with a smile as he raced nude down the corridor.

Tristan looked over his shoulder. He should kill Balladyn now, but he wanted to get to Sammi and make sure she was all right.

Besides, the war with the Dark was far from over.

It was just beginning.

CHAPTER
THIRTY-NINE

Sammi wanted to watch the beautiful dragons—yellow and inky black—as they flew in paths that left her dizzy as they fought the Dark Fae.

Adrenaline kept her moving, but she still wasn't sure if it was real or another figment of her imagination. She burned to touch Tristan, to run her hands over his warm skin and feel the power and strength in his muscles.

She stood and watched the unfolding battle as if she were on the outside looking in. The Dark kept pouring out of seemingly thin air. They reminded her of ants for there never seemed to be an end to them.

The dragons kept most of the Dark back, and the few that got past were soon felled by Ian, Charon, and Phelan. The three fought side by side as if they had years of practice.

They were vicious in their fighting, ferocious in their attack.

Merciless in their dealing with the Dark.

They were Warriors. Immortal Highlanders with

primeval gods inside them. Sammi looked at Phelan's gold skin and claws before sliding her gaze to Charon and his copper skin and the thick horns that protruded out of his temples to curve around his head.

Then her gaze landed on Ian. His skin was a light blue, pale but vibrant. His claws were a darker shade of blue. He turned and she got a look at his eyes. They were the same color as his skin but they flooded his eyes from corner to corner leaving no trace of an iris.

The Warriors might not be dragon shifters, but they could hold their own against the Dark.

Phelan let out a deep growl after he ducked something she couldn't see. He quickly plunged his gold claws into the Dark's throat.

It was a brutal scene, but one she couldn't look away from.

Suddenly the Dark Fae that were battling the dragons turned and looked behind them. Sammi could see nothing but the countryside, but apparently the Fae could see something more.

"It's a doorway, lass," Ian said when he glimpsed her confusion.

A doorway. Of course. She remembered hearing Tristan speak of Fae doorways.

She watched as the Dark began fighting what was behind them in the doorway. And then a naked man rushed through, followed by Tristan.

Sammi struggled to remain on her feet as her knees threatened to buckle. Tristan fought alongside the naked man with a dragon tattoo on his back, but all the while Tristan's gaze scanned the area.

Until his eyes landed on her.

There was no time for words as Con shifted into a magnificent gold dragon. A moment later, Tristan released his dragon.

With the Dark fighting four Dragon Kings and three Warriors, they were soon being driven back. Sammi thought they might continue the fight, but Ian took her hand and began to run with her away from the Dark Ones.

The next instant, Tristan swooped in and scooped them each into one of his hands. Sammi looked down at the fast-disappearing ground to see Charon and Phelan were likewise grabbed.

It wasn't until she felt the heat of Tristan's scales and the wind around her that she knew she was truly away from the Dark. Somehow, Tristan had gotten her freed.

The clouds surrounded them, hiding them from view of the world below. She rested her head on Tristan's hand and closed her eyes as the tears came. With Tristan flying so fast, she could always claim it was the wind stinging her eyes. No one had to know just how scared she had been—and still was.

Scared because she had faced something evil and horrendous deep in the bowels of the Dark Fae castle.

But also because she had acknowledged what she swore to never feel—love.

She loved Tristan with her whole heart, her total being. Her entire soul.

Love infused her, suffused her. She couldn't run from it anymore. It was there, blooming in her fragile heart like a delicate flower.

Sammi didn't know what was going to happen when they got back to Dreagan. Would she be able to tell

Tristan how she felt? It might be better to keep her feelings hidden. How would she ever know if he cared for her if she didn't tell him?

She squeezed her eyes shut and wished she were brave enough to tell him, regardless of how he might feel. He was a Dragon King—commanding, formidable, and dominant. How could she begin to fit into his world?

Did she even dare?

The love growing within her told her she could. Dared her to try.

She must have dozed, because she woke when she felt Tristan begin to descend. Sammi opened her eyes and lifted her head to see the mountains of Dreagan she had come to love. One by one the dragons dove to the ground, landing in a valley where others waited.

Sammi found Jane standing between Cassie and Elena as they stared up at them. Sammi looked over at Ian to see him watching her. He gave her a nod, as if to tell her everything would be all right.

She noticed that Tristan remained in the air while the others landed and released the Warriors they held before shifting into human form. Pants were tossed at them, and even from her height, she could hear the joyous laughter at another round going to the Kings.

And then Tristan landed. He set Ian down first. Sammi watched Dani rush to her husband and shower him with kisses as he held her tight.

Her chest constricted as she wondered if she would ever have that kind of relationship. She might be too damaged.

"Sammi!" Jane shouted as she ran up.

That's when Sammi realized Tristan had set her on her feet. His hand unfurled, releasing her. She tried to turn and look at him, but Jane had her in a bear hug before she could.

"Are you all right?" Jane asked as she pulled back and looked her over. "What did those assholes do to you?"

Sammi would tell Jane everything as well as apologize for the nasty things she had said, but first she had to see Tristan. She turned around to find him still in dragon form. His apple-green eyes were on her.

Conversations ceased, but Sammi paid no attention. She didn't understand why Tristan wouldn't shift into a human. Her heart began to pound in dread. Was this his way of saying good-bye?

"Doona give up," Ian whispered next to her. "He needs you as much as you need him. Both of you are afraid. Who is going to make the first move?"

It was a valid question. Tristan was waiting on her, and she was too afraid to say or do anything. But she didn't want to go through life alone anymore. She wanted someone to plan her days with, someone to hold her in his arms while they watched movies, someone to laugh with—love with.

She wanted Tristan to be beside her at night when she went to sleep. And she wanted to open her eyes and see him in the morning. She wanted to know she could turn to him if she needed him—and she wanted to be there for him.

Sammi took a step toward Tristan. "Don't go," she begged.

Seconds ticked into minutes as they stared at each

other in silence before he let out a breath. In the next instant, he stood before her in all his glory, his dragon tat seeming to move upon his chest.

"I'm sorry," he said. "I should never have put you in danger. You should never have been at the cottage."

"How else were we to get the Dark there?"

"I failed you."

"Plans come apart all the time. I'm here now, thanks to you."

He glanced away. "Barely. Did they . . . did they touch you?"

"Balladyn kissed me."

Tristan's eyes narrowed into slits. His voice dropped dangerously when he asked, "Did he?"

"I'm glad he did." She saw his slight flinch. "Because it proved how much your kisses affect me. I hunger for you even when you're standing right next to me. My mind is filled with nothing but you."

"I'm still learning my place here and why I became a Dragon King. I have a twin and a past life I couldna remember until I touched you."

"You became a Dragon King because of your innate goodness, your nobility and loyalty, your decency and the imposing, masterful warrior that you are. Whoever or whatever turned you into a Dragon King saw what I do."

Sammi squelched the fear rising within her and took another step toward him. "You scare me, Tristan. The way you touch me, the way you kiss me. You didn't let me hide. You made me face what I never have. You opened up . . . everything," she said with a sweep of her hand, "to me. It's overwhelming and more frightening than I can put into words. What I experienced in that awful place with the Dark is something that will never leave. Then I think of you. A part of me is urging me to run away and forget that you battered down my walls."

"And the other part?" he asked softly.

She swallowed, her throat closing at the emotions welling to get free. In his brown eyes she could see a future—it might only last a few weeks or months, but it would be glorious.

Sammi took another tentative step until they were close enough to touch. "The other part is begging me to stay and have more of you. To tell you that I love you. To soar in the skies with you and face whatever comes down the road."

This time he was the one who took the last step. He hooked one of his fingers with hers. "You like flying, do you?"

She blinked. She wasn't sure what she'd expected him to say. That's not true. She had hoped—prayed, actually—that he would say he loved her as well.

Sammi then saw the smile in his eyes and grinned. "Out of all I said, that's all you took away?"

"Well, I can make it so that we go flying every night," he said with a wink. "Besides, I'll only take the woman I love with me."

A sob caught in her throat as he yanked her against him. She buried her face in his neck and felt the warm tears slide down her face. Her heart was bursting with joy.

Just a few hours ago she thought she was going to die. Now she was held in the arms of the man she loved, the only man who could breach the walls of her heart.

Finally, it felt as if her world was falling into place, as if it had been waiting for Tristan to enter her life.

"I can no' live without you," Tristan said. "I doona want to even try."

He placed his hands on either side of her face as he pulled back to look in her eyes. Tenderly, he wiped away her tears with his thumbs and gently placed his lips on hers.

"I doona know what the future holds for us, Sammi, no' with this war starting, but I'll do anything to keep you with me."

"I'm not going anywhere. I've found where I belong," she said with a smile as peace settled around her. "With you."

"Thank God you finally realized it," he said as he took her mouth in a bruising kiss.

He practically tore off her clothes before he lifted her and she wrapped her legs around him, the head of his arousal brushing her sex.

She dropped her head back and looked at the clear blue sky as their bodies joined and pleasure took them.

CHAPTER FORTY

Two days later . . .

Tristan snuggled against his wife in the early hours of the morning. The sun was just coming over the mountains, its red-orange light spilling through the windows across the bed.

Wife. He still couldn't believe she had agreed to become his mate. At first Sammi had been confused about the entire affair, but Jane had quickly put her at ease.

There had been a moment when Sammi learned there would be no children for a mate of a Dragon King that Tristan thought she might change her mind, but she assured him she wanted nothing more than to be mated to him.

Con didn't put up a fuss as he had with Kellan and Denae, but he wasn't happy about it. He had spent hours with Sammi locked in his office with him. Whatever Sammi said sufficed, because she was beaming when she finally exited.

Tristan ran his thumb over the dragon eye that was

now tattooed on her skin. All the mates had it appear after they recited their vows in the sacred chamber deep within the mountain.

He rubbed the red and black mixture of ink, still amazed that she was really his.

All of a sudden, a memory flared. He was standing with Logan, another Warrior, as they tried to reach the Isle of Eigg. Wyrran, the hairless yellow-skinned creatures about the size of a child, appeared around them.

Deirdre had created the beasts. He tried to shout a warning to Logan, but before he could get the words out, *drough* magic infused the air and held him immobile.

Then Deirdre appeared. She was stunningly beautiful except for the evil inside her that turned her floor-length hair and eyes white.

How he hated the Druid.

He tried to break free of the hold, but her magic was too strong. Logan was trying to talk their way out of it, but Deirdre was having none of it.

Then she told him Logan's secret. Logan had gone to her to become a Warrior. He was stunned, completely taken aback by the regret shining in Logan's eyes.

If he thought that's all Deirdre would do, he should've known better. Out of the corner of his eye, he saw a flash of maroon. Malcolm.

He had always liked the mortal, but now he was a Warrior who did Deirdre's bidding. He didn't understand how Malcolm could do such a thing after living at MacLeod Castle for so long.

Deirdre then told Malcolm to take his head.

He glanced at Logan before he settled his gaze on

Malcolm. There was no emotion in Malcolm's maroon eyes as he reared back his hand before he let it go.

Tristan jerked upright in bed, his breathing ragged as the memory of his death as a Warrior became as clear as if it had just happened.

"Tristan?" Sammi asked as she kneeled beside him. "What is it? What happened?"

"I remember how I died as a Warrior."

Without a word, she leaned over to the bedside table and grabbed her mobile phone. She punched in a number and said, "He remembered how he died."

Tristan heard Ian's voice, but couldn't make out the words. Then Sammi tossed aside the phone and wrapped her arms around him.

"Ian's coming. He asked me to phone him if you ever remembered."

Tristan stroked the waves of her sandy hair, which helped to calm his racing heart. A friend had killed him. Logan had kept a dark secret from all the Warriors. Was it his place to tell the Warriors about Logan? He didn't believe it was. It as Logan's burden to carry, not his.

There was a knock on the door, startling both of them. Sammi jumped up and grabbed her robe as she padded barefoot to answer the door.

Tristan was slower to rise. He looked around the cottage. They were supposed to spend a week alone before returning to Dreagan, but they had only gotten a few days.

"Tristan?" Ian said.

He turned his back to the door and grabbed a pair of jeans. "I never thought I had been murdered."

"It's something I live with every day of my life," said a new voice.

Tristan whirled around and saw Malcolm. Remorse shone heavily in Malcolm's blue eyes. The Malcolm he saw in his memories had been cold, stony, callous even.

But the Malcolm standing before him now was a different man. That much was obvious.

"I'm sorry, Dun . . . Tristan," Malcolm said. "I know it doesna make up for what I did, but I wanted to be the one to tell you that I did Deirdre's bidding because she promised to never harm Larena. I . . . I only wanted to protect her. I didna realize Deirdre would make me take your head."

Larena. The only female Warrior and cousin to Malcolm who was married to Fallon. Tristan was remembering more and more.

"That nearly did Malcolm in," Ian said.

Sammi pushed past both men to stand beside him. "What changed?"

Malcolm smiled as he said, "Evie. My wife."

"I know." Tristan swallowed and focused on Malcolm. "I was there helping the Warriors against that final battle with Jason Wallace."

Malcolm winced and let out a sigh. "Which makes me feel even worse. After what I did to you, and then no' knowing it was you up there helping me save Evie. I have a life I doona deserve."

"Deirdre was a bitch," Tristan said.

Ian's eyes widened. "You remember everything?"

Tristan gave a shake of his head and was grateful when Sammi put her hand in his. "Nay. Every once in a while I'll remember something, but I know I was a

Warrior. I know I was your twin. But I am a Dragon King now."

"You are my twin," Ian corrected him with a grin.

Malcolm cleared his throat. "Tristan, I have no right to ask, but can you ever find it in yourself to forgive me one day?"

Tristan looked at Ian who gave Malcolm a pat on his shoulder. His twin had already forgiven Malcolm for his part in it. Why shouldn't Tristan do the same? Besides, he had a feeling Malcolm had suffered enough from his dealings with Deirdre.

"I forgive you," he said.

The relief on Malcolm's face was worth it. Tristan would have to relive his memory of dying forever, but Malcolm had done it for family.

Tristan knew what that meant. He would do anything for Sammi and Ian, and also Dani. She was part of his family now. As were Jane and Banan.

"There was another Warrior with me. Logan," Tristan said.

Ian exchanged a look with Malcolm. "Aye. Witnessing your death while he could do nothing set Logan on his heels. He told us his secret, the one that Deirdre shared with you."

"Everything all worked out?" Fallon asked as he stepped up behind Malcolm and Ian.

Malcolm looked to him.

"Aye," Tristan said.

Ian shoved the others out. "Let's leave the newlyweds alone."

A second later, Fallon had jumped them out of the cottage. Tristan sank onto the edge of the bed as Sammi stepped between his legs and rested her arms on his shoulders.

"Are you really okay?"

He shrugged and pulled the belt of her robe loose. It fell open to reveal her gorgeous body. He leaned in to kiss one pink-tipped nipple and felt it harden against his mouth.

"I am with you in my arms," he said before sucking the nipple deep in his mouth.

A moan rumbled from her as she shifted her shoulders and the robe fell to the floor. He fell backward with her in his arms before he rolled her onto her back. Tristan lifted his head to smile at her.

"You're going to be the death of me," she said with a smile, her powder blue eyes dark with desire.

"Then we'll go together, love, because our lives, our souls are intertwined."

"God, how I love you," she said and ran her fingers through his hair.

"No' near as much as I love you."

All words ceased as their passion became too great. The need to claim each other, to mark each other was all that mattered.

That and the harmony that they had searched for—and found—within each other.

EPILOGUE

Kiril didn't want to gloat as he sat drinking his Irish whisky at *an Doras*. After all, the Dragon Kings had won another round against the Dark Ones.

How many more they would win was anyone's guess, but the air about the pub told him that the Dark were furious. Furious that another Dragon King had gotten loose, and furious that Taraeth had yet to deliver on his promise.

Kiril couldn't wait to talk to Con. The King of Kings had some balls to go into the Darks' palace as he had. But then again, Kiril expected nothing less from Constantine.

Suddenly, a ripple of surprise and shock moved through the pub. Kiril remained in his seat looking disinterested as he tried to pick up on the conversation.

What could have the Dark Ones almost giddy?

One female Dark began to clap her hands and laugh madly, as if her greatest enemy had been killed.

"I can't believe it," a male voice said from behind Kiril.

He couldn't turn and see who it was, but the excitement was evident in his voice.

"What?" said a male voice that was deeper, wearier.

"Balladyn has captured Rhi!"

Kiril's stomach clenched. Rhi had been taken? Why hadn't any of the Dragon Kings told him?

Shouts came from all around the pub as the news spread. It seemed Rhi had many enemies on the Dark side, many that wanted to see her dead.

That wasn't going to happen if Kiril had anything to say about it.

Ulrik molded himself to the stones and waited for the footsteps to retreat. He leaned his head back and looked up at the mountain he had once been able to enter without having to sneak in.

Many of the etchings of the dragons throughout had been done by him, but none of that seemed to matter to any of them.

His enemies.

His betrayers.

Ulrik slid from the shadows, keeping close to the wall as he entered the cavern. Anger infused him as it always did when he saw his Silvers kept caged like some savage beasts.

At least they were sleeping. He walked slowly to the enormous cage and let his hand glide over the silver scales of his dragons.

They couldn't hear him anymore, wouldn't recognize him as their King, but they would always be his in his heart. Until the day he could reclaim his role as a Dragon King and exact his revenge on Constantine.

It was a day he had been looking forward to for so very long. And it appeared closer than ever.

"Soon, my lovelies," he whispered as he walked to each one and stroked them. "Soon we will take to the skies again."

He couldn't linger longer. With a pang of disappointment, he hurried to the entrance of the cavern before he was found. Ulrik paused when he reached it and looked back.

A smile formed when he saw one of the Silvers had shifted its face toward him.

They still recognized him.

"Soon, Con. Verra, verra soon you will pay for what you've done."

Read on for an excerpt from
the next book by Donna Grant

BURNING DESIRE

Coming soon from St. Martin's Paperbacks!

Kiril had one hand in the pocket of his slacks when his gaze snagged on a pair of legs that seemed to go on for miles. Her black skirt skimmed high up on her thighs, and her platform heels only made her legs appear longer.

He paused and let his gaze wander up her legs to her slim hips. Her silver shirt sparkled with sequins as the band at the hem accentuated her small waist. The shirt bloused out while the back crisscrossed showing a wealth of creamy skin. Her black hair was pulled to the side in a messy braid that fell over her left shoulder.

She kept her back to him as she looked in a window of a shop. Her gaze lifted and locked with his through the glass. He was thoroughly mesmerized. Awestruck.

Entranced.

Her beauty left him speechless, dumbstruck. His gaze was riveted. Kiril took a step toward her when she turned to face him.

His lungs locked, the air trapped as he gazed upon loveliness the like he had never encountered. Her oval face was utter perfection. Thin black brows arched over large silver eyes. Her cheekbones were impossibly high and tinted with a hint of blush. Her lips, full and wide, made his balls tighten.

She was Fae, but not even that made him turn away. Kiril had encountered many beautiful Fae, yet there was something entirely different about this one.

He blinked, and that's when he saw her glamour shift. If he hadn't been so enamored, he would have spotted it sooner.

Disappointment filled him when he spotted the thick stripe of silver hair against her cheek and her red eyes signally she was Dark Fae.

It didn't take much for him to deduce that the Dark wanted to use her against him. It was a good thing he could see through glamour, or he might really have found himself in a pickle.

He should walk away, but he couldn't. Nor did he want to. He desired to know the Fae, and by getting close to her she might let something slip that could help him in his quest.

His game just became infinitely more dangerous, and yet, there was a small thrill that made his stomach tighten at the idea of learning more about the female.

She was thoroughly intoxicating to look at, and if the intelligence he spotted shining through her eyes was everything he expected, she was going to completely fascinate him.

His mind made up, Kiril walked to her wearing his most charming smile. "Find anything you fancy?" he asked as he nodded to the window of sparkling jewelry.

She laughed, the sound making his blood heat. "I

love the glitter of the gems. It's a weakness." Her head tilted slightly as her eyes regarded him. "It's not every day that a Scot visits Ireland. What brings you to our green isle?"

"Business. And pleasure."

She let her gaze slowly wander over him. Kiril wished he knew what she was thinking and if she liked what she saw. When her eyes returned to him, her smile of approval said it all.

It was all he could do not to press her against the window and devour her lips in a kiss that would leave them both breathless.

She shifted her small silver clutch from one hand to another. "I've lived in Cork all my life. It's a beautiful city."

Kiril nodded and belatedly noticed the Dark who had been watching him were gone. He had taken the bait, after all. It also made him aware of just how completely he had been bewitched with the female. He was going to have to watch himself for sure lest he find himself bound in chains. "Are you waiting on someone?"

"I was. They're late, and I'm tired of waiting," she said, her eyes posing an invitation her words hadn't.

The offer was on the table. All Kiril had to do was take it. It was tempting, or rather she was. It would be a treacherous obstacle of quicksand if he accepted.

The lies would grow, the deceptions would spread. But if he succeeded, the rewards for the Dragon Kings could be numerous.

Kiril held out his arm. "Would you like to join me for dinner?"

Her gaze lowered to the ground as she smiled shyly and took his arm. "I would like that very much."

They strolled arm in arm down the sidewalk toward the Italian restaurant that was his favorite. The host grinned widely when he spotted Kiril.

"Glad to have you back," he said and motioned them to follow.

Kiril guided the woman ahead of him with his hand on her lower back. He felt her shiver when his fingers grazed her bare skin.

He couldn't hold back his satisfied smile. She had been sent to seduce him, but she wasn't immune to his touch. That could work to his advantage, especially if he managed to flip her to their side. It wouldn't be easy, but he didn't think he was going to mind the effort.

Desire, dark and profound, smoldered through him. It wasn't the desire that alarmed him, but the raw, visceral need to know her, the yearning to taste her.

The hunger to fill her.

That desire swelled and intensified, spread and multiplied with every second they were together. It consumed him, devoured him. He was being incinerated from the inside out with that burning need.

Kiril slid into the half-moon shaped booth beside her and promptly ordered a bottle of wine.

He opened the menu and decided to push her. It was either that or kiss her, and he was afraid if he started kissing her, he wouldn't be able to stop. Kiril didn't think anyone in he restaurant would want to see him have sex. "Why did you accept my invitation?"

Surprise flickered in her deep red eyes. "I was hungry, and you offered."

"Do you often go off with strange men?"

She laughed, the sound going straight to his cock. "You're the first. I'm Shara, by the way."

"Kiril."

"Kiril. A strong name, but also an unusual one."

He set aside the menu and regarded her. It was strange. He normally hated looking into the eyes of a Dark Fae. Something about red eyes that seemed wrong, but he didn't mind it with her.

Shara. What a beautiful name to match such an intriguing, captivating woman.

She cleared her throat and set her napkin in her lap. Her lips parted to speak, but before she could the waiter brought the wine.

Kiril continued to watch her even as he sampled the wine and nodded his approval to the server. Once their glasses were filled and their order given, the attendant walked away.

"You were saying?" he prompted her.

"I was going to ask what kind of business are you in?"

Kiril thought about spinning another lie, and then realized there was no need. She knew he was a Dragon King, knew that he was from Dreagan. One less lie could only help him.

"I work for a distillery. I sample other whisky around the world for comparison."

Her red eyes held his as she lifted the wine glass to her lips and tried the cabernet sauvignon. "Wouldn't it be easier to taste these whiskies at your distillery?"

"It might, but it adds to the taste to try it at the place it's distilled. It's also helpful to sit in a pub and watch what the bartenders pour for their patrons."

"I see." She set down her glass and licked her lips.

Kiril swirled the red wine in his glass thinking how much he wanted to kiss her. "What do you do, Shara?"

"I work in my family's business."

So she didn't lie either. Interesting. "And what is it your family does?"

"Import/export."

Another truth. Dark Fae were notorious for luring humans into their world, but it wasn't pleasure the humans received. The women were taken by the males, and though they might experience brief pleasure, unbeknownst to them their souls were being drained.

As for the human males, the female Dark used them for sex. Sex with a Dark was like a drug, and the humans could become addicted fast. The females rarely lived long enough to know what was happening, but the female Dark's made sure to keep the human males alive for decades while having their fun.

"A lucrative business, I assume," Kiril said.

Shara glanced away. "It is."

Kiril let the questions drop as their food was delivered. The rest of the meal was spent talking of anything that neither of them had to lie about. It was . . . refreshing.

For the first time in days, Kiril almost felt like himself. He was still on guard, but he was more relaxed. Perhaps it was because he knew what he was about.

Or maybe it was because he wanted to shove aside the food, yank her to her feet, and toss her atop the table to have his way with her.